Caught in a Loop

THE SKATERS OF SEQUOIA VALLEY
BOOK THREE

TOMI TABB

Paperback ISBN: 978-1-969184-15-4

Hardover ISBN: 978-1-969184-16-1

First edition

First published by Pas de Chat Publications 2025 Copyright © 2025 by Tomi Tabb

 Formatted with Vellum

Ava and Fernando's World

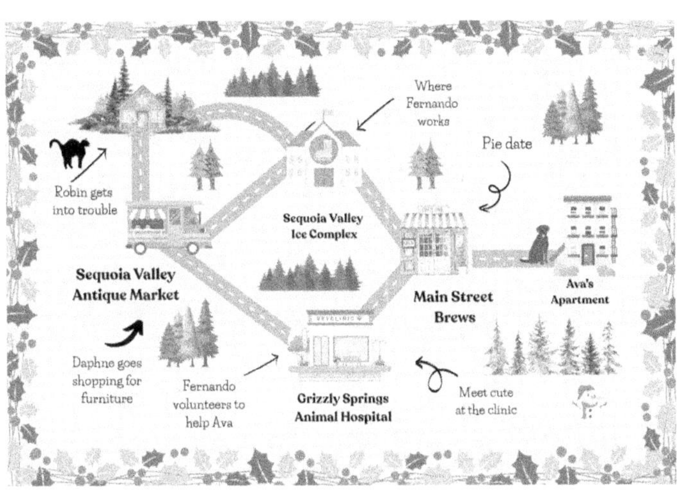

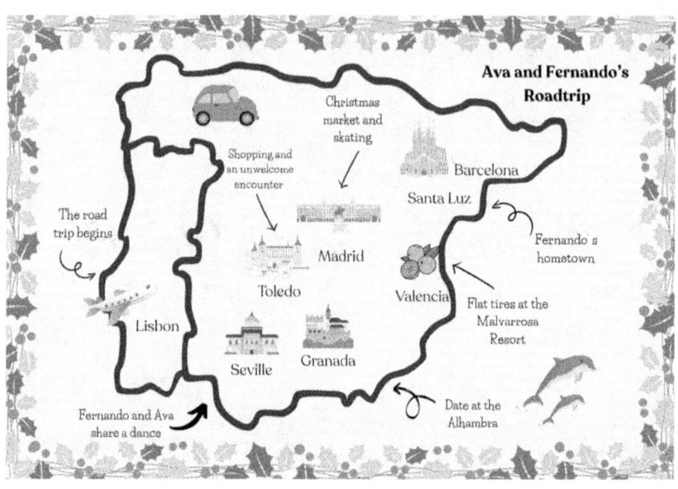
Ava and Fernando's Roadtrip
Christmas market and skating
Shopping and an unwelcome encounter
Barcelona
Santa Luz
The road trip begins
Fernando's hometown
Madrid
Toledo
Valencia
Flat tires at the Malvarrosa Resort
Lisbon
Seville
Granada
Fernando and Ava share a dance
Date at the Alhambra

Chapter One

"This is it. The last box," Dylan says as he stacks it in his truck and closes it. "Thanks for all your help, Ava. I couldn't have done it without you."

This is it. He's leaving. I rub the back of my neck, trying to disguise my trembling hands. "It wasn't any trouble. Are you still set on leaving for Colorado tonight?"

"That was the plan." He checks his watch, then glances back at me. "Since I'm all packed up and I've turned in my apartment keys, there isn't any point in sticking around. I might as well get a couple hours of driving in before it gets dark."

He leans closer to me. My heart flutters. I'm running out of time to tell him the truth.

"This is the hardest goodbye of all." He wraps his arms around me and envelops me in a tight hug. I soak in the scent of his cologne, committing it to memory. It smells of pine needles and the woods. "It's the first time we'll be apart for more than a couple weeks since we met in vet school. When was it? Eight years ago? You know me better than anybody else, and I couldn't ask for a better best friend."

"I feel the same way." I've been dropping hints about my true feelings to him for weeks. I thought by now he would've picked up on something, but apparently not.

"I only wish you were coming with me." He sighs and releases me. "It could be just like old times." His eyes gloss over, lost in the past. "Do you think the bar on Second Street still serves the best ribs? Or that the Asian market near the edge of Colorado State still sells five-dollar sushi on Tuesdays?"

"I don't know. We moved to California four years ago. Odds are some things have changed." I swallow hard. Here goes nothing. "There's, uh . . . something important I wanted to tell you." My voice is barely above a whisper.

"Sure, what's on your mind?" He glances at me with those wide baby-blue eyes, leaning against the driver's side door of his SUV.

All the muscles in my body tense. And suddenly, it's like my tongue has been glued to the roof of my mouth. All I can manage is, "Have a safe drive."

"Thanks. I will!"

Ugh. It's happened again! Crap. Crap. Crap. What do I do?

He climbs into the vehicle, a wide, brimming smile on his face. "Once I get settled, feel free to visit anytime you want. There's always space in the guest room for you."

Come on, Ava, put on your big-girl scrubs and tell him. The words should be easy. I. Love. You.

He starts the engine and buckles his seat belt. "I'll text you when I get to my stop for the night."

I open and close my mouth, still unable to find the words.

As he shifts the car from reverse to drive, he offers me one last wave, then exits the parking lot. I stand on the sidewalk in front of our practice, hands glued by my side, watching as the truck makes its way down State Route Three until it completely disappears from sight.

I clench my fists as anger floods my system. "I love you, Dylan," I say a moment too late. I throw my head back with a groan. "Why couldn't I say that two minutes ago?"

Dylan and I have been friends for the past eight years and business partners for the last four. Two short of a decade. Every single day since I realized I had feelings for him, I told myself I'd pull him aside for a heart-to-heart chat and tell him exactly how I felt.

But no matter how many times I tried, I've never been able to get my brain to connect with my mouth when he's in the same room as me. It's like watching the Titanic hit an iceberg and slowly sink into the murky depths of the Atlantic.

When Dylan told me he was moving back to Colorado, I thought, perfect, here's my big opportunity. But my tongue-tied disease grew even worse. And now, I've lost my chance completely—he's gone.

"Dr. Brown?" Vicki, the receptionist, calls out from inside the practice's front door. "Are you available? We have a call from a guy on line three who sounds panicky. He's one of Dr. Conti's patients."

"And you're not sending it to him because. . .?"

"It's, uh, just you," Vicki says.

Her words send an ice-cold shiver through my body. I'm alone. The transition is officially complete. I'm the sole owner of the Grizzly Springs Animal Hospital. With Dylan out of the picture and on his way to join the research staff at our alma mater, Colorado State University, there's no other vets.

"I'll be right there. Give me two minutes, then send the

call to the back." I take a deep breath and spin around. This is exactly what I need right now.

"Sounds good." She shuffles back inside.

I enter the room we use as an office. My brain jump-starts into doctor mode, running through all the possible scenarios I might be about to encounter: a dog that ate something it shouldn't have; a cat that won't come out of its hiding spot; a bird that's plucking out its feathers. You name it, and I've given advice about it. One thing about working with animals is there's never a dull moment.

I clear my throat and pick up the phone, "Thank you for holding, Dr. Brown speaking."

"Doctor . . ." the accented male voice on the other end says with a rolled R. "I'm sorry to bother you. My friend's left your contact information. It's their cat. I'm worried about it."

"What's going on with it?"

"My friends are out of town, and it's been hiding since I arrived to watch it. I don't know what's going on. He's supposed to be friendly. I thought he'd want to come out and play with me."

Cats are masters at hiding signs of an illness or injury, but since this guy mentioned pet sitting, I have a hunch it's something far simpler. I just need a little more information to confirm it. "Has it eaten? Or used its litter box?"

"I think so? There was a hole in its food bowl this morning. Unless the dog ate the cat's food. Or the turtle. And I think it used the litter box. Do you mind if I go and check?"

"Sure."

I hear the man place the phone down and then foot-steps echoing against a wooden floor.

As I sit, my eyes search the room. My stomach clenches

when they settle on Dylan's empty desk. There's a giant gaping hole where his collection of things he's removed from dogs and cats used to be. It's yet another reminder he won't be coming back.

A moment later, the man returns to the call, sounding slightly out of breath. "Yes, it looks like it did. There's a big dark spot in the corner."

"That's all great news." I sigh. At least this case is an easy one. "Based on what you're telling me, I'm confident your cat is going to be just fine. It's a case of what I call stranger danger. He's hiding from you because he's shy. Cats are creatures of habit. They have rituals and routines they don't like interrupted. When something is off or different, their instinct is to hide."

"OK. But shouldn't he have come out by now?"

"Not necessarily. Cats are like people. They do what they want, when they want, on their own schedules. Until he gets used to you, he'll probably only come out when he thinks you aren't around. Which means when you're out and about. Or at night, when you're asleep."

"You're sure?" he asks.

"Yes, I'm positive. It happens all the time. There's no need to bring the cat in." I give the guy a few tips on cat care and remind him if he's worried, he can always call me back.

"Gracias, Doctor. I know you're busy. I'll let you go."

I disconnect the call and replace the phone in the cradle.

"Dr. B?" Vicki pokes her head in the doorway. She's dressed in teal-blue scrubs with dogs in sunglasses today. Her curly brown hair has been tied back into a low ponytail. "I saw the line click off. Was everything okay? He was talking so quickly that I forgot to ask his name."

That's Vicki for you. She tends to struggle with getting people to get to the point of their stories. She's too indulgent. While it bothered Dylan to no end, I don't mind it. It makes the owners who come and see us feel like we're more than just a business.

"It's fine. And it was just a guy who was cat sitting for the first time."

She laughs. "Phew. That's a relief."

"How does our morning look today?"

"Empty. We had another cancellation come in a couple minutes ago." Vicki shoots me a sympathetic look.

"Another one of Dylan's clients?" I guess.

She nods. "They didn't specifically *say* they were leaving us, but I could hear the Lake Wakahanra Animal Clinic's receptionist in the background. She's got that distinct gravelly voice."

"We knew this was gonna happen." I squeeze my eyes shut. "I just didn't think it would be three-quarters of his patients."

When Dylan and I first opened the Grizzly Springs Animal Hospital, we thought we'd have no problems attracting new patients. It's a small town, and the closest vet practice was two cities over. But as the last four years have proven, I was naive.

Our first year, like most new businesses, we struggled and weren't profitable. But that didn't stop us. We worked our butts off doing low-cost vaccination clinics, performing free spays and neuters, and sending out coupons for fifty percent off first-time visits. And in year three, it started to pay off. We began to break even and pay off a good chunk of our debt.

But we had one problem: Our clients were mostly female and flocked to Dylan. Not me. They wanted the "handsome" and "attractive" vet. Which I can't say I blame them for. Dylan *is* handsome. He's five-ten, and has a year-round tan and the smile of a toothpaste model.

But unfortunately, it meant I became relegated to playing the role of vet tech most days. At first, I didn't mind. We weren't in a position to be able to hire a tech. But as time marched on, I did grow to resent it. I wanted to see patients. Not stand in the background and be the one taking the pet's weight and history to pass on to Dylan.

"Don't worry, Dr. B, I'm sure things will work out. Just because Lake Wakahanra's clinic has all male vets who happen to look like models doesn't mean they're any good. You've been in the area a lot longer than them. Plus, they're three times as expensive as us."

I try to push away the feelings of fear welling up inside of me. We can't afford to lose any more business. "I hope you're right."

"You know I am."

My gaze travels to the medicine cabinets. "I, uh, think I'm going to spend the rest of the morning working on inventory. It's been a good six months since we've done one." Not to mention it's the perfect way to stay distracted. Vicki frowns. "Don't worry," I reassure her. "You're needed up front. I can do this on my own."

"Did I ever mention you're my favorite vet to work with?"

"I'm the only one," I joke half-heartedly. "That reminds me. We'll need to start posting job openings for a vet tech. We've been without one for a couple months now. It was fine when Dr. Conti was still here, but without him, I'll need another set of hands."

If I'm being honest, hiring a vet tech is stretching our budget—I wiped out half my life savings when I bought Dylan's share of the practice—but it's a necessary evil.

Vicki cocks her head to the side. "Do you want me to post on places like LinkedIn?"

"Please."

She fist-bumps me. "Just give me the details and I'll type something up for ya."

"Thanks."

Vicki hesitates in the doorway.

"Was there something else?"

"Um, I was wondering if I could play around with updating our website and clinic flyers. Dr. Conti always insisted they were fine, but if you ask me, they're fugly. They look like something a middle-schooler threw together in Word the night before a project was due. If you redid them and spent some money on marketing—"

I hold up my hand. "Vicki, you have my blessing to do whatever you want with them." The flyers she's talking about *were* done in Word. Dylan and I may be vets, but neither one of us knew how to use any fancy design programs. We just needed something basic with our names, prices, and services on them.

Even though alarm bells are ringing in my head at the thought of spending money on marketing, if it means bringing in some much-needed clientele, I'm all for it. It's my first official decision as the new owner.

"I won't let you down," Vicki shouts, hugging me tightly, causing the chair I'm sitting in to roll backward and hit the wall. "Oops, sorry."

Our bodies shake with laughter. It takes us a moment to catch our breath.

I stand up and scoot the chair back into position. "When's our next appointment?"

"At two. It's Mr. Paul's retriever. She's due for her annual vaccines."

"Got it. I'll set a timer on my phone, but if you could let me know when it's one-thirty, I'd appreciate it." I tend to get carried away once I start a project.

"You bet."

With that, I take a clipboard and notebook, walk over to the storage room, and begin going through the medicines we have on hand. If there's one thing that calms my nerves, it's organizing things.

"D r. B?"

"Is it our Spanish friend again?" I call from the break room, waiting eagerly for the Keurig to hurry up and brew a cup of dark roast coffee. It's late in the day, and I'll pay for it later when I can't sleep, but I need that caffeine boost to keep going.

"Uh-huh."

I rub my temples. I don't mind this guy calling, but it's the fifth time. It irks me a little that he hasn't looked up the answers to his questions on the internet. "You know the drill," I finally answer. The coffee machine makes a clicking sound. Coffee in hand, I cross the hall to my desk and pick up the phone. "Hola."

"Hola, Dr. B. You speak Spanish?"

"Un paquito. Just a little. I took it in high school."

"Ah, that makes sense." The deep male voice laughs. "You have a good accent."

"Thanks. How can I help you?" I take a swig of my coffee. Ick. It's bitter without any creamer or sugar, but it'll do the job.

"I know the last time I called I said it would be the last time, but something's come up."

"Sure. What's your question?"

"It's the turtle this time. I don't know what I'm supposed to feed him. I've used the last of the food my friends left me yesterday. I tried calling them, but no answer. The pet shop owner said crickets were the way to go, but he hasn't touched them."

"Do you know what type of turtle it is?" I twirl the cord of the phone over my pinky.

"Ugh, no."

"Can you email or text me a picture?"

"Sí."

"Great. Most turtles are omnivores, but there are a few species that don't care for insects." I rattle off my cell number to him and take another sip of my drink while I wait. A moment later, my phone chimes. "Got it." I open the message and enlarge the image. It has a high-domed shell, a hooked jaw, and webbed feet. "Hmm . . . it looks like a box turtle to me. They usually enjoy a diet of small insects and veggies like lettuce, carrots, and celery. When did you offer him the crickets?"

"An hour ago?"

"Just like with your friend's cat, give the turtle some time. He'll eat when he's ready. Does it have a sunlamp and access to water?"

"Yes."

"Great. Just make sure it's on during the day and off at night."

"Gracias, I will. Thank you again for all the help. This time is the *last* time, I promise."

"You're welcome." I stand and stretch, knowing this time, he's right. "We're getting ready to close the clinic, but if you think of something else, feel free to text me. You have my number now." I just hope I don't live to regret it. I know it's something I shouldn't technically do, but this guy truly needs help.

"I'll try hard not to bother you."

"You won't—and oh!" I snap my fingers together. "Before I let you go, there is something I wanted to ask you."

"Yes?"

"What's your name?"

I hear a laugh on the other end. It's rich and gives me a few goosebumps. "It's Fernando. Fernando Alvarez."

We chat for a few more seconds, then end the call. "Fernando," I muse to myself, replacing the phone in the cradle. "That's the perfect name for a guy with a voice like that."

Does Fernando have dark hair or light hair? Is he tall or average height? Does he wear glasses? Have any tattoos? As I finish my coffee, I daydream about what he might look like. However, I keep circling back to one image: Dylan's.

Chapter Two

Later that evening, after I've eaten dinner and walked my spoiled chocolate lab, I lounge on the couch with a glass of wine and binge the latest episode of the reality dating show *Cupid's Arrow*. I enjoy all the drama.

If I applied to be a contestant, would I get Dylan's attention? Probably not. I doubt he has any clue about the show. I sigh. Well, if I became a contestant, at the very least, it would propel me back into the dating world. I've been a single woman since my undergrad days.

I've been on dates here and there since then, but my last serious boyfriend broke up with me between our freshman and sophomore years. He claimed I was too focused on studying. Which, in his defense, I was. I was obsessed with maintaining a perfect grade point average. Getting into vet school is more competitive than med school. I needed every advantage I could get.

Once I'd finally made it to Colorado State, I continued to make the university library my second home. I was always cramming for an upcoming exam or working at my internship. I never made time for having a life. That was until Dylan came along.

My brain relives this morning's interaction. My mood drops. Maybe watching a dating show isn't the best idea right now. I click off the Connected Hearts Network and flip to the Hallmark channel. It's the middle of November, and they're already showing their holiday movies.

There's a girl and a guy on the screen sitting in a grand ballroom in front of a Christmas tree. Perfect. I need something low stress and predictable. I may have missed the first hour of the movie, but at least I can count on the couple getting together and being able to magically save whatever business is about to go bust, or one of them learning the true meaning of Christmas.

Padding over to my freezer, I pull out a pint of my favorite dark chocolate, fudge, and cherry ice cream. Hopefully it's still good. Who knows how long it's been sitting in my freezer. Actually, I take that back. I remember buying it about six months ago on the day Dylan mentioned he'd accepted a research position at our alma mater, studying vultures.

I pry off the lid and take a small test bite. A chunk of chocolate hits my tongue at the same time as a piece of the tangy cherry. I chew and swallow. There's a hint of freezer burn, but it's still delicious. As I move around the kitchen, looking for my supply of gummy bears to throw on top, Max lets out a low whine. I laugh. "Don't worry. If I get a treat, you do too."

His tail wags wildly from side to side. I pull a few bone-shaped biscuits from the cabinet and set them in his bowl. Not wasting a moment, he devours them. Only crumbs remain by the time I'm settled back on the couch. Max whines for more, but when I don't give in, he huffs and plants himself on his bed. He knows I mean business.

As I reach for the remote, my phone chimes. I expect it to be Dylan, but to my surprise, it's Fernando.

> Fernando: Hola, Dr. B. I'm sorry to bother you. Does that offer for help still stand?

I thought I made myself clear on the phone. Or else I wouldn't have given him my number. I start typing.

> Ava: Yes. What's up?

> Fernando: The cat has finally come out of hiding, but he's covered in mud. He must've snuck outside somehow when I wasn't looking. I know cats can bathe themselves, but is mud something they can eat?

Yikes. Mud and cats do not mix. I sit taller.

> Ava: In small amounts, mud is okay, but in large amounts, they need help. How bad is it?

> Fernando: Let me send you a photo.

It pops into our thread. The brown goop is so thick that I can't make out what color the feline is.

> Ava: This poor little one is going to need a bath.

What I don't mention is that if it doesn't manage to come out with shampoo and water, the cat will have to be shaved. Which is no fun for anyone.

> Fernando: That's what I was afraid of. Do you know if any groomers are open this late?

Ava: I doubt it. Even if they were, most groomers don't do cats. You'll be better off bathing the cat yourself. You'll need warm water, and if you have it, some cat-friendly shampoo.

> Fernando: I think I saw some dog shampoo in the bathroom, would that work?

Ava: It's not a good idea. Dog and cat shampoos technically do the same thing, but the ingredients in dog versions can have some harmful effects on a cat's skin.

I chew on my lip. Fernando is clearly in over his head. Even for an experienced person, giving most cats a bath is a workout. Not only do felines usually hate water, but unless you hold them the right way, it's easy to become a human scratching post.

Ava: I'll tell you what, why don't you bring the cat down to the clinic and we'll clean him up there.

> Fernando: That would be amazing! Do you have any openings for the morning?

Ava: No appointment required. Doctor's orders. Are you in Grizzly Springs, Sequoia Valley, or Lake Wakahanra?

> Fernando: Sequoia Valley.

Ava: Then it should be easy to get to my
practice. The address is 2200 State
Highway Three in Sequoia Valley. Is a
half hour enough time for you to get
there?

Fernando: You mean you'd be willing to
meet us tonight?

Ava: Yes. We don't want that cat being
muddy any longer than necessary.

Fernando: Are you sure? I don't want to
ruin your evening.

I stare at the ice cream sitting on my coffee table. My evening was already a wash.

Ava: You won't be. I'm not doing
anything.

Fernando: Then I'll be there in thirty
minutes.

Ava: See you there.

I zip through central Grizzly Springs and make it to the clinic in twenty minutes. The parking lot is empty since the other shops in the strip mall are closed. I grab my usual spot right in front of the door. There's just enough time to flip the lights on and prep one of the exam rooms before the front door jingles open.

"Hello? Dr. B?" Fernando's voice calls out.

"In exam room two. Would you mind making sure the

front door shuts completely behind you? I don't want anyone else to think we're open and sneak in." There's a *click*, followed by the squeak of his tennis shoes against the floor. "Thanks," I shout.

"No problem."

I survey my setup one last time. Towels, soap, multiple bowls of warm water, gloves, shampoo, and an electric razor. I think I've collected everything we need.

I step out of the exam room. "Hi, Fernando, it's nice to finally meet you in the flesh."

Waiting for me is a tall man with sun-kissed skin and thick brown hair that looks like it belongs in a shampoo commercial. It's messy in that effortlessly perfect way that no normal human could ever pull off. His eyes are big and warm, deep-brown and framed by long lashes. Cradled against his broad chest is a soft-sided carrier, and from inside, a cat lets out a dramatic meow.

"Likewise, Doctor."

The way he rolls the R at the end of "doctor" sends a shiver up my spine. He reminds me of one of my favorite audiobook narrators. I could listen to him talk for hours on end.

I break eye contact and clear my throat. "Come on in." I need to focus. I have a patient. "Go ahead and set the carrier down on the table. I'd like to examine our friend here first to make sure there aren't any injuries. Then we'll head over to the sink."

"That sounds like a plan."

I slowly unzip the top of the carrier. "The file said her name was Robin?"

"Yeah, that's right."

"It's an interesting name for a feline. It reminds me of the bird."

"Thank my friend Tim. He loves comic books."

"Oh, is this guy named after Batman's sidekick?" I don't know much about comic books, but at least it's a character I've heard of.

"Sí, that's the one."

"Are you a comic-book lover too?" I ask, glancing up at him.

"No. Tim's tried to get me into them, but there's too many different backstories and characters to keep track of. I like the movies though."

"Me too." My attention returns to the carrier. Robin has backed into a corner and made herself as small as possible. The few pieces of fur that aren't caked in mud stick up straight. I lower my voice and speak softly. "Hi, Robin, I'm Dr. Brown and I'm here to help you."

Robin anchors her claws firmly into the bottom of the carrier. Unfortunately for her, I know every trick in the book. I reach inside and gently pry her paws free.

"If you could put that on the floor." I nod toward the case. "We don't want her trying to sneak back into it."

Fernando crouches to set the carrier down, and as he straightens, his arm lightly brushes mine. It sends a tiny spark dancing across my skin. I pretend not to notice, focusing on the cat.

Running my hands along Robin's body, I check over her musculature. "She's in good shape," I say, trying to keep my voice steady. "I don't feel or hear anything abnormal."

"That's a relief," Fernando says, exhaling with a breath that ruffles a lock of hair over his forehead. His eyes meet mine for a second longer than they need to. Just enough to make me feel like I've forgotten how to blink. "If anything were to happen to him, I'd be toast."

I clear my throat and break eye contact, returning my

attention to Robin, who lets out a dramatic *meow*. Like all animals, she's an expert at reading human emotions. *Same, girl.*

I stroke her a few times. Mud comes off on my hands. By now, the pheromone diffusers in the room have kicked in. The poor animal has started to relax. "Is this your first time watching your friend's cat?"

"Sí. My first and probably my last. They told me pet sitting would be a piece of cake, but so far, it's been a nightmare. I have no idea what I'm doing with the cat and turtle."

"For what it's worth, I think you're doing a good job," I reassure him. "You've asked all the right questions and found help when you needed it. By the time your friend returns home, you'll be an expert." I laugh.

"I hope so." He rubs the back of his neck, looking defeated.

"And by the way, you should know that Robin isn't a he. She's a female cat."

"Huh, what do you know." He stares at her in amazement.

Robin lets out a low purr under my hands. "I think we're ready. She's calmed down. Exactly what we want before we rile her up again." Scooping the feline under my arms, I walk her over to the sink and place her inside. The moment her paws enter the inch of tepid water, she squirms.

"Anything I can do to help?" Fernando asks with a hint of concern.

"If you can grab the shampoo and two of the containers of warm water, that would be great. I'm going to rinse her first, then scrub the more stubborn clumps."

Unsurprisingly, Robin is not tolerant when it comes to

baths. By the time I finish washing her hindquarters, I'm drenched, but thankfully, scratch free. I run the towel over her fur one final time. Fernando opens the carrier. I place her inside with a clean towel on the bottom and zip it closed.

"Phew." I sag against the rim of the sink. "That's my workout for the week."

"Doctor, I feel awful about this!" Fernando's eyes rove the mess of towels and puddles of water littering the floor. It looks like we've had a small tornado hit the inside of the exam room.

"It's fine." I wave him off. "Comes with the territory of being a vet. I'll mop and toss the towels into the laundry. I'll have my receptionist tackle the rest of the mess tomorrow."

Fernando shakes his head. "You already did all the work cleaning up Robin. Let me take care of the room."

"You don't have to do that." I frown.

"You didn't ask. I'm offering." He begins rolling up the sleeves of his button-up, exposing forearms corded with muscles. I swallow hard. "Where do you keep your cleaning supplies?"

"In the cupboard." I point to the corner of the room.

"Bueno." He claps his hands together. "Leave everything to me," he insists.

As I open my mouth to protest, my phone starts to ring. Reaching into the deep pocket of my scrubs, I spy Dylan's name flash across the screen. I hesitate. Normally I'd never let a client clean up after their own animal, but I do want to talk to Dylan.

"Go. Answer your phone. I've got this." Fernando winks.

"Hey, stranger." I hold my phone to my ear and shut the door to the office with my hip. A surge of excited energy floods my body and I'm suddenly wide awake.

"Hi, Ava." Dylan's voice, on the other hand, comes out exhausted.

"How's it going?"

"I've been better. I'm only just reaching the Nevada state line. There was some roadwork around Bakersfield that backed traffic up for miles. It took hours to get through."

"I'm sorry." I inhale sharply. "Are you still going to stop in Vegas for the night?"

"Yeah. It's only about an hour away and I've already prepaid for my hotel room. How has your day been?"

"Oh, you know, same ol', same ol'. I did a few routine exams and vaccinations. Things don't change much around here."

He sighs. "That's the nice thing about Sequoia Valley— it's predictable from one day to the next."

"Are you missing it already? You can always come back," I tease.

"Nope . . . well maybe a tiny bit," he admits. "I am nervous about what I'm getting myself into."

"Dylan, you've been talking about the move for months. All your doubts will disappear as soon as you're back in Fort Collins." I sit in my chair and lean back. "Remember how it was when we first moved to California? You had the same sort of anxiety."

"Yeah . . ."

"And what happened here?" I push.

"We opened the practice we always talked about."

"Exactly! If it worked out here, it'll work out in Colorado." I try and sound positive.

"But *you* won't be here." Dylan's voice drops.

"I won't." I dry swallow as a lump forms in my throat. "But I'm only a phone call or video chat away."

"I've been thinking about you a lot over the last couple of hours."

My pulse begins to pick up. "I've thought about you too."

"You're such an important part of my life. You have no idea how difficult it was to leave you in Sequoia Valley."

"Dylan," I start, my body humming with energy. This is it! This is my opening! It's now or never. "Hearing you say that means everything to me. You know . . . this morning there was something else, but I chickened out."

"Ava?"

I lick my lips. "The truth is I . . . I . . . I love you. I have for a long time!"

"What are you talking about?" he sputters.

"You're one of my best friends. We know one another inside and out." My heart is hammering so loudly, it's almost hard to hear. "There's always been a strong connection between us. Haven't you felt it?"

"No. I haven't," he says slowly.

I freeze and nearly drop the phone. It's as if somebody has taken an IV of ice water and inserted it into my veins. "No?" I repeat.

"No, not like you're thinking. You're a good friend and great business partner, Ava, but that's all you'll ever be to me. How do I put this? You're like . . . my favorite bossy older sister."

My mouth opens and closes. I'm at a loss for words. Fat salty tears flow down my cheeks. All these years of waiting and he only sees me as a sister? There's a crackling sound. My heart is being crushed into a million pieces and tossed into the wind to scatter.

"Please don't take this the wrong way, but if I were romantically interested in you, we would've gotten together a long time ago. I'm not saying this to be insensitive to you, but you're not my type. You have a lot of great qualities that I'm sure some guy out there would be lucky to find, Ava, but you're, um, a little too focused on work for me."

The more he says, the more it stings, like pouring rubbing alcohol over a fresh cut. I wish I'd never opened my mouth. I was better off being left in the dark.

"Look, Ava, I, um, have a lot of driving to do still. I'll text you later."

"OK," I manage to say.

The phone clicks and all I hear on the other end is an empty dial tone. I drop my phone onto my desk, and my body shakes with sobs.

"**D**r. B?" Fernando knocks on my door.

I'd forgotten he was still here. "Just a second," I say, using the back of my hand to dry my eyes. They're probably red rimmed and swollen. Maybe in this lighting, Fernando won't notice.

"Dr. B? Is everything all right?"

Well, that was wishful thinking. Fernando stands in the doorway, his brown eyes are wide with concern. They're the color of toffee, one of my favorite candies.

"No, but I'll be fine in a few days." I sniffle.

He enters the room, pulls a box of tissues from the top of Dylan's old desk, and hands them to me.

"Thanks."

"Is there anything I can do to help?"

I shake my head. "No, I appreciate the offer. I just need some time to let everything settle." I blow my nose. "That's a little better." I take a deep breath, stand on shaky legs, and change the subject. I can't take any more emotional pain today. "I feel guilty for leaving you alone for so long. Let me finish cleaning the room. That way you and Robin can head home."

"Actually, I was coming in here to let you know I was done."

He's finished? I know I was in my office for a long time, but it couldn't have been more than an hour.

"I was also going to ask if I could treat you to dinner as my way of saying thank you for all your help, but . . ." He rubs the back of his neck. "That might not be the most appropriate offer right now."

"No, it wouldn't." All I want to do after this is go home, eat my pint of ice cream, and feel sorry for myself. We walk together down the hallway to exam room two. "You don't owe me anything. Just promise me that you'll keep a watchful eye on Robin and try not to let her sneak out."

"I'll do my best."

As I push the door open, I have to blink a few times to make sure I'm in the right room. It looks cleaner than when I arrived. "You mopped, cleaned the sinks, waxed and polished the floors, and did all the laundry?"

"I did."

"I wish I could hire you."

He laughs. "If I didn't already have a full-time job, I'd

consider it. Being around animals every day would be a dream come true."

"Do you have any pets?"

"No." He shakes his head. "Work used to take me on the road all the time before I settled in Sequoia Valley. I didn't have a permanent home. But now that things have changed, maybe it's something I'll consider."

"Well, if you decide you're in a good place to adopt a cat or dog, let me know. I always have leads on animals who are looking for a good home."

"I promise, Dr. B, you'll be one of the first calls I make."

My breathing has become more stable and my voice not as shaky. Fernando may not know it, but talking with him gives me the calm I needed after Dylan ripped through my heart.

Chapter Three

On Saturday, I meet my sister, Daphne, for lunch in the neighboring town of Lake Wakahanra. She's three years older than me and married, with two energetic kids under five. Physically, we could pass for being twins. We both have shoulder-length light-brown hair, stand about five-foot-five, and got the same icy-blue eyes from our parents.

Personality wise, however, we're polar opposites. Daphne has always boasted an easy, go-with-the-flow approach to life, while every step I've taken has been meticulously researched and carefully calculated. Daph always jokes it's a required trait to work in a STEM field, which is partially true. Some people are just born organizers, and others are meant to be free spirits.

I've spent the last half hour bringing her up to speed on the Dylan fiasco.

"Well, all I can say is good riddance, Ava. I never liked him anyway. He always struck me as self-centered and unaware. And it looks like I was right. I don't know what you saw in him. He isn't good enough for you. I hope he

"""

has a miserable start to his new life in Denver." She takes a sip of her tea, laughing into her cup.

"He's in Fort Collins, but close enough."

"Whatever."

"And please don't bad-mouth him. He's still my friend."

"I wish you'd cut ties with him." She wrinkles her nose. "Friends don't treat one another like Dylan treats you. I bet he hasn't even called to apologize for the callous way he broke the news to you."

"No."

"And how long has it been?" she asks.

"Three days. But he might be out of cell range or busy driving," I offer, suppressing a grimace.

"Quit making excuses for the guy. He's a grown man. You're probably more worried about him than he is about you. Anyway, the more important thing is that you move on. Don't waste any more of your brainpower or tears pining over a guy like him."

That's easier said than done. I lean back in my chair and stare out the window, watching some of the boats sail past the restaurant on the lake. It's a beautiful warm fall day. Everyone around us is in a great mood, talking about the upcoming Harvest festival hosted by Sequoia Valley Middle School.

Except for me. All I can think about are past memories of Dylan. It's as if somebody's taken a rubber band and keeps snapping it against my wrist, causing flickers of pain. I still remember the first time we met, crystal clear.

"Hi, I'm Dylan."

"Ava," I say, not looking away from skimming the course syllabus being handed out.

"I must've lucked out to get such a smart and talented woman like you for a lab partner."

I snort. "Nice try at flattery, Dylan, but you don't even know me."

"That's what you think, Ava Brown, but you're wrong. I know exactly who you are." His voice sends a shiver up my spine. "You're the top student in our year, you spend most of your afternoons in the library, and your favorite food is the pho from the student union. Does that sound right?"

I glance away from the syllabus and into the handsome face of the man sitting next to me. He flashes me a Cheshire cat smile. His brown eyes sparkle with mirth. I swallow hard. Dylan Conti. Of all the people I could possibly be paired with, it had to be him.

"It does." My voice quivers.

"Good, because just like you, I don't just want an A in this class. I want us to be number one. I'm prepared to do whatever it takes to get it."

From the starting gate, we were both on the same page. I was afraid Dylan would be one of those guys who slacked off and couldn't pull his weight on a project. But each step of the way, he proved me wrong. He spent more time in the library than I did that semester. And he always came to class prepared, with a fresh set of ideas on how to run our assigned experiments. We spent so much time together that by the end of the term, we'd become good friends.

"Ava, what are your plans tonight to celebrate the end of finals? Are you heading to Joe's party?"

"No, I didn't think I was invited. We're not really friends," I say slowly. "I was planning to relax and binge-watch Project Catwalk *or* The British Baking Championship.*" I stare at the ground. "I actually don't really know anyone in our cohort very well. Except for you."*

"Well, it's time that changes. You have such a bright personality. Everybody deserves to see it shine."

I giggle to myself. It's such a lame pun, but somehow the way Dylan says it makes it sound sexy.

"Joe invited everyone in the class over to his place. That includes you. If you want to go, I'll even pick you up. I know how much you hate driving in the snow."

I hesitate. This is so far out of my comfort zone.

"I know how intimidating it can be to hang out in a room full of strangers, but I promise, the other vet students in our year aren't that bad," he says.

I take a deep breath. I promised myself vet school wouldn't be a repeat of my undergrad years, where I lived like a hermit. Dylan's right. The other students in our cohort wouldn't be here if they weren't as motivated and driven. My throat goes dry. "Okay, I'll go."

He flashes me the cheeky smile I've come to know well. "I'll pick you up at six."

Attending Joe's end-of-finals celebration wasn't the frat party I had pictured in my head. There were no kegs or hot, stuffy rooms full of twenty-year-olds dancing to loud, blasting music. It was a potluck in a dining room filled with adults who enjoyed stimulating conversations. But I never would've known that if it hadn't been for Dylan's urging.

As I return to the present, I wonder how I could have been so blinded by him. I always thought his flattery and flirting were signs he had a crush on me. But I guess I should've picked up on the fact that he always gravitated toward women who looked like Victoria's Secret Angels. Not women like me who dress for comfort and wear their hair in a long braid, with baggy blue scrubs and tennis shoes. "Maybe I should've tried harder. A little makeup wouldn't have hurt," I mutter.

Daphne's head snaps in my direction. "Ava, did I hear you blaming yourself?"

"No," I say quickly. Heat rushes to my cheeks.

"Good. Because you're perfect just the way you are."

I snort. "I should record you saying that for future use."

"If you want, but I'm happy to repeat it." Daphne shrugs. "Anyway, you know what I think would help you take your mind off things?"

"What? A blind date with one of your friends?" I joke.

"No." She rolls her eyes. "You're not anywhere close to being ready to date anyone right now. What you need is a vacation. When was the last time you took one?"

"That depends on your definition of vacation." I pick up my water glass and take a long sip.

"I'm not talking about taking a day off here and there. I mean a solid two weeks off where you escape all your troubles and go off the grid. No phone. No working. No men. Just you and your surroundings."

"Daph, I can't. I'm the only vet on staff." My body tenses. "If I took a vacation, it would mean closing down the practice for two weeks." Not to mention the financial implications.

"Aren't you also the owner?" she challenges. "Didn't you tell me last month you'd managed to buy out Dylan's half of the partnership?"

"I did. But that means I'm under a lot of pressure and have a lot more responsibilities than I used to."

"All I'm hearing are excuses. If you're the boss, you call the shots. Hire a temp, pick a date next month, and go. Your receptionist can handle running all the other stuff."

Dollar signs flash before my eyes. Temps aren't in my budget, but on the other hand, I do feel like I need a mental break from everything that's been going on. "I guess it could work . . ." I trail off as an idea comes to me. "My friend Laura from vet school is always talking about wanting to visit California. If I offered her my apartment for two weeks rent free, maybe I could lure her here."

"I sense a but." Daphne pinches her lips together. "What other excuse are you about to throw at me?"

"Money is tight. I don't know if I could afford to pay her a salary," I admit.

Daph waves me off. "If you need a loan, consider it done."

"But—"

"Look, you can pay us back by babysitting for us every Friday night for the next year. No more excuses. You're my sister. You know Brian and I would do anything for you." Daph reaches across the table and places her hand on top of mine. "Now tell me, what else do you need?"

I chew on my lip. "Do you think I could have you refresh the clinic's reception area? Vicki is working on the website and marketing. Now that it's my baby, I'd like it to reflect me."

"Totally. I've hated the boring beige walls you guys have for years." Daphne smiles to herself. "It's time for some color—maybe something bold like orange and purple."

"Orange?" I sputter.

"Uh-huh. It's a color people won't forget when they walk away. Why do you think Home Depot uses it?"

I open and close my mouth. "I, er, trust your vision, but it's not exactly . . ."

Daph laughs. "I'm joking. Relax. I wouldn't use orange. I'll go with something more relaxing."

Daphne is a talented, highly sought-after interior designer. She's done up many of the houses in the area belonging to the players of the Jasper Ridge Jaguars professional hockey team. Her work has been featured in magazines and in popular architectural blogs. As she's grown in popularity, she's started charging top dollar for her work. But as her sister, I know I can count on getting the family discount—free. That's a price I can afford.

"Thanks, sis."

After lunch, Daphne and I head to the antique market. It's one of the largest in this area of the state. Tents are set up throughout the entire downtown square, packed with families all taking advantage of the nice weather.

"I'll meet you back here in an hour. If I buy something I can't carry, I'll text you and have you bring the truck around," she says.

My eyes widen. "What are you planning to buy?"

She whips out her phone and opens her notes app. "For the arts-and-crafts room I'm working on at the Landis', I need a couch, a coffee table, a wingback chair, and a Tiffany lamp base. The Olsen place is a mid-century modern theme. For the guest room and kitchen, I'm looking for a table, a clock, a—"

"Okay." I hold up my hands. "I get the picture. You need a lot of stuff."

"I do. And I probably won't find most of it today, but if I do . . ."

"I'll be a good sister and help you drive it to your storage unit." Normally, I'd be annoyed that I'm being asked to play chauffeur for her antiques, but since I know my sister and brother-in-law will be advancing me some cash, I owe it to them.

"You're the best." She beams.

Daphne makes a beeline for some of her favorite vendors. While she scavenges through each item on display, like a mouse hunting for a piece of expensive award-winning French cheese, I head in the opposite direction where the food trucks are, in search of something caffeinated and some dessert. After the week I've had, I deserve it.

I take my time studying each of the chalkboard menus before my nose leads me to the Lucky Dog Diner's food truck. The diner is famous for its pies. They have the perfect graham-cracker crusts that melt in your mouth. It's just the right balance of sweet and savory. Add a dash of their fluffy homemade whipped cream, and you have the world's best dessert. The perfect comfort food.

As I walk toward the end of the line, I count at least fifty people ahead of me. Unfortunately, I'm not the only one who wants a slice of pie. At this rate, it might take the full hour to place and receive my order. Time I don't have. My shoulders hunch. I guess I'll have to settle for something else.

Just as I turn and start for the crepe truck next door, I hear, "Dr. B! Dr. B! Over here!" Fernando waves at me near the front of the Lucky Dog line. "Come, join me."

I feel guilty cutting in front of everyone else who has been waiting, but I *really* want that piece of apple pie. I keep my head lowered and try my best to ignore the glares sent my way.

"Hi, Fernando," I say, a little breathless. "Hope you're enjoying your Saturday."

"I am." He nods. "But it's better now that you're here."

He says it so casually, I almost miss the way his eyes

flicker over me for just a second longer than friendly. Or maybe that's wishful thinking.

"How are all the animals doing?" I ask.

"Much better now that my friends Gemma and Tim are home." He laughs.

I noticed the first time we met that Fernando is one attractive man. But I didn't *notice* it. It's like background music becoming your favorite song. He has a strong, angular jaw dusted with a thin layer of stubble. His thick chocolate-brown hair matches the warm, rich shade of his eyes.

As my gaze travels down, it's not hard to miss that Fernando likes his clothing to be formfitting. His T-shirt is stretching over the defined planes of his chest and the broad span of his shoulders. Whenever he moves his arm, the sleeve strains against the curve of his bicep. His jeans ride low on his hips, fitting like they were tailored just for him, hugging powerful thighs and showcasing a firm, sculpted bubble butt.

If my sister were around, she'd say his body reminds her of Chris Evans as Captain America. It's shaped like a Dorito. Heat sears in my cheeks. Ugh. I won't be able to look at those chips the same way for weeks. "That's good to hear." My voice comes out slightly higher pitched than normal.

"I don't know who was happier, the animals or me."

"I'm sure they appreciated having you around."

"Maybe. Maybe not." He shrugs. A few muscle cords in his neck pop. "Either way, I'm relieved to pass off the responsibility. Now I can focus on my upcoming trip home."

We shuffle forward a few inches in line. I force myself to focus on his face instead of letting my gaze wander elsewhere. He has sharp cheekbones softened by a few fine lines that fan out from the corners of his eyes and mouth. They're not age lines, but rather lines from years of laughter and smiles. "And home would be . . .?"

"Santa Luz, Spain."

"Mmm, Spain would be such a nice place to visit right now." I add it to the mental list of places I could go on vacation. "What part of the country is it in?"

"The south. About forty-five minutes from Barcelona." He slips his hands into his pockets. "How about you? Are you from Sequoia Valley?"

"No. I actually grew up in Wilmington, North Carolina. It's a coastal city three times the size of here. Our claim to fame is being close to the Carolina and Wrightsville beaches."

"That's how Santa Luz is too. Most tourists visit us for the beaches. Think white sand. Blue seas. Some tropical fish."

Oh, he's making it sound even more tempting. The beach would be one of my top reasons to visit Spain, except we're going into winter. And even though Spain is on the Mediterranean, it's probably still too cold to swim in. "How long are you going for?"

"About a month. I save up my vacation time all year so I can make it worth my while."

I nod. "That's smart."

"Do you get back to Wilmington often?" he asks.

"Not since college. My parents sold the house I grew up in a couple years ago and moved out here to California. They wanted to be closer to my sister and her kids."

"You're lucky they're close."

"I am now. But it wasn't always that way. When I was in

college and vet school, I could only get home once or twice a year."

We spend a few minutes chatting about our families. I share a little bit about Daphne and my niece and nephew. Fernando mentions that he's an only child, but has a large extended family.

"I'm curious. What made you decide to leave Spain?"

"I caught the travel bug." He grins. "When I was twenty, I was recruited for a job on a cruise ship. I spent a year traveling up and down the Mediterranean and loved being in a new city every couple of days."

We move up in line a few places. "How romantic!"

"If you're a guest on the ship it is, but not for crew members." He laughs. "We had bunk beds in rooms about the size of a walk-in closet."

"Ouch." I wince. "I don't know if I'd last in a space that small."

"Not many people can, myself included. It's why I started looking for another job that'd let me travel six months in," he says.

"Got it." A tingle runs up my spine. "But I have another question. If you're all about traveling, how did you end up here in Sequoia Valley? It's not exactly as exciting as somewhere like London, Paris, or Rome."

"One of the women I used to work with is from the area. When I was looking to change jobs last year, she let me know about an opportunity here in town. I came to visit, fell in love with the scenery, and poof, here I am."

Before I can ask Fernando more questions, it's our turn to order.

"Fernando! What are you doing here?" the guy inside the food truck asks. "You didn't have to wait in line. You're a VIP. You should've come around back and had Gemma or me get you whatever you wanted."

"Part of the food truck experience is about waiting in line." He leans casually against the window ledge. The sun hits Fernando's hair, highlighting a few golden streaks among the brown. "Besides, if I hadn't, I wouldn't have been able to chat with the talented Dr. Brown." He winks.

"Hi Dr. Brown." The man leans out the window as far as he can. He's in a Lucky Dog Diner shirt, and has a hairnet over his brown hair and a baseball tattoo on his arm. "It's good to see you outside the vet's office."

"Likewise," I say, trying to play it cool. I've never met them before. They were Dylan's clients, but now, I guess they're mine. I hold up my hand in a meek wave. I glance to Fernando for help.

"This is Tim, Robin's cat daddy."

"That's me. Thanks for everything you did for her. My girlfriend and I really appreciate it. I swear, if I didn't know any better, I'd say Robin is secretly a mutant cat. She always seems to teleport her way outside. I should've named her Nightcrawler."

I relax, and we shake hands. I have no clue who Night-crawler is, but I remember what Fernando mentioned the other day about his friend loving comic books.

"Gemma is working the pickup window. She'll want to say thanks too." Tim nods toward the opposite end of the truck. "Now, what can I get you guys?"

"I'll have the cherry cobbler and a coffee. Dr. B?"

"The apple pie and a coffee for me."

"Great." Tim hits a few buttons on the register.

"What do I owe you for my half?" I ask.

He waves me off. "You've got the friends and family discount. It's on the house. Gem will call your order number when it's ready." He hands Fernando a receipt, and his eyes dart between the pair of us. "Enjoy, you two."

"Did he just wink at us?"

"Yes. Just ignore him. I do."

Does Tim know something I don't? This is only the second time I've ever met Fernando. We didn't even plan to meet here. It just happened.

"So, Dr. B, I'm curious. What's your first name?"

We head over toward the pickup window to wait for our number to be called.

"It's Ava."

"Ava," he repeats. "That's a very pretty name."

My cheeks warm. "Thank my parents."

He chuckles. "Do you mind if I call you that instead of Dr. B?"

"No, I'd prefer it. It's my only day off, and I'd rather just be a normal person today."

"You work on Sundays?" He blinks in surprise.

"Not always, but I am this week. I do a low-cost vaccination clinic for cats and dogs once a month."

"That's kind of you," he says.

"Vet care is expensive." I glance away with a shrug. "I've made it my mission to make it as accessible to as many people as I can. Pets are members of the family." In a perfect world, I'd do stuff for free, but unfortunately, I have staff and bills to pay.

"How many pets do you normally see when you do a clinic?"

"It depends on how fast word spreads." I lift my chin and rub the back of my neck. "Sometimes we get five or six people, sometimes we get fifty."

"Do you need any help? I'm free tomorrow."

My eyes widen. "You want to help?"

"Sí." He nods. "It's for a good cause, and I owe you for coming to the rescue with Robin."

I spend a moment studying him. He appears to be sincere in his offer. The old Ava would find a way to politely thank him and refuse his help. But business owner Ava has to be willing to accept assistance whenever it comes my way. Tomorrow is going to be the first time it's just Vicki and me. We could desperately use another set of hands. If Fernando is there, he could check the clients in, and Vicki could act as my vet tech.

"If you come, it'll be early. Seven a.m. early," I warn.

"Early is fine." He brushes me off. "My normal workday starts at five."

"Five?" I blanch. "What time do you have to wake up?"

"Three-thirty. It's not so bad once you get used to it."

And here I thought I had it bad having to get up before seven. "Where do you work that you have to get up *that* early?"

"Order number 144," a woman calls in a thick Scottish accent.

"That's us." Fernando eagerly rushes to the window, ignoring my question.

Fernando and I find a spot under a shady tree and sit as we enjoy our pies.

"I've tried hard to bribe Tim into giving me the secret recipe for the Lucky Dog pies, but haven't had any luck yet."

"I don't blame him. It's a trade secret. Desserts like this are the reason the diner is so popular, and the customers keep returning." I lick the last bit of filling off my fork. "So good." I sigh in contentment. "This reminds me of the pie my grandma used to make."

Her house was a colonial-style home with bright-blue shutters and a matching front door. Whenever she was cooking, she'd leave the front window open. As you approached the house, the smell of a fresh pie or whatever else was in the oven would hit you. "I wonder if my mom still has the recipe," I muse.

"If she does, would *you* be willing to share it?" Fernando prods.

"Sure, but there's not really anything special about it. It's a recipe that came from one of her favorite cookbooks."

"That's even better. It's been tried and tested." He finishes his own pie and places the plate on the ground. "If I were to go online, sure, I could find a million different recipes, but sorting through them is like diving blindly into a pool. The only way to see if they're any good is to test them."

"You don't trust the reviews on a site?"

"Nope. I've been burned before."

My body shakes with laughter.

"It's true. Last year, for instance, I found five different recipes for a basic lemon loaf. They all had a four-star rating or better. I tried them all to see which one was best."

I picture Fernando working in a kitchen as if he's conducting a serious science experiment with each recipe. "And? What was wrong with them?"

"They were either too sweet or too artificial tasting. Ask Tim, even he agreed."

"I'll take your word for it. I don't bake." Suddenly, my phone begins to ring. I fish it out of my purse and see Daph's name on the screen. I'm half tempted to ignore it. I've been enjoying my time with Fernando and don't want it to end. But I did make a promise to her. I reluctantly swipe to answer. "Hi, Daph."

"Ava! You won't believe it." I pull the phone back a half inch from my ear. My sister sounds like a chipmunk with how excited she is. "I found three antique writing desks that are in great shape for cheap! The only thing is, we may have to make a few trips from here to storage."

Funny, I don't remember any desks being on the list. This is why Daph keeps having to rent storage units. They're too crammed full of stuff. She buys things she thinks she'll use on future projects. At this rate, she'd do better if she rented a small warehouse. "Will they fit in my truck bed?"

"I hope so. One might be a little tight, but I have the trailer we can attach to it at the storage site."

"Okay." I sigh. "I'll meet you in a few minutes."

"Thanks!"

Hanging up on Daphne, I look to Fernando. "Your sister?" he asks.

I nod. "I have to go."

"No problem. I should get going too. I have a few errands to run on my way home." He gets up and practically takes all my weight as he pulls me up to my feet as if I'm a marionette puppet. How much can this guy bench press?

"It was nice seeing you again. Thanks for letting me cut to the front of the line."

"It was my pleasure, Ava. I'll see you tomorrow." His hand lingers a little longer than necessary. As he steps back, his fingers brush lightly over mine, sending a zing up my arm.

"See you then," I say softly.

He grins and starts whistling to himself as he strolls out of the market area and toward the parking lot.

I stare at his retreating form, admiring his powerful stride and the way his bubble butt shifts side to side. My phone chimes again, bringing me back to reality.

Daphne: The guy I bought the desks from just added a sofa and a side table for free! This is my lucky day!

That's right. I was helping Daph before a certain Spanish man waylaid my thoughts. I'd better move it before she buys more stuff.

Chapter Four

On a whim the next morning, I swing by Norma's Cafe on my drive into Sequoia Valley and pick up few boxes of bagels, some cream cheese, and two large thermoses of coffee for our clients, Fernando, Vicki, and me to enjoy.

Between the blueberry, cinnamon raisin, cranberry orange, everything, and plain options, there should be something for everyone. Hopefully Fernando likes one of them. At least I know Vicki will eat anything.

I pull into the parking lot and climb out of the car around six-thirty. The clinic won't start until eight, but it takes about an hour to get everything set up. I rub my hands over my forearms. It's about fifty degrees. Many of the leaves have fallen from the trees around me. There's a thin layer of tule fog in the air that'll burn off by the afternoon. I have a zip-up fleece jacket over my scrubs and could still use another layer.

Walking around to the other side of my truck, I pull open the door and shuffle the boxes around as a blue sedan pulls up alongside me. Fernando is in the front seat. He removes his sunglasses and rolls down the driver's side window. His eyes are lit up with excitement. "Good morning, Ava! Or should I say Dr. Brown?"

His hair is slightly damp from the shower. A few notes of his aftershave hit my nose. It's a clean scent—cardamom or amber, I think. "Hi, Fernando. Ava is fine. You're here early."

"I was up at my usual time. I can't ever sleep in. I hit the gym, then figured I'd play some games on my phone until you got here. But since you're early too, you might as well put me to work."

Ah-ha. That's one reason he gets up early. He must be a gym rat. Unless he works there. I can picture him being a personal trainer. Heck, working with him would inspire me, and I haven't even set foot in a gym since high school.

He rolls up his window and exits the car. He's dressed casually in jeans and a short-sleeve black T-shirt, fitted just as snugly as the one he wore yesterday. "Can I help you carry anything in?"

I redirect my attention to my passenger seat. "Please, I have some coffee that's a little heavy. If you could get one of the jugs, I'll come back for the other after I take the bagels in."

Picking up the pink bakery boxes in one hand, I fish the keys to the clinic out of my pocket with the other and unlock the front door. The lights hum to life. I place my load on the receptionist counter, rubbing my hands together. "I should turn the heat on for a bit." Fernando, a step behind me, places the two jugs of coffee next to the boxes. My gaze travels to his bare arms. "Do you want to borrow a jacket? I think there's one in your size in the back."

"No, I'm fine." He waves me off. "It's a lot warmer than we keep it at work." He chuckles.

I place a hand on my hip. "Is that the gym?"

"No. The mafia," he deadpans.

He's thrown me for a loop. I have no idea how to respond to that. I haven't had my coffee yet, and my brain is moving at the speed of a sloth. "Uh . . ."

"I'm only joking. I work in downtown Sequoia Valley."

There goes my personal-trainer theory. I wish he'd stop playing games with me. "No, what I meant was—"

"Hey, Dr. B." Vicki enters the building, interrupting us. "Oh, you brought bagels! You rock!" She crosses the room and immediately makes a beeline for the breakfast food. "Have I ever told you you're my favorite boss—oh hi!"

She notices Fernando and stares for several seconds, a hand hovering over the bagel box.

"Good morning." He grins, flashing a cheeky smile and rolling his Rs as usual.

"Vicki, this is Fernando. He's going to be helping us out this morning," I interject.

"Fantastic." She smacks her lips together.

I feel a twinge of jealousy. "Fernando, if you don't mind, can I have you grab our refreshment table? It's in the closet of the exam room we gave Robin the bath in."

"Si, anything you want, Ava."

Vicki's eyes continue to follow him until he's out of sight and earshot, and then she lets out a low whistle. "Is that the guy from the other day? I recognize his voice! I didn't think he'd be so handsome in person." She fans herself. "I can't believe you scored a date with him! Does he have a brother? Or a friend?"

I furrow my brow and glance toward the back door. "Vicki!" I admonish, lowering my voice. "It's not like that.

Our relationship is strictly professional. He's volunteering here today as a way of paying me back for all the help I gave him over the phone. That's all."

"So you're not dating him?" she says slowly.

"No," I answer quickly.

"Would you mind if I asked him out on a date, then?"

I don't know why, but I feel possessive of Fernando. It's not like I'm looking to date anyone. After the Dylan fiasco, it's the last thing I want. "Be my guest," I murmur, forcing a smile onto my face. "But I have no idea if he's single."

The words come out more bitter than I intended. It's not like I have a claim on him. But some irrational part of me wants to pull him aside and say, *Actually, he's helping me today. Maybe he's here for me.* Ridiculous, I know. I don't do spontaneous or bold. "Don't worry. I'll find out," I tell her instead.

"Where would you like this?" Fernando reenters the room.

I point to a spot opposite the door, near the wall over-filled with bags of dry cat and dog food. "Right there would be great."

I watch as Vicki confidently strides up to Fernando, breakfast in hand, and initiates a conversation about his favorite types of animals and whether he has any pets. It's like watching a Hallmark movie meet-cute play out.

My mouth suddenly feels like I've stuffed a bag of sour Warheads into it. I don't know what's wrong with me. This isn't supposed to matter. I can't watch. I need to get away. "I'm gonna go and look for the tablecloth, cups, and other stuff," I announce.

Vicki shoots me a silent "I owe you one for letting us be alone" look, and as quickly as my feet can carry me, I flee to the safety of the back.

Inside the break room, I whip out my phone and decide to spend a few minutes scrolling through Photogram. I pulled out all the supplies we need last night. They're in a box on the counter behind me. The app loads and greets me with some adorable puppy photos, my niece and nephew, Mom's dinner, then finally, Dylan.

I freeze and stare blankly at the snapshot of him standing in front of a white door, dangling a set of keys. The caption reads: *"The next adventure begins now. Couldn't be more excited to be back home again."*

I frown. He arrived in Fort Collins already? And he didn't text me to let me know? I back out of Photogram and pull up my texts. Nope, he didn't. It's not like him. I know things might be a little weird between us after I confessed my feelings for him, but I didn't think the dynamic would change so quickly.

Leaning against the door, I take a few slow, deep, steadying breaths. I fight the urge to send him a text. I can't get worked up about this. Maybe he was just busy or too tired. He's had to drive for three days straight, after all. Yeah, that has to be it. I'm still hurting deeply, but I do want us to continue being friends.

A couple minutes later, in a slightly better headspace after my second cup of coffee and a few Reese's Pieces from my secret candy stash, I reenter the lobby. Vicki is sitting behind the computer, while Fernando is laying out some clipboards and pens on another folding table that's been set up opposite the door.

"Did you find everything?" Vicki asks without looking up.

"I did. Took a little while though." I set the box of supplies on top of the table. "We'll need to pick up more utensils before next month. I raided the break room to make sure we had enough.”

“I’ll add it to the Costco list.”

As I begin to open the tablecloth, Fernando slides up next to me. There’s some heat rolling off his body. No wonder he prefers short sleeves. “What’s next, Dr. B?”

“The plan is to cover this.” I gesture to the table. “Then set up the food and have Vicki give you a brief crash course on how to sign people in.”

Hearing this, my receptionist looks up, cocking her head to the side. “And what am I going to be doing?”

“You’ll be my tech.”

“Yes! Finally!” She fist-pumps. “Dr. Conti never let me do anything, but you can count on me, boss! I’m ready.”

“I won’t have to use a computer, will I?” Fernando’s large eyes widen with concern.

“No.” I shake my head. “Clinics are usually just good ol’ fashion paper and pens. A lot of the people today we’ll only see as a one-off. Your job will be to make sure all the paperwork is filled out to make it easy for Vicki. She’ll be the one ringing the clients up, processing payments, and recording the vaccine info. The next time you’re here though, we’ll add in the computer,” I joke, fully expecting this to be his one and only time he volunteers.

He wipes his brow with mock relief. “Sí, next time. I’ll be ready.”

“Come on, Nando, we only have about fifteen minutes ’til the doors open.” Vicki gently pushes him toward the reception area.

I can’t believe Vicki’s already given him a nickname. I shake my head and wander back into exam room one.

"I'd count today as a major win, Dr. B," Vicki exclaims as we sit in the lobby munching on some of the leftover bagels.

"What was the final count?" I ask.

"Thirty-four. We had twenty-six dogs and eight cats."

"That is a good turnout," I agree, happy to finally sit after being on my feet for most of the morning and afternoon. I've definitely got all my steps in for the day. Another reason I don't need a gym membership.

"It felt a lot busier than that." Fernando sips on his coffee. "I could've sworn you helped a hundred patients."

"I'd need to clone myself for that." I laugh. "I think it might've felt busier to you because the reception area was full the entire time. When there's that many animals around, it's chaotic."

Vicki nods. "Totally."

"Do you have a date in mind for the next clinic?" Fernando asks.

I glance at the wall calendar. "Um, probably the second Sunday in January."

"We aren't doing a clinic in December?" Vicki frowns.

"No. I'll tell you all about it tomorrow."

She shrugs, surprisingly not asking more. As my gaze follows her, I notice her watching Fernando with longing eyes as he checks his phone. Ah-ha. She's too preoccupied to have processed what I said.

"If the date changes, Ava, let me know." He glances up from the screen. "I've saved the weekend for you."

Hearing him say that warms my body. "We haven't scared you off? Are you sure you want to come back after today?" I stand and stretch, brushing a few crumbs off my pants.

"No. Even if it was hectic, it was still fun. I'll be back." My stomach flutters in delight. He stands too, tossing his cup into the trash. "I need to get going. I wish I could stay and help clean up, but . . ."

I place a hand on his shoulder. "You've done more than enough. Thanks again for everything."

"It was my pleasure."

Our eyes lock, and for several long moments, I wonder if there's a thunderstorm headed our direction because my body feels like it's filled with static electricity.

It's only when the sound of Vicki's voice fills the room that we break apart. "Boss lady, I'm going to reconcile the receipts. Do you mind if I leave a little early, too, when I finish?"

"No, um, that's fine." My cheeks sear with heat. I hope she didn't notice us. "You've given up a lot of your weekend already."

"Adiós, ladies." Fernando waves and exits the clinic.

"Bye," Vicki calls out, watching him through the front window as he slides into his car and drives away.

"Did you have any luck scoring a date with him?" I ask as I close the box of leftover bagels and screw the lid on top of the coffee jug.

"No." Vicki's shoulders hunch. "That gorgeous hunk of a man said he isn't on the market right now. I knew there was a good chance he'd be taken, but I was still hoping I had a shot." She exhales deeply. "At this rate, I'll never find a boyfriend."

A part of me is gleeful that I won't have to worry about Fernando and Vicki becoming an item. But I'm also disappointed that he's taken. Another part of me *kind* of wanted to ask him out too. "You'll find someone, Vicki. Don't worry."

"I hope so. I'm tired of being the third wheel whenever I go out with my friends." She sits down at the computer and prints out an end-of-day report.

"Do you want to take any of the leftovers home with you? Or should I leave them in the break room?"

"Leave them here. If I take them to my apartment, my roommates will eat up whatever's left before I get up in the morning. At least if they're here, I'll have breakfast, snacks, and maybe even lunch for a day or two."

I arch an eyebrow. "I don't pay you *that* poorly that you have to eat like a college kid, do I?"

"No, boss lady, you pay me well." Her eyes widen. "I just have expensive taste. I spent my next three paychecks treating myself to VIP concert tickets, a cute outfit, and a hotel." She counts on her fingers. "I had to cut back somewhere to pay my bills, and this month, it's the food department."

"Well, if it ever gets so bad you're sick of Top Ramen, let me know. I'm happy to spring for lunch." I'm poor too, but I don't want my one and only employee to starve.

"Thanks, Doc."

Over the next hour, I clean up. Vicki heads home, and soon I'm alone. It's about four p.m. by this point. Sitting in my office as I take a break, I open my phone and check my texts again. Nothing.

Why am I torturing myself? Dylan will text me when he's good and ready. I rub my temples. A headache begins to form at the base of my skull.

"Dr. B?"

I jump at the sound of Fernando's voice. My hand flies to my chest. As I glance behind me, I see the man leaning casually against the door frame. "Fernando, you scared the crap out of me." My pulse is still racing at the speed of a jackhammer.

"Sorry," he says. "I tried calling your name a few times, but I guess you didn't hear me. I forgot these." He holds up a pair of sunglasses. "Are you still cleaning?"

"Yeah, but I'm almost done." I quickly stand and pick up the trash bag that I set to the side. "I just need to take this out to the dumpster on my way to my car and lock up."

He tucks the sunglasses into the collar of his shirt. "I'll walk out with you."

I pop a hand on my hip. "Didn't you have somewhere you needed to be?"

The faintest patch of pink appears on his cheeks. "Not really. Sundays are my catch-up day. I, uh, wanted to get away from Vicki. She's a lovely woman, but . . ."

"She made you uncomfortable with her flirting," I guess. "Well, don't worry, she got the message that you're, quote, 'off the market.'"

"That's a relief."

The way he says it makes me wonder if he was telling the truth or if he was lying. Is he really single?

Wait. No. I don't want to know. This isn't what I need right now.

I grab my purse, sweater, keys, and the trash as we exit my office for the front. "If she made you uncomfortable, you should've said something. She's a big girl. She can handle it."

"I didn't want to be rude."

I wave him off. "Well, for future reference, you don't have to be nice. Being direct with Vicki is the best way to get a message through."

"Noted."

Outside, the air has warmed since this morning. The stores on the other side of the mall are hopping with people shopping for holiday supplies at Hobby Land. They have a week to go before the Thanksgiving.

"Thanks again for all your help today," I say as I lock the front door.

"You've already said gracias to me more times than I can count. You don't need to say it again." Fernando winks.

A warm, fuzzy feeling envelops me. I open the lid off the trash and toss the black bag inside, then squirt a little hand sanitizer on my hands and rub them together. The scent of pineapple and mango fills the air.

"I, uh, guess I'll see you in January. You're going on your trip home soon, right?" My mind has gone blank. I suddenly have no idea what to say to him.

He places the sunglasses on the bridge of his nose. "Sí. In a week."

"Well . . . travel safe."

"Thanks."

He walks me to my truck. I open the door and slide inside. Alone, I'm able to exhale. Some of the tension leaves my shoulders. "At least I played it cool," I mutter.

I click my seat belt on and insert my key into the ignition. Turning it over, I hear the sound of it catching, but not the roar to life I'm used to. As I glance down to the dashboard, sure enough, the orange warning light for the engine is glowing. No repair shop in town is going to be open on a Sunday. Looks like I may have to call Daph for a ride.

<h1 style="text-align:center">Chapter Five</h1>

My thoughts are interrupted by the sound of Fernando tapping on the driver's window. Since I can't roll it down, I open the door.

"Do you have a problem, Ava?"

Reluctantly, I nod. "I think the battery's dead."

"That's no bueno." His eyes flicker from my car to his. "I have cables in my trunk. Do you want me to try jumping it?"

"That'd be great. That way I can at least get it to the garage on the other side of town. We don't have decent roadside service up here like we did back in Colorado."

"I learned that lesson the hard way. I had a flat my first week here. I found out pretty quickly it's better if I fixed the issue myself," he says.

"Do you know how to fix cars?"

"Not everything, but enough. My abuelo owned a garage. Growing up, I helped him out over the summers and picked up a couple of skills."

"I wish I could do stuff like change a tire. My dad tried to teach me when I started driving, but I'm hopeless with it.

I can operate on any animal, but give me a car and all I can do is use my phone to call someone else."

An image of Dylan appears in my mind. The last time I had a major problem, he was the person I called. It was actually one of the few times we got into a major argument. He didn't like the fact that I still drive the same car I've had since high school, calling it a safety hazard. He may or may not have been right.

As long as my truck is kept in decent running condition, I don't see a reason why I have to give up on it. We didn't speak for a few days. That was the longest period of time we'd gone being mad at one another. Until now.

"Do you mind popping the hood?" Fernando asks.

"Sure." I reach under the dash.

"Gracias. Let's take a look at what's going on." I watch as he walks to the front, props the hood upright, and leans forward to inspect the engine. "You've got an interesting mix of parts," he calls out. "How old is this truck?"

"Twenty or twenty-five years? It was my dad's before it was mine. I had it in North Carolina and Colorado before here."

He lets out a low whistle. "They don't make them like they used to."

"They don't," I agree.

He inhales sharply. I hear him muttering under his breath.

"What? Did you find something?" I stumble out of the driver's seat and to the front.

Fernando nods grimly. "It's not your battery." He points to a crevice and some gears. "It looks like your timing belt snapped."

I stare, not having a clue if that's an easy fix or not. "Uh . . ."

"The timing belt keeps all the parts of the engine running in sync. When they get old, snapping is common. You just need a new one. Everything else looks like it's in good shape."

"That's a relief." I rub the back of my neck. I just hope it doesn't cost an arm and a leg to fix. It's never the parts that cost a ton, it's the labor.

"Unfortunately, that means your car will have to be towed to a garage." Fernando unlatches the hood and closes it. "It's not drivable without the part."

My heart sinks. I'll have to rent a car to get through the week. Another expense I didn't account for. Daphne and Brian need their vehicles for work. I can't see my parents lending me theirs. Mom does a lot of volunteer work and won't want to cancel anything.

"Can I give you a ride home or anywhere else?" Fernando asks.

"I've already taken up so much of your day." I sigh deeply. "I'll call my sister."

"Ava, it's fine. Like I said earlier, I really didn't have any plans today." He leans against the car. "I'm already here. Let me make things a little easier for you."

Do I take him up on the offer or do I refuse like a normal polite person? It's an internal tug of war. I *hate* being an inconvenience on him. But I'd like to get out of here and sort out my transportation for the remainder of the week ASAP.

"Only if you let me buy you lunch so we're even—assuming you haven't had lunch."

"I have, but I wouldn't mind coffee and a dessert."

"Deal."

He flashes me a smile that would make me buy whatever toothpaste he was selling. I dry swallow. "Great. Dessert it is."

The tow-truck driver quotes me a three-hour wait. I'm not happy about it, but it's Sunday afternoon and I live in a small town. What are you going to do about it? While we wait, Fernando and I head across the street to Main Street Brews.

"Have you ever been here?" I ask as the hostess seats us in a booth next to the window. It's quiet, and only two other couples are occupying the adjoining booths. Soft piano music plays overhead.

"No, but I've driven by a few times. I usually grab my coffee at Norma's on the way to work." He cracks open a menu and studies it. "What's your favorite thing to order?"

"This time of year, it's definitely the pumpkin or pecan pie."

"That good, huh?" He arches an eyebrow and glances over the top of the menu. "How would you compare it to what the Lucky Dog serves?"

"Um . . . I guess I'd say it's a dead heat."

Fernando chuckles. "I'll have to let Tim know he's got some competition."

"How long has he worked at the diner?" I ask, wondering if what his friends do might give me a hint at what Fernando's job is. He's mentioned working with Gemma.

"I have no idea, but I can tell you it's not his day job. Tim's a middle-school teacher."

"Oh." Another theory out the door. Fernando seems to have a calm demeanor that's great for being around kids, but he doesn't strike me as the teaching type. Especially when he's taking a month-long vacation. "Why was he working in a food truck if he's a teacher?"

"Tim's one of the Lucky Dog's best customers. He's good friends with the owner too. Last fall, the guy asked if he wanted to become an investor. He was thinking about expanding into the food truck scene."

I blink. "And Tim said yes?"

Fernando nods. "Mm-hmm. Once the truck was bought, Tim got curious and wanted to see how it all worked. So he jumped in one weekend to help out."

"And . . . he liked it?" I guess.

He nods again. "Thought it was a blast. Now he and Gemma work one weekend a month on the truck. Just for fun."

"That's too funny."

He glances over the menu again. "Have you ever tried the apple pie here?" he asks.

"Yeah, but it's been a while," I admit.

He snaps the menu closed, eyes sparkling with mirth. "Then we should refresh your memory." He drums his fingers against the table. "What if we order one of everything on the seasonal menu. That is if you don't mind splitting them."

"Sure." I take a sip of water. Seeing all the pies in the display case when we walked in made my mouth water. I'm hungry and I have no shame. I'm totally willing to try some of everything. After all, pies are a much better lunch than the mac and cheese I was planning to make.

A waitress approaches us. "Hi. How y'all doing today? Can I get ya started with anything?"

"I'd like to try that apple cider latte." Fernando hands

back his menu. "And one of every pie on the seasonal menu."

"And you, ma'am?"

"A pumpkin spice latte please. No food for me. We're splitting."

The waitress jots everything down and promises she'll be right back with our order, extra plates, and cutlery. In total, we're about to sample eight different pies. Thank goodness my scrubs have a stretchy waistband.

"Whatever we don't finish, I'll take back to the office. Vicki will love it," I joke.

"That's thoughtful of you." Fernando opens a napkin and spreads it on his lap.

"Not really. It's more that she loves free food."

"She sounds like some of my coworkers. The high schoolers are always looking for leftovers from the weekend birthday parties."

We both laugh. Then he excuses himself to use the bathroom.

So he does work with kids. Hmm. What type of job would have insanely early hours and involve teenagers and birthday parties? I stare out the window, watching some of the traffic on Main Street pass by. Could it be a place like Chuck E. Cheese?

My brain conjures an image of Fernando in a giant mouse costume, roller skating around the restaurant from table to table. I shake with silent laughter. As amusing as that is, being the top mouse wouldn't be a job that pays enough to be a full-time career. Unless he's a manager or franchise owner. That's a possibility.

Just as Fernando returns, the waitress rolls up with a small cart holding our desserts. "Here ya'll are. I have the boysenberry, the pecan, the sweet potato, the peach crumble, the pumpkin, the Dutch apple, the triple berry, and the mince pie."

My eyes discreetly rove Fernando's body as he moves his arms, organizing our plates. I take in how his biceps flex and extend through the fabric of his shirt. They're large enough to impress a Marine sergeant drill instructor. It strikes me that Fernando would fit right in with the buff male vets from the Lake Wakahanra Animal Hospital. Is he actually a vet? Could he have been playing me the entire time to get the inside scoop on my clinic?

"These look delicious! Good call on the pies," he says, flashing me a schoolboy grin. It's cheeky and unassuming—the same look he gave me the day we met. My breath hitches. No, he can't be a spy. I'm positive he didn't know what to do with his friend's cat.

"Would you like some whipped cream?" the server asks.

"No, thank you," Fernando and I both answer at the same time.

"I don't blame you. If you need anything else, let me know."

My attention returns to our food. I stare at our selection with wide eyes and wonder if perhaps we are being too ambitious. "I think my eyes might've been bigger than my stomach."

"That problem will be solved once you take a bite of each. Don't feel like you have to eat all of them, just pick your favorites. The rest, like you said, can go to Vicki or to the teens at work." Fernando meticulously cuts each slice in half with the precision of a surgeon. "Shall we go from sweet to savory or savory to sweet?"

"Savory to sweet, you neanderthal. Who eats sweet to savory?" I answer without thinking. My hands fly to my mouth. Oops.

"I do." He winks. "But this time, we'll do it your way." He reaches for the pumpkin first. "On the count of three. Uno. Dos. Tres."

Our forks slice through the adjoining edges of the pie like putty and I take a small bite. I taste it all, the nutmeg, the cinnamon, the pumpkin puree. It's a symphony of flavors in my mouth.

"I don't think I want to eat anything else. This is so good." I groan, remembering why this dessert is my favorite.

"Then it's yours." Fernando scoots the plate closer to me. "You don't have to sample the others, but it might be fun to." He takes a sip of water. "I have to agree with you. This is one of the best pumpkin pies I've ever had. It's light and tastes homemade."

"You might even be able to get the recipe from them," I tease.

"Maybe."

We try each of the remaining pieces. Fernando declares he likes the mince best, with the Dutch apple coming in second. We ask the waitress to box up everything else while we sit and finish our favorites.

"So, Ava, I wanted to ask you earlier . . . I'm curious, why are you skipping your December clinic? Is it too much with Christmas?"

"No." I set my fork down and sigh. "I've been talked into taking a vacation by my sister."

"Vacation? That's usually a good thing." He cocks his head to the side. "You make it sound like a punishment. You clearly work hard. You deserve some time off."

"A day or two, sure. But two weeks? That would be the longest stretch of time I've taken off in . . . let's just say a long, long time."

I flash back to the visits Dylan and I took to every bank

in the Central Valley when we were ready to open the place. There were only two institutions willing to offer a start-up loan to two vets who had only just graduated from veterinary school. And only one that offered us an interest rate we could stomach.

We ended up taking it, but it didn't cover everything. That's where Brian came in. He gave us the best deal we could ever hope for—no interest. Brian's generosity is what allowed us to pay off that bank loan in three years. And what allowed me to be able to buy Dylan's share of the business.

Fernando's large brown eyes take a moment to appraise me.

"I know I'm being silly. The person I'm planning to ask to fill in for me is a rock star. She has more experience than me. I shouldn't be worried."

"I think your fears are natural. It's hard to give up control of something you've worked so hard for."

I pick up my fork and shuffle a few crumbs around the plate. "The truth is, I don't really want to go at all."

"Then why are you? I'm sure your sister would understand."

"Probably, but I know she's right. A change of scenery is the best thing for me right now. So much has been going on lately that I'm on the verge of burning out." I give Fernando a brief rundown of how Dylan and I started the clinic from the ground up as partners and how I recently acquired full ownership. I gloss over the part about my love life crashing and burning. "The transition is finished. There are still a few loose ends to tie up, but Vicki can handle them."

"It sounds to me like you've made up your mind."

I rub the back of my neck. "Huh . . . I guess I have."

Fernando takes a long sip from his latte, then places his cup down and changes the topic. "Have you decided on where you're going to spend your vacation?"

"A little," I admit. "I've been thinking about a safari in South Africa, but for my first time outside the States, I think it's too ambitious. So for now, I'm focused on somewhere in Europe."

"That's a smart choice." He takes a bite of the apple pie. "Let me know if you have any questions. I've been to every country on the continent."

"I forgot you said you used to travel a lot for work." I take a bite and chew slowly. "Maybe I will pick your brain. If you were gonna recommend the best country for a travel novice to visit, what would it be?"

"That's a trick question. Travel is personal. Where you go depends on your interests and your comfort zone." He relaxes against the back of the booth. "When I first started on the cruise ship, I'd get anxious whenever we arrived in a port city where I'd have to speak English. Which is most of Europe." He laughs.

I blink a few times. "But your English is so good!"

"It is now, but it wasn't when I was twenty." He shakes his head. "Learning basic English in school is one thing, but when you're suddenly asked to use it around native English speakers, you realize how little you actually know. Thankfully, being forced to use it nearly every day helped me learn fast."

I sip my pumpkin latte and smack my lips together. Fernando has some good points to think about. I have some high school Spanish at my disposal, but I don't want to worry about not being able to communicate with the locals. I'll be nervous enough traveling solo.

"How about we do it this way: Off the top of your head, name three cities. Ready? Vamos." He points to me.

"Um . . ." A catalog of images floods my mind. "Paris, Rome, London, and Barcelona."

"That's four," he jokes.

"I know, but you put me on the spot." I laugh nervously. I hadn't meant for Barcelona to slip out. I don't want him to think I've picked a city in Spain just because of him. Even though I have.

"If you choose any one of those four cities, you won't be disappointed. They each have something for everyone."

"Like what?"

"Hmm . . . in Paris, it's definitely the food. There are three bakeries on the Rue Monge in the fifth arrondissement that have the fluffiest croissants, and in the sixth arrondissement near . . ."

As I sit here and listen to Fernando's vivid descriptions, I start to daydream and picture myself eating and sightseeing my way through each locale.

"And in Barcelona there are just as many things to see and do, but if I were you, I'd consider spending time on Spain's west coast, near cities like Granada and Toledo . . ."

He glows as he describes the architecture, the people, and all the other amazing things Spain has to offer. He clearly loves his home country. And his enthusiasm is rubbing off on me. Spain now sits at the top of my list. It looks like I'll be booking my tickets as soon as I get home.

Chapter Six

Later that night, as I lie in bed scrolling through blog posts and videos of people who have traveled to Spain, an alert pops up on the top of my screen that Dylan has posted on Photogram. I shouldn't click it, but I can't help myself.

The page reloads and I inhale sharply. The lighting is dim. Dylan is dressed casually in his normal jeans and button-up shirt. A five o'clock shadow graces his face. It's a look he pulls off so well and still sends my pulse racing. His eyes are looking directly at the camera as he sits on a bar stool at one of our favorite former haunts in Fort Collins, toasting the camera. I'd recognize the backdrop of colorful bottles anywhere.

I scroll down the page and read his caption: *"Treating myself after a long day at CSU with the company of @queenofvultures. Can't imagine a better way to spend the night. Here's to the start of something special."*

Under Dylan's comment is a comment from the Queen of Vultures that reads. *"I've waited so long for you to be back here. Can't wait to see how our adventures together unfold.*" At the end, she's added heart emojis.

My phone falls from my hand. I have so many questions. Who is this Queen of Vultures? Just what do these heart emojis mean?

I click on her Photogram account. It's set to private, but I can still see that her name is Rainy and that she's a vet, vulture advocate, mountain biker, and dog mom. Her profile picture is small, but I can make out that she has shoulder-length electric-blue hair and brown eyes.

Okay. So this Queen of Vultures, Rainy, is somebody Dylan must work with. The research position he's taken is studying vultures. But what about the hearts?

I read her comment again. *"I've waited so long for you."* My stomach sinks. Is Dylan romantically involved with her? Is she his type? I frown. Of all the women I've seen him date, nobody has come remotely close to looking like Rainy. She doesn't tick the tall, model-esque box. She's a vet, just like me. And a dog mom, also just like me.

Ugh, I have to stop this. I'm starting to obsess over Dylan to an unhealthy level. I need to get him out of my head. He doesn't want me. He told me point-blank there will never be an *us.* The only person who's miserable and suffering is me.

I rub my temples. It's like the inside of my head is a Swiss clock and there are two figures inside striking a rubber mallet against the base of my skull. I climb out of bed and walk out of my room to the kitchen. Max trails behind me, his paws clicking against the wooden floor.

As I fill a glass with water from the tap, I bend over and scratch his ears with one hand. The soothing motion relaxes me. I'm beginning to wonder if Dylan even cared all that much about our friendship. He still hasn't texted me. I know it's a two-way street, but he's the one who said he'd get back to me. Clearly, I'm not a priority anymore. Maybe I was always just a business partner to him. A means to an end.

If I want to help myself, I need to completely disconnect myself from all that's going on. Setting my cup on the counter with a thud, I march back to my bedroom, grab my phone, and one by one, delete each app.

Opening a blank text message, I type to Daphne:

Ava: You'll be proud. You wanted me to go off the grid for this vacation. So I am. I just deleted all my social media apps. The cleanse starts now.

I don't expect to hear from my sister. It's late and she's probably fallen into bed, exhausted from working a full-time job and caring for her family.

Now I only have one more task to do. I google plane tickets and come up with one airline that's about a grand cheaper than all the others. Pulling up the Pacific Skyways web page, I plug in the dates for a week from now. My hand hovers over the "Book Now" button. Pacific Skyways used to be a decent airline, but their reviews lately say otherwise.

Is it worth taking a chance? I blow out air. A thousand dollars is a lot of money. Especially when my budget is tight. What I save could go toward my hotel, food, train tickets, or souvenirs.

Decision made. I'll do it. Taking a deep breath, I click the button. The screen changes, flashing a confirmation number. I've just booked myself a non-refundable round-trip business-class ticket to Spain. I'll worry about figuring out the rest of my trip in the coming days.

"Well, Max, there's no going back now. I'm really doing it. I'm going on vacation."

He barks and wags his tail as if he's telling me, "About time."

Monday morning, I receive a reply from my sister.

> Daphne: Good girl. Not accessing social media is hard at first, but don't give in to the urge to download anything again.

> Ava: Is this coming from personal experience?

> Daphne: Duh. I had to do a social-media cleanse when the kids were born. I wanted them to be the focus, not me taking pictures of how cute they were and sharing them with my internet friends.

> Ava: Huh. I never knew that.

> Daphne: Now you do.

> Ava: How long did you last?

I stare at the screen as three dots blink. Daphne has decent self-control, but she's not as strong as I am. Her phone is always attached to her hand, as if it's an extension of her body.

> Daphne: About a week.

I snort.

Ava: At least that's something.

Daphne: In my defense, I needed access to Photogram for work.

I roll my eyes. My sister took eight weeks off work when my niece was born, but I choose not to remind her of that.

Ava: I have one more thing to share. I booked my airline ticket last night too!

Daphne: Oh! Where are you going?

Ava: *Spanish flag emoji*

Daphne: *Big eyes emoji* You're going overseas?

Ava: Yup. *Grinning emoji* I'll tell you about it later. Can you meet for lunch at 12?

Daphne: Sure. I'll bring something to your office.

Ava: Sounds good.

Tucking my phone away, I enter the break room and find Vicki munching away on a bagel.

"Morning, boss. You ready for a new week?" she asks in a cheery tone.

"I am," I answer honestly.

She sits up taller. "You're in a good mood. Did you have a double shot of espresso in your coffee? Or meet a hot barista on your way in?"

"No, it's nothing like that." I shake my head, chuckling. "I booked myself a vacation."

"Way to go, Dr. B!" She reaches over and we high-five one another. Our hands make a satisfying slap. "Cool beans. So does that mean we're closing while you're gone?"

"No. I sent a text to my friend Dr. Owens this morning. If everything goes according to plan, she'll be covering for me the last two weeks in December." I bite the inside of my cheek and force myself not to wonder what'll happen if she says no since it's such short notice, and I lose out on the money from my airline ticket.

"You deserve it, boss lady. Since I've been here, I don't think you've ever taken a day off. Even when you were sick."

"I haven't," I admit, running my hand over the back of my neck. "This is my first one in a long time. And I'm hoping I can count on you to keep everything running smoothly. Dr. Owens will be in charge of the exams, but you'll be in charge of everything else."

"You betcha! I'm your right-hand woman."

"There's one other thing. My sister is going to be working on redecorating the reception area and our branding. I know you've mentioned wanting to shadow her before."

"Yes, yes! I'd *love* to work with her. Even if it's for a short time." Vicki squeals and jumps up and down. "Your sister is one of the hottest interior decorators in the state. Have I ever mentioned it was one of my majors for two whole semesters in college?"

"Was that before or after political science and psychology?" I ask. Like Daphne, Vicki is another free spirit. They should get on well. They're a lot alike.

"Neither. It was after biology and before graphic design, but close enough. Good memory."

"It comes with the territory of being a vet."

I let Vicki know I'm planning to be gone beginning

next Monday and not to book any more appointments until Dr. Owens confirms her availability.

The remainder of the morning passes in a blur. I take care of a parrot in need of a beak trim, meet a newly adopted pug who needs a routine exam, and give a warm bath to a snake that's had trouble shedding its skin.

"Just adding a humidifier to his tank will make all the difference. Any brand will do," I advise my client on the way out.

"Got it, Doctor. Thanks again for fitting us in today. You're the only vet in the area who does snakes."

"Of course. I'm more than happy to help. If you know anybody else who needs an all-species vet, send them my way."

"I will!" The snake's owner picks up her pet and lets it coil around her neck.

They pass Daphne entering the clinic as they're leaving, causing my sister to turn her head and blinks a few times. "Was that lady wearing a live snake?" she asks.

"Uh-huh."

She shudders. "Why?"

"Why not? Snakes can be great pets." I start listing out a couple reasons just to mess with her. She's been frightened of them since we were kids. "They're super intelligent, they only eat every couple of weeks."

"I know better than to have this conversation with you. You think all animals are amazing."

"I do," I say with a laugh.

She shakes her head and holds up a brown paper bag. "I brought sushi and some bento boxes for lunch. Hope you don't mind. I've been craving California rolls for ages, but Brian doesn't do anything that's fishy."

My brother-in-law is a steak-and-potatoes kind of guy. "You know me, I'll eat anything."

"Where's Vicki?" she asks, setting the bag down on the reception counter.

"At lunch. She had a hair appointment, so I let her go a couple minutes early." Walking over to the door, I lock it and flip the "Open" sign to the "Will Return at 1:30" side.

"How did she take the news about your vacation?"

"She was gung ho." I peek inside the bag and the scent of teriyaki chicken tickles my nose. "All right, you got my favorite dish! We can eat in the break room."

"You only order one thing from Samurai Sushi, it wasn't exactly rocket science. I know the rolls I like won't fill you. You eat like a college student."

We sit down, spread out our lunches, and I fill Daphne in on Dylan and the Queen of Vultures.

"I'll continue to say it every time you bring him up. I'm sure that man was using you," Daphne tells me emphatically. "Does that mean you're finally going to cut him off?"

"Not completely." I play with a bit of rice caught on the edge of the plate. "I've decided if he wants to talk, he can contact me. The ball is in his court."

"Well, it's a start." Daph presses her lips together. "At least a vacation will get your mind off him. I just never thought you'd go all *Eat, Pray, Love* on me and choose Spain of all places. I didn't even know you had a passport."

"I got one last year when Dylan and I were supposed to visit Banff National Park in Canada."

"And you didn't go because . . ."

"His mom needed help moving."

"How convenient." Daphne mutters the word "flake" under her breath, then clears her throat. "Well, I think

Spain is a great choice. It was one of the places Brian and I visited on our honeymoon cruise. We loved it."

"That's right." I snap my fingers.

"Where are you thinking about going?" Daphne pops the last roll into her mouth.

"Fernan—I mean, one of my friends gave me a couple of recommendations. There are the big cities like Madrid and Barcelona. And a few smaller cities like Granada, Toledo, and Seville. I need to figure out how to get around, but I was thinking that—"

Daphne swallows hard and holds up her hand. "Hold on a second, you said your *friend* recommended these places to you?"

"Um, yes?" I sputter.

"As in a *male* friend?"

"Uh . . ." My cheeks begin to burn as if I've been sitting outside in the sun too long.

"Ava. Please tell me you aren't going on this trip with a rebound guy you just met."

I release a breath. "No. It's nothing like that."

My sister relaxes. "Then who is he?"

"Just someone I met a week ago. He needed some help with a friend's cat."

"Uh-huh." She looks me up and down. "How many times have you two spoken? It must have been quite a few. I know you. One, you're on a first-name basis with Ferdinand, and two, there is no way you'd be so casual about taking suggestions from him unless you trust him."

"His name is Fernando," I automatically correct.

Her eyes gleam with mischievousness, challenging me to try and sneak a lie past her. We hold one another's gaze for several seconds before I give in. Daph has always been able to get whatever she wants out of me. She's so darn stubborn and would never back down from a challenge when we were kids.

My shoulders hunch. "We crossed paths at the antiques market on Saturday. And yesterday, we went out for dessert after he helped me out with my monthly clinic. My car wouldn't start, and he offered me a ride. I felt like it was the least I could do."

"I was wondering where your truck was. You could've called me or B for a ride."

"I didn't want to inconvenience you two." I play with a stray piece of hair. "I know how much you have going on. Between soccer, hockey, swimming, and all the other activities the kids do, you guys are always busy."

Daphne stays silent for a few moments. "I'll give this Fernando the benefit of the doubt for now. Just promise me you'll be careful. Guys have motives. They don't do favors without wanting something in return."

"I don't know, he seemed genuine to me."

My sister wrinkles her nose. "Just trust me. I don't want to see you get hurt again."

I close my eyes and shake my head. On this, I'll just have to pretend to agree. "Fine, I'll be careful."

"Good. Now about Spain . . ."

Chapter Seven

"Ma'am, I'm sorry to wake you, but I need you to return your seat to its upright position. We're making our final descent."

I feel my body being gently shaken. I blink a few times and stare up at a flight attendant in a bright-teal uniform, confusion filling my brain before I realize I'm on my way to Spain. I remember being tired and deciding to rest my eyes for a little bit. The flight is supposed to be about thirteen hours. I've never slept that long in my life. But then again, there's a first time for everything.

"Sure," I tell her.

She flashes me a tired but grateful smile as I touch the button on the armrest and adjust the seat as the cabin lights flicker on.

Suddenly, the plane gives a violent shudder. Passengers around me yelp. I grip the sides of my seat tightly and swallow hard as my pulse hammers against my chest. A few seconds later, it happens again.

An intercom dings, followed by a man's voice. "Hi, folks. This is the captain speaking. Apologies about the turbulence, but our radars are showing that it's going to continue being a bumpy ride until we can get down on the ground in Denver. I've asked our flight attendants to remain seated for the duration of the flight. There is a mechanical issue with the plane that needs to be resolved before we'll be able to continue on to our final destination. I'm still waiting to hear back from HQ, but it sounds like we may be stuck there overnight. I'll have more details for you shortly. Thanks for your patience."

I lean my head against the back of the seat. Denver. Of all the places in the world, it has to be Denver. I'm going on this trip to get away and forget about Dylan. Not to get closer to him.

As the bad weather continues to strike the plane, I wonder if the universe is trying to play a sick cosmic joke on me. The plane shakes a third time. I squeeze my eyes tightly together. The sooner we're on stable ground, the better.

Except once we land, the situation goes from bad to worse.

First comes the announcement from the flight attendant. "Ladies and gentlemen, if you'd please gather your belongings and exit the plane, you'll receive further directions from the Denver gate agents."

Like a trail of ants invading a picnic, one by one, people retrieve their carry-on bags from the overhead bins and exit the plane a row at a time. The atmosphere is tense and filled with curious whispers and crying babies.

We file into an empty gate area, where there's a rush to claim seats. It reminds me of a game of musical chairs. I'm too tired to deal with it all and opt to sit on the floor against the wall. It's what most of the passengers end up doing since there's about three hundred of us and only a hundred chairs.

From my perch, I watch as about twenty people flock to the lone Pacific Skyways gate agent at the counter, demanding answers to what's going on. I can't hear what he's telling them, but it isn't hard to read his lips. His supervisor is working on it, and everyone needs to be patient.

An hour passes, and everyone's energy intensifies. The pilots and flight attendants trickle off the plane, speaking to one another in hushed tones and avoiding eye contact with passengers as they walk quickly toward the terminal's exit. My heart sinks. They know something is up and don't want to be here when the bad news breaks.

A half hour after that, three additional gate agents arrive to support the poor man who's been fielding questions since we landed. That's when we finally receive the announcement. "Hi, folks, thanks for your patience. If you're here from Pacific Skyways flight 723 with service to Madrid, we regret to inform you that the flight has been canceled."

It's like a bucket of ice water has been dumped over my body. I'm on pins and needles. The gate area is filled with angry shouts and expletives.

"If you'd all form an orderly line, the Pacific Skyways staff will begin the rebooking process and get you on the next available flight to wherever your final destination may be."

"What about a hotel for the night?" a man near the front shouts.

"You aren't sending a replacement plane for us?" a woman cries.

The agent ignores them, hanging up the mic and walking over to the nearest computer. That's when it hits me and everyone else in the gate area that we'd better get in line. The mad scramble begins.

It's a giant mess. The line of three hundred people stretches two gates long. I'm stuck toward the middle back. Another two hours pass, and by this point, we're all tired and hangry. Nothing in the airport is open. It's three in the morning and there are still twenty-five people in front of me. All I want is a nice soft bed.

My eyes rove the gate area, wondering if it's worth continuing to wait. I have no energy. If I pull out my phone and book myself a hotel, all I'd have to do is order a rideshare, and in five to ten minutes, I could be curled up under a nice warm blanket. Except I don't have the spare funds for it. I've already paid a thousand dollars for nonrefundable business class tickets and prepaid for some of my hotel rooms in Spain. I sigh deeply. My neck, lower back, and feet ache beyond belief. I only have to tough it out a little longer.

By four a.m., I'm two people away from the front. My eyelids and limbs are heavy. I contemplate sleeping on a row of seats in the gate area when this is all over, like the guy over there with a red hoodie and noise-canceling headphones, snoring his head off. Jealousy floods my system. I want that to be me.

"Ma'am? Are you ready?" I hear a woman's exhausted voice say.

I realize it's finally my turn! I stumble forward as if my legs belong to a baby giraffe and shove my passport and ticket onto the counter. "Sorry, yeah. Here you go."

The agent yawns, then swipes my passport and starts typing. In a monotone voice, she says, "On behalf of Pacific Skyways, we apologize for any inconvenience today's canceled flight may have caused you. Your final destination is Madrid, is that correct?"

I fight my own yawn and nod. "Yeah, it is."

She clicks a few more keys. "Well, it looks like the next available flight I have for you is Thursday night."

The shock of her words sends a rush of adrenaline through my body. I'm suddenly alert. "That's *four* days from now! You don't have anything sooner? Not even a replacement flight?" I'm keeping a tight lid on my emotions. Right now, I'm about ready to flip a table and kick down all the nearby trash cans.

"No." Her tone is flat. "They're all full."

Jaw clenched, I ask, "What about if I flew in economy instead of business?"

"Oh, I didn't even notice you had a business ticket, just a second." She perks up slightly.

I stop just short of saying something snarky and tell myself she's probably just as tired as me. It's a simple mistake.

"The next business-class opening I have is for next Tuesday."

"That's even worse!"

She shrugs. "Everything is full."

"Then give me a refund. I'll find another airline that can get me to Madrid."

She types on the computer. "Your ticket is nonrefundable," the agent says flatly. "You're only eligible for flight credit."

My brain lets out a banshee scream. I cheaped out on trip insurance. And I stupidly used my debit card instead of my credit card to book my ticket, so I can't do a charge-back for an unused flight.

I guess I could try to use my credit card now to book a

new ticket. But the same thoughts as earlier hit me. A last-minute ticket will cost a fortune. Probably triple or quadruple what my current one cost. Money I don't have.

I pinch the bridge of my nose. "I can't believe I'm even entertaining this, but would the airline pay for however long I'm stuck here in Denver until the flight departs? Or reimburse what I've paid for my hotels?"

"No. We'd only cover a room for tonight and provide you with a fifteen-dollar voucher for a meal here at the airport. For any other expenses you'd like to request reimbursement for, you'd need to contact our customer service department to open a case."

One night and one meal? No wonder my ticket was so cheap. Pacific Skyways doesn't care about its customers. It's the last time I'll fly with them. "What about other cities? I'll settle for anywhere in Spain."

We go back and forth until she finally finds me a business-class seat to Lisbon, Portugal, leaving this evening at ten p.m.

"Since your flight is leaving tonight, Pacific Skyways won't be providing you a hotel room."

To this point I've tried hard to keep my cool, but I've had enough.

"No," I say in a deadly cool tone. "I've been waiting patiently for over four hours for you to take care of me. I'm a business-class customer who paid good money for my seat. I've watched your team send others to local hotels for the night and I deserve the same treatment."

"Ma'am—"

"No." I cut her off. "It's not ma'am. It's *Doctor* Brown." My eyes narrow. "If you can't help me, I'd be more than happy to take it up with your manager." I turn and gesture to the remaining fifty people behind me. "And I'm sure all of them would too."

A few of the people behind me applaud and throw their two cents in. I've always despised entitled people and always try to be kind and understanding, but at this point, I'm beyond caring. My request is reasonable. I need to sleep, eat, and shower.

The agent cringes, but steps away from her computer to speak to a heavyset man in a yellow safety vest, crumpled white shirt, and black slacks leaning against the door that leads to the disabled plane.

I drum my fingers against the counter and send my best annoyed glare in the man's direction. He glances at me, then nods to the agent. Good. We're on the same wavelength. The old Ava would never do this, but the new me is proud. This Ava isn't a pushover. She's got an iron backbone.

I sleep for ten hours, order room service, take my shower, and return to Denver International Airport later that evening. Sleep has revived me. I'm able to think clearly again. My emotions have calmed down, but I'm still livid with Pacific Skyways.

As I arrive at the gate for Lisbon, I have quite a few problems I'm gonna have to tackle. One, I have no idea how I'm going to get from Portugal's capital city to Madrid. I don't even know how far apart they are. I was too tired to care last night. Or rather this morning.

Two, I need to get in touch with my original hotel and let them know I'm still coming but have been delayed.

Three, I need to find an app that can help me learn a few words of Portuguese.

I search for a place to sit and start on my list. Ironically, I pass the same sleeping man in the red hoodie from last night lounging near the corner by the window. The headphones are still in place, but the hood has slipped back. There's no mistaking the dark brown locks and sharp jaw.

I throw my head back and start to laugh at the ridiculousness of it all, receiving a few curious looks from passengers in the waiting area. "Well played, universe. Well played."

Marching over to the man, I tap him on the shoulder. "Hi, Fernando."

Slowly, he turns, peeling off his headphones. A smile pulls across his face, which is coated with a day's worth of stubble. His eyes are red rimmed and bloodshot. "Ava."

"Let me guess, you were on the canceled flight too?"

"Sí, I was."

"I saw you sleeping stretched out on a couple of chairs this morning." I sit down next to him as he removes a duffle bag from the seat beside him. "Have you been here the whole time?"

"Uh-huh." He nods. "I'm like a cat. As long as I have my headphones and something to toss under my neck, I'm good to go. My friends used to make fun of me for it."

I let out a small snort. "I'd consider it a superpower. I'd love to be able to sleep on demand, but I'm the total opposite of you, a light sleeper. Even my dog Max walking against the wooden floor wakes me up."

He chuckles again.

"Why'd you pick to fly to Madrid instead of directly to Barcelona?"

"I *was* booked for Barcelona last Wednesday, but my flight got canceled when I got to the airport," he says.

I wince. I've only been delayed a day. He's been waiting over a week. I guess I'm lucky. It could be a heck of a lot worse. "Two canceled flights in a row?"

He nods. "Now I'm headed to Lisbon. Hopefully, third time's the charm."

"I'm headed there too."

"That's a happy coincidence." Fernando tucks his headphones into his carry-on and glances at his watch. "Are you in the mood to grab some dinner before the flight? We have two hours."

"I'd love to, except I'll just be keeping you company. I'm not in the mood to drop twenty-five bucks on something like a burger and fries. I'll eat on the plane." Sure, the airline gave me a fifteen-dollar voucher last night, but I spent that on a water and magazine from one of the gift shops. It didn't go very far.

"I don't blame you. Airport food is a rip-off. But I was thinking we could go to one of the airport lounges. It's too bad it was closed when the flight canceled. I could've slept there, but at least we can get dinner. Their food is free when we get inside. I haven't flown much this year, but I still have platinum elite status with Pacific Skyways until the end of next month, and I've got two guest passes. It's use them or lose them."

I bite my lip. Free is one of my favorite prices. "If you're sure, I'd be happy to join you."

We stand and Fernando stretches. "Most of the time, it's nothing to write home about, but Denver has a flagship lounge and it's pretty great."

I adjust my backpack and let him lead the way. I've

flown out of Denver plenty of times, but lounges are a brand-new experience for me. "Besides food, what do they have?"

"Unlimited drinks, fast Wi-Fi, showers, and a masseuse."

"A masseuse?" I sputter.

"Uh-huh. If you're a platinum elite or flying first class, you can get a free twenty-minute massage. I take advantage of it every time I can." He laughs.

I have a new theory. If Fernando flies so much, he must be a consultant. I don't know why I didn't consider it earlier. That would explain the travel. And if the head office is on the East Coast, it also explains why he's up at the crack of dawn. It all fits. I pat myself on the back for solving that mystery.

We follow the signs for the Pacific Rim Club and take an elevator up a level. As the doors open, two women sitting behind a large marble desk greet us.

"Welcome," one of them says. "I can help you guys over here. Do you two have your boarding passes and IDs?"

Fernando approaches the counter. "We do." He pulls out a fancy metallic card and hands it to the woman. She swipes it. "And I'd like to use one of my guest passes today."

The woman's cheeks color. "Oh sorry, Mr. Alvarez, but this lounge no longer accepts the guest passes. They were discontinued at the end of September. Unless your friend has a business-class or first-class ticket, she'll have to pay the fifty-nine-dollar fee if she wants to enter."

Fernando's face falls. "I was told the passes were good through the end of the year."

"It's a, er, newer policy the airline implemented."

Another nail in the coffin for Pacific Skyways.

"But I never received any notification."

She hesitates as if there is something she wants to say, but thinks the better of it. I can tell she's been put in a difficult position by her company. It's one of the many reasons I'm grateful to be my own boss.

"Business-class ticket holders can use the lounge?" I ask.

The woman nods.

"I wish somebody had told me that earlier," I mutter under my breath.

"They should've at check-in," she says.

I keep my thoughts to myself and instead place my hand on Fernando's arm. "I appreciate the trouble you're going to for me, but I can use this." I hand over my ticket and passport. "Here."

Crisis averted, we enter the lounge and grab a table near the window overlooking one of the runways. It's a larger place than I'd imagined. In some ways, it reminds me of a mall food court.

Chairs, tables, and a few private booths are spread out across the room. Taking up the entire far wall across from us are the kitchen and cafe area. I see a refrigerator stocked with soft drinks, a barista, two rows of steaming hot dishes, and a dessert bar.

"I'm so sorry about that, Ava, if I had known it would be so much trouble—"

I hold up my hand to interrupt him. "Don't worry about it. It's no big deal. I've never been inside a lounge before and didn't know what I'd be missing. It's more about spending some time with good company."

My gaze travels up to a man in a business suit carrying a steaming plate of spaghetti and meatballs. I can smell the garlic and spices, causing my mouth to water. "But now that we're here, how about giving me a tour. I'm curious about what else is in this place."

"Of course."

As we turn, someone tugs on my bag. "Ava, what are you doing here?" Dylan asks from a nearby table.

Chapter Eight

My eyes widen and my feet refuse to move. It's as if I've been petrified and turned into a statue by Medusa.

"Ava, are you okay?" Fernando asks in a concerned tone. "You're ghost-white."

I open my mouth, but no words come out. From behind Fernando's broad back, Dylan looks up, and for the briefest of seconds, our eyes meet. He looks the same as the day he left Sequoia Valley for Fort Collins, with a little more scruff coating his jawline.

"I'm, uh, just passing through Denver," I say softly. "What about you?"

"I'm here with my girlfriend," he says matter-of-factly. "We're headed to Europe."

Porcupine quills are being jabbed into my skin. If my sister were here with me, she'd tell me to hold my head high and walk away, making sure I'm not giving Dylan the satisfaction of knowing that he's bothering me. But I'm also filled with morbid curiosity. Who is she? How long have they been together? I can't get myself to stop watching him.

"Oh," I manage. "How . . . how long have you guys been together?"

"Officially? Three months, give or take."

"How did you guys meet?" I ask.

"Oh, she interviewed me for the research position."

I frown. Talk about a conflict of interest. I know Dylan is qualified, but it makes me wonder if the reason he was hired was because Rainy was interested in him. Or if he flirted with her to get the job.

I don't have to wait long to meet the mystery woman. A few moments later, the Queen of Vultures joins him at the table. There's no mistaking her electric-blue hair. She's about our age, in her early thirties, but a little shorter than me.

"Friends of yours?" she says, setting down two plates of cookies and stroking his arm in a tender motion.

"Yeah. This is Ava, my business partner from California," he offers.

Business partner. Another ouch. Not even a friend? My heart pounds as hard as golf-ball-sized hail shattering a car windshield.

I wave a hand. "Hi."

Rainy smiles tightly and nods back to me. "Hi."

Tension fills the air as she studies me. Dylan, however, remains oblivious to it as he closes his laptop and pushes it to the side, giving his girlfriend his full attention.

"I was, uh, surprised you didn't text me," I say.

"Oh sorry." He turns his head, glancing at me. "I've been busy. You know how it is. New job. New apartment. There's so much to do and never enough time."

I *do* know how it is, but the photos he's been posting say otherwise. He's had enough time to go out. "Yeah, I get it." I take a deep, steadying breath, my legs shaky as a jellyfish.

Fernando slips his hand into mine and squeezes gently, reminding me he's standing right there.

"Who's this?" Dylan juts his chin out.

I turn my head and stare. "Oh this is, um . . ." My mind has momentarily gone blank.

"Fernando," he says with a stronger accent than normal. "I'm Ava's boyfriend. And we need to get going. It was nice to meet you."

I let him lead me toward the dessert offerings, fingers laced through mine. "An ex?" he says in a tone so low that it's barely audible.

"Sort of." I swallow hard. "It's complicated."

He leans his head right next to my ear. "Do you trust me?"

I hesitate for a moment, then answer, "Yes."

His arm travels up to the small of my back, supporting all my weight. Bringing me into his body, he places a warm, gentle kiss on my mouth. Whoa! This is the last thing I thought he'd ever do!

I melt into his arms, deepening our kiss as my eyes flutter closed, eager for more. His lips are silky soft. I smell the scent of zesty orange and gingerbread. My arms wrap themselves around his neck. It's like I've been wrapped up with the world's softest weighted blanket and I'm so comfortable that I don't want to ever leave.

Eventually, we break apart. Fernando's brown orbs are large and filled with so much warmth, they could heat a freezing room. His voice is raw and throaty. "Let's see if they have some pie. I know how much you love it."

"Mm'kay," I manage, breathless, floating wherever he leads me. My mind has gone fuzzy. All thoughts of Dylan have fallen by the wayside. Fernando may not know it, but he's just spoiled me for all other men. I don't know if anyone could match a kiss like that.

He grabs a tray at the dessert case. "I couldn't stand how they were treating you. For the record, they're watching us. Your ex is probably wondering why he was stupid enough to let you go," he whispers into my ear. "I'm sorry if I crossed the line, but he clearly needed to be put in his place."

I don't bother looking back at Dylan. I don't care. "Don't be." I enjoyed every moment of it. In fact, my body would love it if he gave me another one right now.

"Oh look, they have mince pies! Let's take two. I know I promised you dinner, but there's no rule that says we can't start with dessert first." He winks.

"No, there isn't."

Desserts in hand, we relocate from our original table to a private booth at the opposite end of the lounge, far away from Dylan and Rainy. Having a few minutes to calm down has helped my brain and my body return to reality. Although my nerves are still on edge.

"Thanks for the, um, kiss back there." I pick up my fork and take a bite of the pie.

"You're welcome."

"Seeing Dylan caught me off guard."

"You don't have to explain, Ava. I understand better than you may think." For a moment, Fernando's eyes gloss over, and a flash of sadness passes over his face. It's gone, however, as quickly as it appeared.

"No. I think I should." I take a deep breath. "Dylan isn't technically an ex-boyfriend. He's the guy I used to own the clinic with, and until very recently, was my best friend. Right now, I have no idea where we stand."

"Yeah, I heard his lame excuse about not texting you." He presses his lips together.

"It's weird. We used to text back and forth at least once a day, and then when he left Sequoia Valley for Fort Collins, he forgot all about me." Over pie, and later, soup and sandwiches, I share a few select snippets of my college years to give Fernando a little context on some of the more recent events.

". . . When I finally worked up the courage to tell him how I felt about him, he said I wasn't his type. And that I'd find someone eventually." I rub the back of my neck. "Since then, he's dropped me. It's like eight years of friendship have been erased."

Fernando inhales sharply. "Ouch."

"Yeah." I stack a few of my dirty dishes on top of one another.

"Real friends don't do that. They find a way to work things out," he says, sending a glare in Dylan's direction.

My heart warms at the support. "I don't know anymore. Maybe all this time I've been blind, and we were never as close as I thought we were."

"I agree with your sister on this one." Fernando nods. "This Dylan is a waste of your time. As much as it hurts, I think you should give him the same treatment he's giving you. Cut him off and don't worry about him."

My shoulders hunch. "I've been trying, but it's a lot harder than it looks."

"It is," he agrees. "There's always a lot of emotional baggage involved."

We both sit in heavy silence for a few moments. Another flash of sadness passes through his eyes. I wonder if someone might've broken his heart too.

The couple of times we've hung out, Fernando has

always been kind and considerate. He's the type of person who's easy to talk to and keeps the conversation flowing. And that kiss. My body is still hot thinking about it. It's hard to believe someone like him is single. At least, I think he's single. He never confirmed he's not off the market.

Deciding I'm tired of such a heavy conversation, I change topics. "So Lisbon . . . have you been there before?"

"A few times." He leans back in his seat, relaxing. "My abuela on my madre's side is from Porto, Portugal. I used to visit her a few times a year as a kid before my mom persuaded her to move to be closer to us."

"Since you're the resident expert again, any tips on getting from Portugal to Madrid?" I fold my hands and rest them on the table. "Should I take a plane, train, or bus?"

"If you value your time, flying is the fastest option." He pulls out his phone and shows me a map of Spain. "The two cities are about seven hundred miles apart."

I stare at the long line connecting two black dots on opposite ends of the screen for a few moments, cursing Pacific Skyways again for making me so exhausted yesterday that I missed a small detail like this. Okay, maybe not a small detail. A wooly-mammoth-sized one. "I didn't realize Lisbon was that far away. I was thinking it would be like going from San Francisco to LA, about a six-hour drive."

"If only." Fernando laughs. "The train would be my second choice if I were you. The bus takes too long."

"Hmm, I guess flying it is." I puff out my cheeks. "It's too bad. Now that I'm headed to Lisbon, it seems like a waste to not take advantage of the opportunity to see the city."

He drums his fingers against the tabletop, studying me. "How flexible are your plans?"

"They're pretty open. Aside from the B&B I booked

for Madrid, all the other places I'm staying at are refundable as long as I cancel twenty-four hours in advance."

"Did you book any train or museum tickets?"

"No. I was having trouble figuring out the websites. I was hoping a hotel concierge could do it for me."

"Well, I'm glad you didn't." His Adam's apple bobs up and down. "If you're open to it, I have another idea."

"Oh?"

"How would you feel about spending the day with me? I'd love to show you Portugal's capital city."

"What?" I sputter, knocking my hand into my glass of water and spilling a little on the table. "I can't ask you to play tour guide! You're on vacation too. And a few days late, I might add."

"We're both headed to the same destination, and my parents won't mind if I get into Santa Luz a little later than expected." He waves me off. "Actually, you'd be doing me a favor. Whenever I go home, Mamá lets me hang out around the house for about a day before she puts me to work. There's always a long list of things she wants fixed, cleaned, or built."

I slowly pat the spot of water dry with a napkin. It's tempting. And I want to say yes, but should I? Or am I playing with fire? Is Fernando my rebound guy? "I don't know . . ."

He glances to the other side of the room, then winces. "This isn't a date or anything like that. I just thought . . . well never mind what I thought. I clearly wasn't thinking and—"

To Hades with it. One day won't matter. "Fernando, quit apologizing. I know you're just being nice. You just caught me off guard."

"Does that mean you're game?"

I take a long drink of water. This trip is all about embracing my inner Daphne and learning to loosen up. I can't stress out when my plans change. Especially when they're outside my control. Besides, the last few times Fernando and I have been together, I've had a great time. The thought of spending more time alone with him sets my heart aflutter. "I'll do it."

"Fantástico!" He smiles widely.

We get up and deposit our dirty dishes near the trash cans. We have about twenty minutes before we're supposed to board. Fernando excuses himself and says he'll meet me at the gate. He has an errand he needs to take care of.

As I walk toward the boarding area, I'm relieved to have a little time to myself. My mind has been running on overload the last hour or so. I'm only just processing all that's happened.

I'm taking Fernando's words to heart. I do deserve more. I still can't believe he came to my rescue like that in front of Dylan. That kiss and the warm, dizzying sensations of delight it sent through my body linger at the forefront of my mind. Sigh. That'll live rent free in my brain for a good couple of months.

Finding an empty seat, I set my backpack down and shuffle around a few items. Fernando joins me a couple minutes later. "Did you take care of what you needed to do?" I ask as he slides into the seat next to me.

"Uh-huh." He slips a plastic bag from one of the airport book stands onto my lap. "This is for you."

"Thanks, but you didn't have to get me anything."

"I know, but I wanted to." From another smaller bag, he holds up a pack of cherry-red Swedish Fish. "Don't worry, I got myself something too."

"You didn't go for the chocolate raisins? Or the yogurt

ones? Those are so much better. The Swedish Fish always get stuck in my teeth."

He wrinkles his nose. "No. Those sound disguising. Raisins shouldn't be covered in chocolate. Or yogurt."

"You're missing out."

"Nope, I've got the only candy I need right here." He tears open the bag and takes a couple. "Go on. Enough stalling. Open it."

Reaching inside my own bag, I expect candy, but instead, my hand closes around a book. As I slide it out, my breath catches. "You got me a guidebook on Portugal and Spain?"

"Sí. I didn't have much time to look at all the books in the shop, but this one seemed to have the best maps. I figured that since you're a planner, and the flight is a little over twelve hours, you might want to pick out what you want to see."

I run a hand over the glossy cover of the book, my heart thumping a few extra beats a minute. "Thank you. I will." I clutch it to my chest.

"Ladies and gentlemen, we're ready to begin boarding. We'd like to ask if you're holding a business-class ticket to go ahead and join the queue on the left-hand side. For everyone else, please wait until the section and zone number printed on your boarding pass are called."

"Shall we, Ava?"

I nod. "Let's go."

Ignoring the passengers hovering around the gate area, we join the queue on the left and make our way onto the plane. Our adventure is about to begin.

Chapter Nine

Fernando and I are seated at opposite ends of the cabin. There isn't much chance for us to talk or interact during the flight. Not that it matters. Every time I walk past him to use the restroom, he's sound asleep. He really is like a cat. I've never met a person who can sleep as long as him. I try to catch a little sleep and watch some movies, but the excitement of traveling to a new country keeps me wide awake.

We land in Lisbon a little ahead of schedule, around eight a.m. local time. Nervous energy floods my system as I step off the plane and wait for Fernando. It may be early, but the airport is plenty busy. I smell coffee, and the aroma of something sweet. I ate breakfast on the plane, but now I'm starting to get hungry again. Food is my love language.

There are people speaking in English, Portuguese, Spanish, French, and several other languages I don't recognize. A grin tugs at my lips—I'm really here. In Portugal. Pulling out my phone, I snap a photo of myself with a Portuguese sign in the background to send to Daphne later.

"Thanks for waiting, Ava." Fernando swings his duffle bag over his shoulder.

"No problem. It gave me a second to take everything in." I sniff the air. "Do you know what smells so good?"

Fernando's eyes light up. "Sí. Follow me" He leads me to a nearby café. "Pastel de nata," he says, gesturing toward a tray of small custard-filled tarts with caramelized tops. "These are a must-try. Let's grab a couple and a coffee. I slept through breakfast. These should hold me 'til we get through passport control."

We join the queue. "How long did you sleep? The entire flight?"

"No. I woke up once to eat dinner."

"That was like two hours into the flight," I tease.

"What can I say, I need my beauty rest." I shake my head. "How did you pass the time on the flight?" he asks.

"Other than watching movies, I read up on Lisbon." We move up a few places in the queue. "There's a lot more to see and do here than I thought. It's too bad we don't have more time, or even a car. There're a couple places outside the city I'd love to visit."

"I have the time if you want to explore. And renting a car is no big deal. Driving is the best way to get around if you want to maximize what you can see and do. Are you up for it?"

I inhale sharply and bite the inside of my cheek. The thought of spending time in the car with him sends a hum of delight through my body.

"Ava, don't feel guilty if it's something you want to do. When I say I'm flexible, I mean it. I leave the planning to my mamá and my tías," he teases.

"You're sure?"

"Positive." He nods.

"Will you let me pay for the car and gas?"

"Nope. We'll have to split it fifty-fifty."

I blow out air. From the tone of his voice, I doubt he'll budge on it. At last count, he was ahead in the "doing me favors" category three to one. Now four to one. I owe him big time. "Fine, but I reserve the right to buy you breakfast."

"Deal." At least he agreed to that.

We reach the front of the line, and Fernando places our order in Portuguese. Heat rushes to my cheeks as I stare at him, then quickly look away. Here's another skill I didn't know he had.

Once we have our bag in hand, we find an empty table, and each take one of the crispy desserts from inside. It's warm and creamy, a perfect mix of sweet and just a hint of spice, and I'm instantly hooked. I groan in delight. "Okay, if all Portuguese food is this good, I'm in trouble."

"Spoiler alert, it *is* all delicious. But Spanish food is even better." Fernando grins.

"Biased much?" I elbow him lightly.

He chuckles, taking a swig of his coffee. "So here's what I'm thinking: I say we rent a car, throw our bags in the back, and spend the first part of the day exploring Lisbon on foot. When we're done, we pick up the car and hit the road. We'll spend as much or as little time as you want here."

I agree, and we toast our coffee cups together to seal the deal.

As we make our way out of the airport and into the city, the citizens of Lisbon are bustling around us. The morning sun glints off the intricate tiles beneath our feet, and the air is filled with the smell of freshly baked pastries and a hint of salt from the nearby river.

We begin a stroll through the streets of Alfama, a labyrinth of narrow alleys and colorful buildings with tiled facades. It's just like the pictures in the tour book, except they're real.

Fernando gives me a smile that feels both mischievous and inviting. "Are you ready to get going?"

"I was born ready. Lead the way, Señor Tour Guide."

"Full disclosure, don't count on me to be a very good tour guide." He rubs the back of his neck. "We'll probably get lost within the first five minutes."

"It can't be that bad. You said you've been here before."

"I have, but my friends were in charge of the sightseeing." He shakes his head. "I'm, uh, terrible with directions and keeping track of time. I set timers for everything. When I moved to Sequoia Valley, the first week was a nightmare."

"Sure," I deadpan.

"No, I'm serious."

"Sequoia Valley is a small town. It's hard to get that lost. There are only three main roads," I challenge, placing my hands on my hips.

"You'd think so, but when I tried to get to my cabin from Millie's Steakhouse my first week in town, I ended up near the Jasper Ridge Canyon."

I let out a sharp laugh. "That's about forty-five minutes in the opposite direction."

"Believe me, I know." He face-palms. "Gemma and Tim

wouldn't let me forget about it for months. I still have no idea how I managed to end up there."

"Didn't you notice you'd been driving for more than ten minutes?"

"No. I got distracted by my music," he says. "The, um, same thing happened a couple days later." His cheeks flush. "Instead of going to Lake Wakahanra, I ended up in Fresno."

I laugh even harder. Fresno's three *hours* out of the way. "I guess that means I'm in charge of the navigation."

"It would be for the best," he admits.

"I can relate to getting lost in what you're doing." We turn the corner and head past a large open square where vendors are beginning to set up their market stalls. "When I'm in vet mode, I'm fully focused on my patient. Nothing else matters but me being able to give them the best possible care I can."

"That's what makes you an excellent doctor."

I dry cough. "Maybe and maybe not. Working slower means I can't see as many patients in a day as other clinics. When Dylan was around, it didn't matter as much since he worked twice as fast. Even though he made a few mistakes, his patient load made up for mine. Going forward, I'll have to learn to pick up my pace."

It stings a little knowing I won't be able to be as thorough as I'd like. I don't want to miss any important symptoms my patients might have. The littlest thing like losing some hair might make a big difference. Especially since animals can't speak. Well, not counting parrots and other species of birds that can mimic and repeat human words.

Fernando cocks his head to the side. "Why do you have to work quicker? I would think a lot of people would appreciate you really taking the time to listen to them and understand their concerns."

"They would, except less people means less revenue. And my bills won't stop just because there's one less vet." We slow our pace as we ascend a hill. My breathing increases. I can't believe I'm sharing this with him. I haven't really admitted my problems to anyone, although I'm sure Vicki has an inkling. "I could raise my prices, but vet care is already expensive enough."

"I see."

"This stays strictly between us, but when Dylan announced he was leaving, many of our female clientele left too."

Fernando stops for a moment. "I'm sorry?"

"It's exactly what it sounds like. We used to have a lot of clients who came only to see Dylan."

"He wasn't *that* good-looking," Fernando mutters under his breath. "Some people are so shallow."

"I take it you have some personal experience with flirta-tious women?"

He grimaces, and a dark look passes over his face. "More than you know."

I think back to how polite he was with Vicki and remember how he couldn't wait to get out of the practice as soon as he was done with the clinic because of her. What happened in his past?

We start walking again. Fernando returns the subject to me. "It sounds like we need to find you some more clients."

"That's always the goal." I rub the back of my neck. "It was a major stressor before the vacation. I'm trying to block it out now, but it's still in the back of my mind. I'll have to come up with a really good marketing strategy. I have my sister to help, but compared to the Lake Wakahanra Animal

Clinic, my advertising budget is pennies." And they have a few very handsome male vets I also can't compete against.

"No stress allowed. You're on vacation." We make another left on a street so narrow that we're forced to walk single file. "All you need is a little help. If you're open to it, one of my bosses, Leslie, is a marketing genius. I'm sure she'd love to help you out. She'd be all over helping another female business owner." He glances over his shoulder. "Leslie and her brother built up the business at the Sequoia Valley Ice Sports Complex from scratch. She's the reason there's always a waiting list for our hockey program."

Ding. Ding. Ding. He just admitted he's a hockey coach! I was close on the consultant thing. "She sounds like a force to be reckoned with," I muse as I soak in the scene before us.

"She is, believe me."

"If you think she'd be willing to offer some advice, I'll take it."

"Perfécto. Remind me and I'll give you her contact information as soon as you're back."

"I will."

At the top of a hill, we reach a majestic vista point overlooking the city. The view takes my breath away: red-tiled roofs stretching out to meet the Tagus River, the bridge arching over the water in the distance, and beyond it, the soft rise of the hills.

"Beautiful," I whisper.

"Sí, it is."

We stand in silence, each lost in our thoughts. I should be soaking in Lisbon, but my mind is whirling with thoughts about Fernando. I steal a glance in his direction. His sculpted arms are resting on the safety railing. The morning light is half hitting his face like a spotlight, highlighting the sharp angles of his jaw and lightening his dark-brown locks. If I saw a photo of him like this on a dating app, I wouldn't hesitate to click on his profile.

I study his body again. He has massive legs to go with his imposing upper body. I bet he was an international star. I don't know much about hockey, but I might have just found a reason to start watching a few games.

We spend the next couple of hours hopping from one place to the next without any clear plans or destination in mind. We see the famous Belém Tower, its stone arches and turrets rising proudly against the backdrop of the Tagus River, and the beautiful Gothic spires and intricate stonework of the Jerónimos Monastery.

By the late afternoon, we're in the heart of the old town, Praça do Comércio. It's a massive open square by the river with views that stretch to the hills. Street musicians play softly nearby, the warm breeze carrying the melody as we sit on a bench, sharing more pastel de natas.

"How are you doing, Ava? Is my aimless wandering stressing you out?" Fernando asks, polishing off the last pastry in the takeaway bag.

"I'm enjoying myself more than I have in a long time. I thought I might get FOMO, but Lisbon is a lot more fun when you don't have to rush from site to site," I answer honestly, watching some ships slowly sail past us in the distance.

This morning, it was a struggle to not look at a map or pull out my phone every time we got lost, but now that it's been a couple hours, it's starting to feel more natural.

"What's FOMO?" Fernando wrinkles his forehead. "I've never heard that before."

"The fear of missing out."

"Ah, that makes sense." He chuckles. "Even after all this time, there's still some English words that are foreign to me. Usually, it's something the kids at work say, like bruh or rizz. By the time I learn what it means, those slang terms are out."

"Do you ever try to use them in a sentence?" I joke.

"Once or twice, but all I got were blank stares."

"If it makes you feel any better, I have no idea what either of those words mean." As I finish my snack, I take inventory of my body. My eyes itch, my feet are sore, and I can't stop yawning. "I think after this, I'll be ready to head to the car. The jet lag is starting to catch up with me."

"You're the boss." He starts to collect some of our garbage. "I'll leave it up to you, but when we leave Lisbon, there are two different routes we could take. We could travel up Portugal's coast toward Porto, or we can travel south and into Spain."

"Fernando," I whine. "That's stressful. Can't you make the decision for me?"

"Nuh-uh. This adventure is for *you*. You're the one who makes the call."

I huff and rub my temples. "I'm starting to get a headache just thinking about it. I guess I'd better check the guidebook."

"No." He places a hand on mine to stop me from reaching inside my bag. It's warm and sends a few tingles up my arm. "You don't want to give yourself FODO. Go with your first instinct."

"It's FOMO, and way to use my words against me."

He shrugs in a silent apology.

I take a deep breath. Most of the reading I did on the plane was on Portugal. It has so much unique history and quite a few cities and places I definitely want to visit again in the future. Spending the rest of the day driving up Portugal's coast could scratch some of that itch, but I came here for Spain. I've already lost a day thanks to the flight cancellation. I don't want any more of my short time here to get eaten up. "We'll go southeast into Spain."

Chapter Ten

Fernando and I arrive back at the airport around five and pick up our luggage from storage and get our rental car.

"Is this right?" I blink a few times as we approach a two-door Smart car that's less than half the size of my truck back home. "The guy said we were getting a compact car, but this looks like a toy. Can you even fit in the driver's seat?"

"We're supposed to have a model with four doors, not two," Fernando says flatly, squinting at the rental agreement in his hand. "I agree, this is too small. Wait here. I'll see if I can get this sorted out." He drops his duffle bag from his shoulder, leaving me in charge of it, along with my backpack and our three rolling bags.

"I don't think the trunk will fit even one of our suitcases," I say to myself. The back of the car looks like it's pressed completely flat and can only hold two or three grocery bags at most.

Knowing there's nothing I can do until Fernando is back, I flip my rolling suitcase over, sit on top of it, and pull out my phone, taking advantage of the airport's Wi-Fi. Opening my email, I start a message to Daphne.

To: DaphnesDesigns@email.com
From: DrB23@email.com
Subject: Hello from Portugal
Hey Daph,

How is everything going back home? Just thought I'd shoot off a quick email to you to let you know I made it to Portugal.

No, you're not reading this wrong. I'm not in Spain. Yet.

To make a long story short, my original flight was diverted, then canceled. Rebooking was a nightmare and a flight to Lisbon was the quickest way I could get over here.

I've spent most of today exploring Portugal's capital city and having a blast. I'm already planning a return trip to this beautiful country. I'm attaching a couple pics as proof.

Can you please pass the message on to Mom and Dad that I made it here safely? I'll call sometime midweek.

Give my love to everyone!

-Ava

Satisfied with what I've written, I select two of my favorite images Fernando snapped today—one of me blowing a kiss to the camera in front of the Praça do Comércio and another of me biting into a pastel de nata.

They're both images I'd like to think show me happy and carefree. I want my family to see that there's nothing to worry about. Which is also why I choose not to say anything about Fernando.

If Daphne knew . . . well, my phone would be blowing up with concerned calls and messages. As much as I appreciate her fussing over me, there's no risk of suffering a broken heart with Fernando. We're just friends. Nothing more.

Although if he *was* ever in the market for a girlfriend—wait, no. What am I even thinking? I scrub my eyes with my hands. I don't need nor do I want a boyfriend. Come on, brain. Get with the program. This trip is about taking a vacation from men and all things related to romance.

I hear footsteps approaching. As I lift my head, I spy Fernando. The muscles in his forehead are knitted into a deep V. He's shoved his hands into his pockets, and his shoulders are hunched.

"Bad news?" I ask.

"Yes," he grumbles. "The rental company overbooked all their standard cars and gave ours away to a family with a reservation."

"Can they do that? We already paid."

"Apparently it's in the contract."

I take a deep breath. "Is there a way we could upgrade to an SUV? Truck?"

"Believe me, I asked. All that's left are Smart cars unless you'd rather we take a Vespa."

"Not especially." I stand and brush off my butt and knees. "What about another rental car company? Do you think . . ."

I stop when I see him shaking his head. "All the counters closed at five. We're out of luck and out of options."

"Great."

Fernando approaches the car and clicks the button on the key fob, glaring at the trunk. "We'll have to fit what we can and ship anything we don't need ahead." His attention travels to his luggage. "If you give me a couple minutes to repack, I can squeeze most of my stuff into my duffle bag. I'll have a courier send my rolling luggage to my parents' place."

"Nuh-uh. We're not shipping stuff if I can help it." I pick up the largest of the bags and shove it into the back. "All we have to do is play around a bit. There has to be some way we can fit everything."

"Ava, it's wishful thinking." He crosses his arms. "It won't work."

"Maybe, but I'm not willing to admit defeat until I've given it a try." I pick up another bag and shove it in tightly standing up. Unfortunately, it tumbles out of the trunk and to the ground. The bags are too wide for the space.

Time for plan B. Let's try this sideways.

It takes about ten different configurations and some maneuvering of items from one bag to another, but Fernando and I successfully squeeze everything in.

Slamming the trunk shut, I lean against it, and shout, "Victory! I told you I'd make it work!"

"I'll never doubt you again." He bows to me. "I'm not worthy to be in the presence of greatness."

"Oh stop. It's just a big game of Tetris. Nothing fancy."

We open the doors and slide into the car. Just as I start to relax, I look over and see Fernando and start laughing. It's like something out of a *Saturday Night Live* skit. His legs are so long, they're crammed close to his chest and touching the steering wheel. His arms spill over the invisible border between the two seats.

He rests his head on the steering wheel, his own body shaking with laughter. "There's more room in the trunk than in the front."

"Best moment of the day." I have a few tears streaming down my face as I hold my stomach to relax the sore muscles. "Don't move. Before you adjust anything, I need a couple pictures." I take out my phone and point it at him.

"I hope these won't end up on Photogram."

"Nope," I say, reviewing what I have. "They're just for me. Okay, all good."

Fernando pops the car door open, extends one leg out, and pushes the seat as far back as it'll go. It moves about six or seven inches, but the luggage blocks him from going any farther.

"How does it feel now? Any better?"

He slides back into the driver's seat. It's still a tight fit, but at least he no longer looks like a clown in a tiny car. "It's manageable. Let's just say I'm glad this is only for the day." He starts the engine and passes me his phone with the map app and an empty destination tab. "You're in charge of this."

"What should I put in here?"

"That's up to you." He glances at me. "How far do you want to go? What are you in the mood to see?"

"I don't know," I answer honestly. "I was thinking we could aim for Seville? It was going to be one of the cities I visited from Madrid." The muscles in his face twitch. It's a similar expression to the one he wore when I asked how far Barcelona was from Lisbon. "From Madrid, Seville was about two hours and forty minutes away by train. But I'm guessing it's a little farther than that."

He nods, his lips curving up. "Seville is four or five hours from here."

"Oh." My face falls. It's a good thing I'm not a contestant on *The Amazing Race.* At this rate I'd be eliminated in the first episode.

"We can drive there, but I'd rather not make the full trip tonight. I'm getting tired. Are you okay if we stop halfway and get an early start for Seville in the morning?"

"Totally." I bob my head up and down. "Especially since you're driving. I should offer, but I'm not confident driving outside the States."

"I'm happy to do it. I enjoy driving." He strokes his chin. "Off the top of my head, I think the city of Tavira is about two hours from here. That's where we should spend the night."

"Sounds good to me." He backs the car up while I pull up directions. It brings up a route in red. "The traffic doesn't look bad. Your phone says it'll take us two-and-a-half hours."

"That, I can handle," Fernando says.

I hit the Start button on the map and let the cool female voice fill the silence. We follow some signs out of the airport area and onto a highway that resembles the ones back home.

"So, um, there's something I've been wondering about all afternoon," I say.

"What's that?" His eyes are focused on the road, but shift in my direction for a second.

"How long did you play hockey before deciding to become a coach?"

"Hockey?"

"Yeah." I wave my hand toward him. "Don't try and deny it. You have the build and competitive spirit. Not to mention you spilled the beans about coaching earlier today."

For a moment, he looks completely baffled, and then his face splits into a grin that quickly turns into laughter. "I'm sorry, I just . . . hockey? Really?"

I cross my arms, feeling slightly defensive. "What's so funny?"

His body shakes even harder, doubling over the steering wheel slightly. "Hockey," he repeats, as though he's savoring the word. "I hate to break it to you, Ava"—he takes a deep breath—"but I don't play hockey. I tried it as a kid, but I was awful with handling the stick and found chasing the puck to be boring."

It takes a second for his words to sink in. "Then if you don't play hockey, what do you do?"

"I'm a figure skating coach."

"Figure skating?"

"Uh-huh." His voice wavers slightly.

I glance to him. Something isn't right based on his tone of voice. "As in jumps, twirls, and the stuff you see on TV during the Olympics?"

"That's the only kind I know of."

"Now I feel like an idiot." I face-palm. "I just assumed that with you being so fit and mentioning ice, you played hockey—"

"You're not an idiot, Ava," he interrupts. "The stereotype has always been that figure skating is a women's sport, and hockey is for men. I can see where you'd assume I was a former player. It's happened before."

The highway hums softly beneath the car as Fernando's words hang in the air. I glance out the window, trying to process the new information. It feels strange to picture him —this tall, muscular guy—doing something as graceful and precise as figure skating.

"I've tried to ask about your job a bunch of times, and

we always seemed to get interrupted. Did you do that on purpose?"

"Yes." His hands tighten slightly on the wheel.

"Why?"

"It's complicated," he says, lowering his voice.

I turn toward him, frowning. "I don't understand. You skate and you coach, what's so complicated about that?"

He exhales slowly, his gaze still fixed on the road. "Let's just say not everyone is as open-minded as you about it. I tend to keep a low profile."

My mouth forms an O shape. I think about what he said earlier about stereotypes. "Were you bullied as a kid?"

"Sí, I was." He fidgets in his seat. "Nowadays, nothing bothers me too much, but when I was younger it was tough. Nothing physical ever happened, but I've been called just about every insult you can think of."

I blink, caught off guard by the rawness in his voice. "Seriously? That's ridiculous."

"Maybe," he says with a shrug. "But it sticks with you, and after a while you begin to question your self-worth."

I lean back in my seat, surprised by how vulnerable he's being. For someone who seemed so confident all day, this is a side of Fernando I didn't expect. I bite my lip, unsure of what to say. "But you stuck with it?"

"Yeah." His lips curve into a faint smile. "Because I loved it. And I was good at it. The speed, the precision, the challenge of landing a jump perfectly. I wasn't going to give it up just because of things people said."

"That's brave," I say softly.

"I don't know if I'd call it brave or being stubborn."

"How did your parents take to it?" I ask.

"My madre was supportive."

"And your dad?"

"He accepted the idea eventually." Fernando hesitates for a beat too long. "He had hopes of me becoming a footballer, playing basketball, or even tennis. But figure skating . . . it was a shock to his system." He takes a deep breath. "We don't talk about it much."

My chest tightens at the sadness in his voice. "That must've been hard."

Fernando shrugs again, but it feels forced. "It is what it is."

The car remains silent except for the sound of the GPS warning us to look for a junction ahead in ten kilometers.

There are so many more layers to the man sitting next to me than I ever imagined. Just as I feel like I'm beginning to get to know him, he surprises me. "For what it's worth, I think it's awesome that you ice skate. Maybe someday I can talk you into giving me a lesson. I'm terrible."

His grip on the wheel loosens. "Thanks," he says quietly. "And I'd be happy to anytime."

"It might come sooner than you think. My niece and nephew go every holiday season, and I don't know if I'll be able to get out of it again this year. I'm running out of excuses," I joke.

His eyes shift in my direction. "When was the last time you went?"

"I think I was in high school? So ten-plus years?"

His eyes widen. "That long?"

"Yeah. I'm not very coordinated. The last time I went, it was like I had a pair of bananas tied to my feet. I fell so many times, even gripping the wall."

"I can fix that," he says with an air of confidence.

"You sound sure of yourself."

"I am."

"How do you know I'm not a lost cause?"

His eyes glimmer. "Because I'm a great coach."

"Mm-hmm." I chuckle. "We'll see about that." I'm not exaggerating when I say I'm not good. I'm terrible. After my last time, I swore I'd avoid ice skating again at all costs, but the competitor inside of me is always up for a challenge.

Chapter Eleven

We make it to the small town of Tavira in two hours. I enjoy our conversation so much that I don't realize we're here until Fernando's phone says, "Arrived at your destination."

We agree to stop at the first hotel we find that looks halfway decent along the main road. Luckily it doesn't take long. We promptly book two rooms, bid one another good night, and crash. My body is so exhausted by this point that I don't even bother removing my clothes before I fall asleep.

It's around ten the next morning by the time we're ready to get back on the road.

"How did you sleep last night, Ava?" Fernando asks me.

"Like Sleeping Beauty. I could've slept a hundred years." I cover a yawn with my hand. "I'm still tired now."

"That's the jet lag talking. Trust me, from experience, once we get to Seville and you start walking around, you'll be wide awake," he says.

This morning, Fernando hasn't bothered to shave. His jaw is coated in a thin layer of stubble. It's a good look for him. I take a deep breath and admire the way the maroon cable-knit sweater and jeans fit him. Late December in Spain is just as cool as Sequoia Valley. It's in the low sixties.

"Would that be from the experience of traveling for competitions?"

"Yes and no. I did some traveling when I competed, but most of what I know comes from skating with Dreams on Ice. We'd go to a new city every few days. It wasn't bad in North America, but in Europe it could be tough. There are a lot of time zones spread out over a small area."

I take a long sip from the cold hotel coffee I brewed an hour ago. Its bitter taste settles on my tongue. "Dreams on Ice . . . is that the show with all the fairy-tale characters like Sleeping Beauty and Cinderella?" I vaguely remember Daphne taking the kids to see something like that in Fresno a couple months ago.

"Uh-huh. Gemma was Cinderella. And my other friend who lives in Sequoia Valley, Frankie, she was Belle."

"And who were you?"

"I think the better question is who didn't I play. I've been Prince Charming, the Beast, Aladdin. The list goes on and on. We had more girls than guys, so we always had to double up our roles."

"Go figure," I say, trying to picture him in one of those costumes. "You're full of surprises."

"Yes, I am," he boasts, puffing his chest out.

There are so many questions floating through my head. Skating professionally sounds fascinating. "How long did you tour?"

"Ten years, give or take. One with the cruise line and nine with DOI. It was the best way to get out of Spain and see the world. It's funny, I never saw myself becoming a coach, but there aren't many alternative jobs if I want to stay involved in skating."

I knit my eyebrows together. "Oh. I thought you'd enjoy coaching."

"I do now, but when I was younger, I couldn't stand the thought of be being stuck in a rink teaching my students the same things day after day. I wanted to get out in front of a crowd and perform."

I nod. "I can understand that. I spent so many hours locked away in libraries studying when I was an undergrad and in vet school that I couldn't wait to be done and get out into the field. Even if somebody paid me a million dollars, I'd never want to go back to a classroom and become a teacher or researcher. I've done enough studying to last a lifetime." I take another drink of my awful coffee. It gets worse with each sip. "I guess my next question is what changed your mind?"

"I matured. The last couple of years I was with Dreams on Ice, I ended up teaching the incoming skaters some of the tricks I'd picked up over the years. And I enjoyed it. I learned I was dead wrong about coaching. You don't do the same things every day. Every student is an individual. They have different skill levels and learn at different paces."

"I'm happy it's worked out for you."

"Me too. So far, living and working in Sequoia Valley has been better than I ever could've imagined."

Arriving in Seville around midday, we find another hotel and grab some lunch before setting out to explore the city.

"I don't know what I was expecting, but Seville is so different compared to Lisbon." I take out my camera and snap a photo of a couple of orange trees, their branches filled with baby fruits. Fernando, however, is less impressed, mentioning that his hometown has oranges that taste much sweeter.

Just like our last city, we forego using a map and ramble around. Our first stop ends up being one of Seville's main squares, the Plaza de España. My eyes widen as I take in the wide canal and brightly colored mosaic tiles on the surrounding walls. "How many are there?"

"Your guess is as good as mine, but I think there's close to fifty." Fernando rubs the back of his neck. "From what I remember, each scene is supposed to represent a different aspect of the region's food and culture. It was built for a World's Fair back in the 1920s."

"When was the last time you were here?"

"When I was fifteen or sixteen. Mamá loves this city. We used to vacation here once a year."

I study his facial features, noting the lines on his forehead. "You didn't enjoy it much?"

"It was all right. We came in summer, and it was hot, hot, hot. I remember always feeling sick everywhere we went and counting down the minutes until we could go back to our hotel room, not that there was much relief there either. Most hotels in Europe don't have air conditioning." He grimaces. "I don't like the heat. I'm cold-blooded, like a reptile. I guess that's why I love skating."

"Ouch. I'm not a fan of hot weather either."

He nods. "One thing I love about living in America is that there's AC everywhere. I don't know how I went so long without it!"

I make my own mental note to avoid a return trip to Europe in the summer. Crowds and heat are not my vibes. There's a reason I've always preferred living in the mountains.

We stroll along the water's edge, passing rowboats drifting lazily under the arched bridges. The sunlight reflects off the water, casting rippling patterns on the ceramic tiles. I stop every few steps to snap photos, each angle more beautiful than the last.

As we turn the corner, we hear the sound of flamenco music. A small crowd has gathered in front of a talented street performer playing a guitar. A few people are dancing.

The upbeat melody has me tapping my hand against my thigh to the beat. "This guy is good."

"He is," Fernando agrees, tossing a few euros into his guitar case. The man tips his cap to us in thanks. Fernando turns to me. "Would you care to dance, Ava?"

"Dance?" I sputter. I can't imagine a worse way to embarrass myself in public. "Like I said the other day, I'm not coordinated." I point to my sneakers. "I was born with two left feet."

"It's just for fun. Trust me, nobody here knows who we are, and they won't judge us. You don't need any skills, just the ability to move your body to the music." He gestures to the crowd around us. There are some kids, an older couple, and two people our age. "So what do you say?" He dips his chin and offers me his hand. His eyes are daring me to dance.

I don't dance. Or play sports. Period. It's always ended badly for me. Like the time I managed to give myself a concussion learning how to do a plié in ballet. My parents and I are still mystified about how I did that. But it tells you all you need to know about me. Daphne was always the athletic one, not me. Growing up, I was happy to watch from the sidelines. But that was then, and this is now. I want my *Eat, Pray, Love* moment.

I swallow hard. If Fernando is going to be my partner, I

guess his ice-skating grace can make up for my missteps. A few beads of sweat pool down the back of my neck and under my arms. "All right," I tell him. "But only this once."

Fernando's face breaks out into a wolfish grin. It's the feature of his I'm the most attracted to. He takes hold of one of my quivering hands and places his other on the small of my back. "Relax," he says. "Pretend your entire body is Jell-O and follow my lead."

I hope he doesn't feel the dampness back there. I move in closer to his body. My heart is hammering against my ribs. On beat with the music, he steps forward, forcing me to take a step back. We repeat this easy motion. His grip is light, but reassuring. It takes my brain a few moments to figure out that all we're doing is an easy on-two step.

"There you go, Ava, you've got it." His voice is low and soothing, like a hot cup of tea on a rainy afternoon. "Now you can look up here, instead of at your feet."

"Oh, um, sorry," I mumble, lifting my chin. Then I misstep, stomping on his right foot. I inhale sharply and abruptly stop. I hope I haven't damaged it! He needs his feet in one piece. I drop his hands and take a step back. "I'm so sorry, I . . . I . . . I didn't mean to."

"I know you didn't," he says calmly. "You were doing great up until you started to second-guess yourself. Let's try again. And this time, trust your body. Focus on me. Let your mind go blank and listen to the music."

"I can't believe you want to try this again."

"Everybody has to start somewhere," he says.

Taking hold of my hands once more, he guides me through the one-two step again. "There it is," he whispers. "I have you. I won't let anything happen to you. Now look at me."

Dry swallowing, I hesitantly lift my chin, locking gazes

with him. His brown eyes are wide, like an owl's. They're laser focused on me. He does have me. He won't let me fall.

"Yes," his voice nearly purrs.

My eyes close and I open my ears. I hear the guitar and its soft melody. I let go, fully give in to Fernando's instructions, letting my body do what it wants. My brain empties and I become that smooth Jell-O.

It's only the two of us. I'm fully aware that his large body is pressed right up to mine. His hands are wrapped around my waist, helping me glide back and forth. I hear the low, soothing rumble of his voice counting out, "One-two, one-two. Yes. Just like that."

The longer we dance together, the higher the temperature of my internal furnace climbs, and the more rapidly my stomach somersaults. Being near this man has awakened my body. It's alive and buzzing with enough energy to power a small solar system. I haven't felt this way since I discovered my feelings for Dylan.

Before I know it, however, the music ends. We stop moving and there's clapping. My eyes open. "Well done, Ava. I knew you could do it."

It's back to reality. I'm hot and clammy. I step back, releasing him. "Thanks, Fernando, that was, er . . . what I mean is, um, thanks.

"You said that already," he teases. "Are you thirsty? I sure am." He lifts the hem of his shirt and pats his brow, exposing a flash of skin and two little squares of muscle that disappear into the waistband of his jeans. I dry swallow. "How about some orange juice? It's what Seville is famous for."

"No surprise, given all the orange trees." I laugh nervously, fanning myself, all too happy to have a distraction. "Do they make a shaved ice or ice cream?"

"I'm sure they do."

I will myself to focus on the oranges, but I'm failing miserably. I'm dying for another flash of what's under Fernando's shirt.

"Are you okay? Your cheeks are all pink."

"I'm good," I chirp, my ears burning. "I must've just been out in the sun a little too long. I'll be fine once we rehydrate."

Ugh, that sounds so lame. But it's the best excuse I can come up with.

We stroll side by side from the main plaza into a beautiful green park with a quaint café nestled under a canopy of palm and orange trees. The tables are shaded by bright umbrellas, and a chalkboard menu out front proudly advertises *zumo de naranja fresco*—fresh orange juice—and *helado de naranja*—orange ice cream.

"Here we go. Let's try this place," Fernando says, leading the way to an empty table.

We place an order and settle into our chairs. A server brings out a large juice for Fernando and a bowl of orange sorbet for me. For a moment, we're content to sit in companionable silence, enjoying the cool treats and the dappled sunlight filtering through the trees. He wasn't kidding about the flavor. The ice cream is delicious, not too sweet or tangy.

"Have you had a chance to get in touch with your parents yet? I know you said they wouldn't mind if I stole you for a day or two, but I still feel guilty about it," I say.

He leans back in his chair and stretches. "It's on my list of things to do this afternoon. I sent Mamá a text, but who knows if she'll read it today or a few days from now. At least if I call her, I know she'll get the message."

"What about your dad? Is he just as bad with texts?" I

ask, taking another bite of the sorbet and letting it melt on my tongue.

"Worse. He owns a flip phone and only carries it and turns it on when my madre makes him. She's always worried he might get stuck on the side of the road or have some other type of emergency, but he insists he'll be fine no matter what."

I giggle. "It seems like a typical thing a man might say."

"I get my stubbornness from him," Fernando jokes. "What about your parents? Are they tech savvy?"

"Kind of. They know the basics of how to use a smartphone and computer, but that's about it. Anytime there's a problem with the Wi-Fi, or they get a new device or something like that, it falls to my sister or me to fix or set it up." I sigh.

"I should call today too. I'll just have to be careful not to mention you." Quickly, I realize what I've said, and I sit up taller in my seat. "It's nothing personal," I sputter. "I just don't want them knowing that I'm alone with a guy."

"It's okay. I understand." Fernando nods. "Have you told them about what happened with the guy from the airport?"

"My sister knows, but not Mom. I haven't gotten around to telling her yet. She liked Dylan a lot. He always turned on the charm around her. It wasn't a secret that she hoped we'd become an item since we were friends for so long." I rub my temples. "I've been able to avoid the lecture on letting men get away from me for a while, but once she knows he's gone, it's game over. I'm really not in the mood to hear it from her."

"Is she one of those mamás who wants you to hurry up, get married, and start a family?"

I nod glumly. "Yep. Mom thinks my career should take

a back seat to my love life since, according to her, my 'biological clock is ticking' and 'there'll be plenty of time in the future to practice veterinary medicine.'" I can hear her voice echoing around in my head as I shake it. "I get that she loves me and means well, but I want to do things on my own timeline."

I draw a few small circles on the table, once again not believing how much I'm sharing with the man across from me. More than I've shared with my own sister at times. He seems to have a knack for being able to get me to open up.

"There are some things that are universal among mamás. Wanting their single children to be in a long-term, lasting relationship is one of them."

I lift my head. "You too?"

"Yes." He runs a hand through his hair, messing up some of the curls. "Mamá isn't subtle about dropping hints that it's time for me to settle down. But my aunts are the worst offenders."

"How bad is it?"

"Bad." He strokes his jaw. "Last year, the tías set me up on a series of dates. But they conveniently forgot to tell me. Every time they asked me to run an errand for them, it involved a beautiful woman. I didn't connect the dots until the third or fourth time it happened."

I try hard to hold in the laughter, but I can't. It bursts out like a donkey's bray. And a moment later, he's laughing too. "I can't believe the lengths your family will go to!"

"I'm dreading what scheme they've come up with this year. I wish they'd just accept that I'm happy being single and I don't want to be in a relationship. All it leads to is pain."

His tone is flat, and as soon as I hear it, I want to ask what happened in his past. He's handsome, funny, and kind. If I were looking for a guy to date, he'd check all the boxes.

Despite my morbid curiosity, it's not about me. It's about him. Now isn't the time or the place to pry. He needs to vent, not face an inquisition. He's trusting me, as a friend, with a part of himself, and I want to respect that.

We sit in silence again for a few more minutes and I finish up the sorbet. Then Fernando changes the subject. "Have you thought about how you're going to get from here to Barcelona?"

"The train?" I shrug. "I haven't checked the schedule, but I'm sure they run pretty frequently."

"They do. But I've had another idea." He clears his throat. "What would you say about taking the rest of the week to drive there?"

My eyes widen and I blink a few times. "Drive the rest of the way? Together? All seven hundred miles?" My pulse is taking off as fast as a hummingbird's wings, fluttering a thousand times a second. I've had a blast with Fernando so far. The thought of spending even more time with him in the car is like discovering one of Willy Wonka's golden tickets. I'm on the verge of shouting yes, but stop myself at the last second. "What about you and your plans?"

He rests his elbows on the table. "I was just thinking it would give you a lot more flexibility to see everything on your list. And now that you know about my family, you know why I'm not in a rush to be set up on a series of dates."

"I should do the polite thing and refuse . . ." I hesitate.

"If I told you I was going to drive anyway, would that help you say yes?" he asks softly.

His eyes glisten with amusement as I study him and dry swallow. I'm getting lost in his rich cinnamon-colored eyes to the point of being hypnotized. My brain is telling me, "Say yes. Just say yes." We *are* both going to the same place. If he's driving anyway, I guess it's not any extra trouble. "Okay," I whisper.

"Brilliant." He sits up tall. "Be prepared to see a side of Spain most tourists never get to."

"I'm more than ready." I shoot him a tight smile, wondering what I've just gotten myself into.

<h1 style="text-align:center">Chapter Twelve</h1>

We spend the night in Seville and leave for Granada a little after six. It's about a two-hour and forty-minute trip.

"If it's okay with you, there's one sight in Granada that's a must-see, the Alhambra. It'll be busy by the afternoon, so I was thinking the best plan of attack is to get there right at opening. How does that sound?" Fernando asks.

"You're the tour guide. I trust you." I check the navigation screen, making sure we're still following the correct route.

His eyes dart over to me. "Have you ever heard of it?"

"No," I admit. "I haven't gotten that far in the guidebook. Is it a museum?"

"Not quite, but close. The Alhambra is a Moorish fortress perched high on a hill above the city. There's some hiking involved, but the architecture, grounds, and views from the top are spectacular. They more than make up for the work of getting there."

"That sounds awesome. I can't wait." I glance at my feet and hope my shoes are going to hold up. I noticed yesterday that I'm starting to develop a hole in the heel from all the walking we've been doing.

At last count, my phone said we were averaging about 18,000 steps a day. That's what I get for getting a cheapo brand from Val-U-Mart. At least it's not blisters. I'll have to pick up another pair of shoes sometime today.

We park in the main lot outside the gates and follow the line of tourists wandering toward the main entrance, waiting for the site to open.

"So, I've been doing some thinking," I say as Fernando pulls up our tickets on his phone.

"About?"

"Your matchmaking family."

"Mm-hmm," he grunts, continuing to stay interested in what's on the screen.

All night, my mind replayed our conversation yesterday, recalling how uncomfortable Fernando was about his family's interference with his love life. I've been looking for a way to repay him. Here's my big opportunity. "Now this may sound a little crazy, but hear me out."

He lifts his head, clicks off the device, and shoves it in his pocket.

"Back in Denver, you did me a solid by acting like my boyfriend in front of Dylan."

"Uh-huh." I can see the wheels in his head beginning to turn, wondering where I'm going with this.

"I was thinking, what if we did a one-eighty and changed roles? I'd be your fake girlfriend. I can't stay here as long as you since I need to get back to my practice, but I thought if we could put on a show for your family, for let's say a week, it might be enough to convince your mom and aunts to leave you alone. What do you think?"

A few moments of silence pass between us. His Adam's apple bobs up and down. "Ava," he starts, his voice coming out slightly hoarse, "I appreciate your thoughtfulness, but the answer is no. It'd be a waste of your vacation. I'm not worth it."

"Yes, you are." I knew there was a good chance he'd put up a fight. Luckily, I have a few counterarguments. "Look, I'll get a good amount of sightseeing in this week. I don't need to see everything in Spain. Besides, it's my time. I'll spend it how I see fit." I cross my arms.

"It'll be stressful, like a modern Spanish inquisition," he warns. "Mamá and my tías will ask you lots of personal questions. They'll want to know everything there is to know about you."

"I can handle a few days of that," I challenge.

"You also won't have any alone time."

"Again, I can handle it."

He places his hands atop his head and blows out air, staring at me for a full minute. "Is there anything I can say to convince you how terrible this idea is?"

"No."

"What if I bribed you? Name your price."

"Fernando, stop. I want to do this for you," I urge, placing a hand on his forearm.

He studies me before saying slowly, "If we do this, I want you to know you can change your mind at any time. All you have to do is say the word and we'll end it."

"Got it." I nod.

He relaxes as he wraps his arms around me and squeezes. "Thank you, Ava. You have no idea how much this means to me."

"You're welcome." His body is warm and inviting. The scent of his citrusy cologne lingers in the air. I don't want him to let go. It's like relaxing against a top-of-the-line recliner.

As he releases me, he mutters, "I can't believe I'm agreeing to this," and scrubs his eyelids with the back of his hand.

I've faced vet school, the exam boards, complicated surgeries, and my fair share of difficult patients. Could dealing with Fernando's family really be tougher than all of those experiences? I guess it won't be long until I find out.

"I'll try and find ways for us to spend as much time as possible outside my parents' home. Letting my mamá know it's your first time in Spain should help. She'll insist I personally show you everything there is to see around Barcelona and Santa Luz," Fernando says.

We advance up a few places in line as nine o'clock hits and the Alhambra opens.

"We'll have to make sure we're on the same page, too, about how we met, how long we've been together, and all the stuff that couples usually know about one another. With you being here with me, the tías are going to expect we've been together a while and that it's serious. It's been a long time since I've brought a woman home."

I place a hand on his forearm. "We still have a few days before we get to Santa Luz and plenty of time to iron out all the nitty-gritty details. I won't let anything slip by. Remember who you're talking to." I wink. "You may be a great coach, but I'm an excellent vet. Being able to recall the tiniest details is what I do on a daily basis."

"You're a great friend, Ava. I was lucky the day I called your clinic."

My cheeks warm at the thought of being called a great

friend. I push it to the back of my mind. I shouldn't be feeling this light around him. I shouldn't be noticing the curve of his smile or the warmth in his laugh, or the way I feel safer beside him than I ever did next to Dylan. I can't risk falling for another friend.

The Alhambra is majestic. I've taken over a hundred pictures so far and won't be stopping anytime soon. I hope my SD card has enough memory. Every time we enter a new room, I feel like a person who is seeing a sky full of stars away from the bright lights of the city for the first time. There is so much to look at that I don't know where to focus.

Take, for instance, the room known as the Court of the Lions. There's a gorgeous ornate fountain that has twelve marble lions shooting water from their mouths, elegant slender columns with delicate carvings resembling lace, and a series of ancient Arabic inscriptions written on the walls.

Or the Hall of the Abencerrajes, which has a breathtaking dome containing an intricately carved canopy of stars. Skylights stream down from the ceiling, creating golden beams that dance across the floor. Each detail seems so delicate, it's as though the patterns have been spun from silk rather than stone.

"I can't believe humans made all this. It doesn't seem possible," I say to Fernando as we linger just outside the Generalife Gardens, their manicured hedges framing a series of bubbling fountains that stretch toward the horizon. The fragrance of orange blossoms and jasmine drifts through the air.

Fernando smiles, his hands resting casually in his

pockets. "That's why I had to bring you here. It's one of the closest places we can get to a fairy-tale setting in this region of Spain."

"I'm glad you did. I would've kicked myself if we'd missed it."

We find a bench and sit down, taking a moment to rest our feet. It's about one p.m. We've spent the last couple of hours exploring. I cross one leg over the other and massage my tight calf muscles. "What are those mountains in the distance?"

"The Sierra Nevada."

"Just like back home in California."

We exchange a quick laugh. "Sí, there are a lot of things California has that often remind me of Spain."

"Do you ever miss it here?"

He takes a moment to consider my question. "Sometimes. There are elements of Spain I miss, like my family, and the food, but overall, I'm happy with living in the States. I've created a life for myself that I wouldn't trade for anything."

"Can you tell me a little bit more about your friends, like Gemma and Tim? I feel like I should know them inside and out. If we were in a real relationship, we'd spend a lot of time hanging out with them."

"Sure, but only if we can take turns asking one another questions. I want to know all about your friends too."

"That's fair." I snort.

Being a gentleman, Fernando lets me ask the first set of questions. "How did you become friends with Gemma?"

"She and our other friend Frankie were the two women I partnered most of the time I was with Dreams on Ice. We spent most of our waking hours practicing, performing, and traveling together."

"And you didn't want to date them?"

He makes a face. "No. I love them like sisters. And I have a strict 'no dating other skaters' rule."

"I see," I say, soaking in the information. Did something go wrong in his past?

"Who would you consider your closest friend?" he asks.

"If you asked me a few months ago, I would've said Dylan, but you know where that ended up." Mentioning his name still leaves a bitter taste in my mouth, but I'm not as affected by him now as I was back in Denver. I hope this is a sign I'm finally on my way to being over that man.

"And your answer today?"

"Daphne, my sister." I exhale deeply. "I'm a workaholic, so I don't have anybody else I could call or watch a movie with if she isn't around."

"I get that. When I toured, I was on the road ten months a year. I didn't have time for non-skating friends. I'm lucky I had Gemma and Frankie around. Besides, I'm not great with talking to people outside my skating bubble."

"I disagree. I think you do really well with everybody. When we first met, you were great with me and Vicki."

"That's different." I watch in amusement as the tips of his ears redden. "I needed help with Gemma and Tim's cat. We talked about medical things, not personal stuff."

"If you want to get technical, that's how it was at first, but we crossed the professional line a long time ago." I laugh.

"Touché."

"My turn. What's one thing about Gemma and Frankie you think I should know?"

"Never place a bet or wager with either of them," he deadpans.

I arch my eyebrow. "Dare I ask why?"

"They always win. No matter what." His eyes crinkle. "I never learned my lesson. Those two got me into so much trouble with our stage manager."

"What type of bets would you make?"

"It varied. Sometimes it might be something skating related, like who could do the cleanest double Axels or most triple toes in a row. Other times it might be something connected to clothing, like who could go the longest wearing an inflatable T-Rex costume without someone saying anything."

"Please tell me somebody took pictures!" I giggle.

"I can neither confirm nor deny their existence," he says with a straight face.

"Ha! That means there are some out there!" He zips his mouth closed and throws away the key. I shake my head.

Fernando and I continue to exchange questions. By the end, I start to form a better image of his two best friends. Frankie may be competitive, but is also fiercely loyal to her friends and family. The entire reason she quit show skating was to move home and care for her elderly dad. Gemma, on the other hand, is more laid back and soft spoken. She's the type of person who wears her heart on her sleeve.

"They both sound like amazing people. I hope I get the chance to know them a little better." I think back to our short interaction at the antiques market a few weeks ago.

"You will. Trust me, it won't take long for them to adopt you. Just don't be too surprised if either of them tries to set us up, even though I've told them no many times before. Those two live for romance. Especially the show *Cupid's Arrow.*"

"I'll keep that in mind." I locate a hair tie and pull my

hair back into a ponytail. I'm excited to have something in common with them.

We stand and stretch. My feet still ache, but I'm not willing to let a little pain ruin spending the rest of the day in the town of Granada.

"We should take a few photos of us together in case your aunts end up wanting to see what we've been up to."

"You're right."

We take a moment for some selfies. His long arms make it easy for us to fit more than our faces into the shot.

"What do you think we should say if they wonder why we only have photos of us together from the trip?" he asks, as we continue toward the parking lot.

"We could tell them a half-truth," I suggest. "That our relationship is new, and we only decided to make things official recently. We can even use the story of you bringing the cat in to see me as our meet-cute."

"I like it, except what's a meet-cute?"

My lips twitch. "In romance books and movies, it's the moment a couple has their first meeting, usually in some sort of adorable way."

"I see." He scratches his head. "I didn't realize it had a name."

"It does. Most romances follow the same formula. There's a meet-cute. The fun-and-games slash getting-to-know-you stage. The climax. The dreaded third-act breakup. The makeup. And finally, the happily ever after. It's why junkies like me keep coming back for more. We crave the predictability."

"Is this something I should be taking mental notes on for our own story?"

"No. We're not in a book or a movie." I place a hand on

his shoulder. "Your job is to focus on selling *us* to your family. Leave the details to me."

"Phew." He relaxes. "That's good because memorizing things is not my forte."

"I feel like there's a story behind this." I grin.

"There's many stories."

We arrive back at the car. He clicks the key fob.

"What's the most recent blunder?"

He opens the door and pauses. "If I tell you, you have to promise not to make fun of me."

"I won't." I hold up my hand. "Cross my heart."

"I was asked to give the best man's speech at my cousin's wedding."

"Uh-huh, and . . .?"

"I put it off until a week before the event. Even though I practiced, when it was my turn to stand and deliver, my mind went blank."

"Did you have a paper copy of the speech or index cards you could use?"

"No." He palms his forehead. "I was so confident I could do it without. I left them at home."

"So how did the speech end up? What did you say?"

"I pulled a few song lyrics together from Taylor Swift and tried to pass them off as my own advice."

"That's actually pretty clever, but I can't imagine people fell for it." I shake with laughter.

"No, they didn't. One of my biggest mistakes was telling Frankie about it. She wouldn't stop singing or playing Swiftie songs every time we coached together. It was a miserable few weeks."

"Remind me never to get on her bad side," I muse, climbing into the car.

"Deal."

As we back out of the parking lot and make our way toward the city center, I find myself feeling increasingly connected to the man sitting next to me. Being in this fake relationship is going to be a piece of cake. I won't have to pretend very hard to be attracted to him or play off his personality. I almost wish I'd suggested it sooner.

Chapter Thirteen

We're into day three and a half of our road trip. Although we'd initially planned to travel along the coast to Murcia, the capital of the region, Fernando talked me into changing our itinerary. We traveled north toward the cities of Toledo and Madrid. As he put it, aside from some Roman ruins and the world's largest palm grove, there wasn't much to write home about in our original plan.

Toledo, on the other hand, is famous for its jewelry, the one thing I have a weakness for. I don't have a large collection, but the pieces that I do own are all things I've inherited from my grandma or pieces of fine jewelry that I've treated myself to whenever I hit a milestone, like graduating from vet school. The way I look at it is that one pair of diamond earrings will last you a lifetime, unlike the less expensive imitation stuff.

"What did you think of the factory tour?" Fernando asks as we leave the jewelry maker's workshop and enter the retail showroom.

"I'm mind blown. The craftsmen have so much talent. I

can't believe they can make such tiny, intricate items by hand."

During the tour, we watched as an artisan carefully inlaid threads of gold into blackened steel, creating the intricate jewelry Toledo is famous for. First, they sketched designs directly onto the metal surface, then chiseled delicate grooves to hold the fine gold or silver wires. We watched how they hammered the wires in place, then polished the entire piece until the designs gleamed.

"Agreed." Fernando nods as we pause in front of a glass case filled with intricate necklaces and earrings. "One of the tías you'll meet in Santa Luz worked as a head designer in a factory similar to this one."

"I'll have to ask her more about it." I shake my head. "If I ever have a midlife crisis and change careers, I think becoming a jewelry designer would be my job of choice."

"Are you going to do some shopping while you're here? Or do you want to look around some of the other shops?"

"I think most of what they have here is similar to what I'd find in other boutiques. If you don't mind, I'll shop now." I immediately reach for a black-and-gold pendant on the shelf in front of me with a gold bird surrounded by a few flowers. It'll be perfect for Daphne. "Do you think your mom or aunts would go for some jewelry from here too? I'd like to have a hostess gift for them."

Fernando's face softens. "You don't have to get them anything. They'll be happy just to see you."

"Yes or no?" I hold up a pendant similar to the one already in my hand, looking them over for any flaws.

"Yes."

"And how many aunts do you have?"

"Too many."

I roll my eyes.

"There's three I'm close to who you'll see every day that you're in town." He lets out a tired sigh. "Ava, if you insist on getting them gifts, why don't you let me—"

"Nope. These are from me. I'm paying for them." I clutch them to my chest. "If you want to give them something, it's on you." I school my face into my best doctor stare to let him know I mean business.

"Fine. Have it your way." He takes a step backward. "I'll meet you outside when you're done. I'm gonna go find a coffee. Do you want one too?"

"Yes please." I beam. "Give me about ten minutes."

Fernando nods and heads out of the store. Over the last three days, I've realized that like many men, he doesn't enjoy shopping. He admitted yesterday that sometimes he gets claustrophobic if there are too many people confined to a small space. If it's an outdoor market though, he's fine. For his sake, I've tried to keep the shopping to a minimum, but sometimes, it's hard to resist the call of tourist trinkets.

As I select a few more items from the display shelves, I spy the familiar tall form of Dylan and his blue-haired girlfriend. I lean my head back and squeeze my eyes shut. What are they doing here? Maybe I'm imagining things.

When I open my eyes, he's still there. With any luck, they won't see me. I take a few steps behind one of the taller display cases, giving myself a pep talk. "I'm not going to let them ruin this trip. I don't have to speak to them or acknowledge their presence. I *can* do this. Dylan no longer has a hold on my heart."

Admitting this to myself sends waves of exhilaration through my body. I'm still working through my emotions, but I'm happy to say I don't feel like a pile of mush when I see him. It's a big step up from where I was a few weeks ago.

Squaring my shoulders, I walk up to the cash register,

pretending Dylan and the Queen of Vultures don't exist, then head straight out the door. It's better if I don't engage with the enemy.

"That was fast," Fernando says as I meet him outside. "Did you have enough time? I don't mind waiting a little longer."

"I'm good. I got something for all the females in your family and my sister. I'm ready to get going," I say, slightly breathless.

He frowns, looking me up and down. "Did something happen inside?"

"It's fine," I say quickly.

"Ava, you don't look like you're—" he starts, but is interrupted by the ringing of his phone. Glancing at the caller ID, he says, "It's Mamá, I . . ."

"Go on, answer it."

He nods and steps off to a private corner, just as Dylan and his girlfriend exit the store. "I knew you were planning a trip to Spain for a reason!" she says. "And now I know why! I can't wait to call everyone and tell them we're engaged! They won't believe it when—"

"Ava!" Dylan shouts, freezing in place.

My fingers dig into the flesh of my palm. I will myself not to say something snarky.

"Oh, um, hi again," the blue-haired woman says, grabbing Dylan's waist and pulling him closer to her.

My jaw twitches. "Congratulations," I manage.

"Thanks," he says.

"I didn't know you guys were so serious." My gaze travels to her hand. Her long, slender ring finger contains a two- or three-carat aquamarine on a gold band.

"When we met, everything clicked. I just knew she was the woman for me. I didn't see a point in waiting. When you know, you know." Dylan, recovered from the shock, kisses the top of his fiancée's head.

My pulse quickens as I struggle to remain in control of myself, counting down in my head from five. I feel like I'm standing in the middle of my own silent scream painting. He's known this woman for less than six months and he's engaged to her? My mouth opens and closes. "I . . . I . . . I hope you guys enjoy the rest of your trip," I manage weakly.

"Thanks, we will," Dylan says.

As they turn to leave, I feel the weight of Fernando's hand on my shoulder and the tense muscles in his arm. "I heard the whole thing. Are you okay?"

"Not really, but I will be."

"Fernando, whose voice is that?" I hear a woman ask.

My gaze travels to the device clutched in his hand. "Is your mom still on the phone?"

"She is." He clenches his jaw. "But I'll tell her we'll talk another time. You don't need this right now."

"No, I can do this." I pry his fingers off the device and take hold of it. The woman on the screen has a round face, and the same olive skin and brown eyes as Fernando. I take a deep breath, picture a room full of puppies, and smile as widely as I can. "Hola, I'm Ava. Your son's girlfriend."

Her eyes widen to the point that she reminds me of a cartoon character, darting up and down, as if she can't believe I'm real. "A girlfriend? A real girlfriend?" she murmurs, then shouts, "Yulia, Yesenia, Maria, come here. Quickly." There's some excited chatter in Spanish in the background. "Fernando has his girlfriend on the phone." Three other people cram themselves into the picture, squeezing shoulder to shoulder.

"Hi, I'm Ava," I repeat.

"Ava! What a beautiful name," one of the aunts says.

"Oh, she's American. I knew there was a reason your son moved away from here," voices another. "Now we know why."

"Shh . . . not all at once, you'll scare her away," Fernando's mom clucks. The women in the background immediately quiet. "Ava, we're delighted to meet you. I hope to see lots more of you soon. You are coming to Santa Luz, aren't you?"

My eyes flutter. My brain is slow to process what she's saying, still stuck on Dylan.

Fernando leans over my shoulder. "Mamá, I told you earlier, she'll only be in town for a short visit. She has her own itinerary of places she'd like to see and to do. It's her first trip to Spain, and I want her to make the most of it."

I hear the stress in his voice. His patience is slipping. Like a shot of caffeine, it makes me alert. I focus my energy on the man standing next to me, lacing my fingers through his free hand and squeeze reassuringly. "Don't worry Mrs . . ." I rack my brain for Fernando's last name. "Mrs. Alvarez, I'll be there."

"Mamá, we have a lunch reservation. I'll call you soon." He says his goodbyes and hangs up. Shoving the phone into his pocket, he closes his eyes and takes a deep breath. "I'm sorry about all that. The timing couldn't have been worse." When his eyes open, they appraise me with concern. "Is there anything I can do?"

"Not unless you're able to wipe my memory." I hunch my shoulders. "I'm sick and tired of falling to pieces every time I see him. I'm trying hard to move on, but my heart isn't computing what my brain is telling it."

"It'll get easier with time," he says quietly. He bends to the ground and picks up a carrier with two coffee cups and a brown bag of churros. "Here, this might help."

We walk away from the shop down a narrow cobblestone alley. I take a sip of my coffee. It's gone cold, but the sweet, crunchy churro more than makes up for it.

"How are *you* doing?" I ask Fernando. "I noticed how your mom and aunts stressed you out."

"I'm fine. Mamá and the tías are just being their normal selves. I should be used to it by now." He takes a long swig of his coffee. "Mamá caught me off guard when she called and started asking a bunch of questions about why I was in Toledo and why I keep changing the date I'm coming home. She thinks I'm avoiding her."

In a way, he is. But I keep that thought to myself.

"I panicked, and before I knew what I was saying, I blurted out that I wasn't alone. It all went downhill from there." He sighs deeply. "I wanted to wait a few more days before I brought you up, but now that the cat's out of the bag, there's no turning back. The tías have already started to blow up my phone with texts asking about you."

On cue, I hear his phone vibrating like mad. We stop walking. "Fernando, I'm the one who suggested we go through with the fake-dating thing." I place a hand on his forearm. "I'm a big bad vet. I can handle this. Trust me."

"You're not big or bad, but I do trust you." He lowers his chin. "I just feel guilty. I'm asking too much of you."

"Don't. You've saved me when I had the car problem, from Dylan at the airport, and by giving me a vacation so far that I won't ever forget. Even after we get home again, I'll still be in your debt."

"You don't owe me anything." He wrinkles his nose. "We're friends. And when friends get stuck in sticky situations, they help each other out."

Hearing him say we're friends causes my heart to

twinge. "What you've done is equal to if not more than what Daphne would've done."

The muscles in his face twitch. "Does that catapult me to the top of your friends list?"

"Hmm . . . I don't know yet. But for now, let's say you're solidly in the middle of the pack."

He starts walking again. "What will it take for me to top your sister?"

"I don't know," I answer honestly. "Daphne's a special case. We've been besties since the day I was born. Twenty-nine years. I'll have to get back to you." I take another bite of my churro. "What about me? Where do I sit on your friends list?"

"In the top five."

"Out of . . .?"

"A magician never reveals his secrets," he quips, biting into his own sugary treat.

I huff. Well, it has to be at least five people long. I'm probably below Frankie and Gemma. And maybe Tim. Not that I blame him. We're only going on knowing one another for a few weeks.

"What I will tell you, Ava, is that every day we spend together, you're earning more brownie points. Who knows, there's a chance you could rise to the top of the leaderboard."

My pulse races. "I like those odds."

As we continue through the maze of Toledo's streets, my mood improves. I forget about Dylan and begin to imagine myself as Fernando's numero uno friend. After three straight days with this man, I'm starting to get a good feel for his quirks and mannerisms.

Take this morning's trip from our hotel to Toledo for example. His driving routine is always the same. He climbs into the car, ducks his head, attempts to scoot the seat back an inch, and cleans his sunglasses before reaching for his seat belt. Once I've shuffled into the car, he'll hand me a coffee and ask how I slept.

The smile he flashes me when I grunt that I slept well sends a shiver up my spine, fully waking me up if the coffee hasn't done its job. The corners of his eyelids crinkle, his top lip disappears slightly, and he flashes me a wide smile.

My favorite moment, however, is when he rolls his Rs as he says, "Wonderful, Doctor. Let's hit the road," and slides his sunglasses on. I could listen to that man speak for hours on end. Who needs a British accent when you have a Spanish one!

As I look over at him under my lashes, my throat goes dry. Yesterday, I thought the fake-dating thing would be a piece of cake. Well, I should've known I was lying to myself. I'm incredibly attracted to him. I just hope I can guard my heart and keep from falling for him.

Chapter Fourteen

It's day four of our road trip. The fatigue from our ambitious schedule is beginning to wear on both of us. We were so exhausted after yesterday that we decided to sleep in this morning. Madrid is only about an hour away. There's no need to rush.

We arrived at the train station around ten and are now en route to Spain's capital city.

"I know it's more than three weeks away, but have you ever been to a Christmas market?" Fernando asks as he places his phone on the tray table.

"Not unless a school craft fair counts. Remember"—I point to myself—"this is my first big trip overseas. Christmas markets aren't a big thing in America. And until very, very recently, I didn't do things outside my comfort zone."

He raises an eyebrow. "Care to share why you're not comfortable at a Christmas market? Do you not enjoy the holiday?"

I had no intentions of ever saying anything to anyone about it, but Fernando has a way about getting me to share things about myself that I'd never willingly let anyone else in on. There isn't a barrier between us. I instinctively know I can trust him to be respectful and not tease me the way Dylan might have.

"I like Christmas. But I've never enjoyed the lonely feeling it brings." I stare out the window at the passing scenery. It looks like we're in for a rainy day as droplets of water hit the train's windows, creating abstract patterns.

"What do you mean?"

I continue looking away. "The holidays are about being surrounded by your friends and loved ones, but when I lived in Colorado, it was isolating. I'd only be able to go home for two or three days at Thanksgiving or Christmas. It reminded me of what I was missing. I was always on my own, away from everyone I cared about."

"What about you know who?"

"Dylan was from Colorado." I keep my voice even. "He wasn't around during our breaks. He always went home."

"And he didn't think to invite you?" Fernando's voice is growing raspy.

"He did once, but otherwise, no." I take a deep breath. "I didn't ask either. I never wanted it to seem like I was fishing for an invitation."

As I raise my head, I see his nostrils flare. "If the jerk knew you were going to be alone, you shouldn't have had to ask. An invitation should've been a given."

"I guess," I say slowly.

"No, Ava. No guessing. It's not normal for friends to leave other friends hanging. Especially for someone you claim was your best friend." Fernando mutters under his breath in Spanish. His eyes have darkened. It's almost as if they're swirling storm clouds on the verge of coming together and forming a hurricane. "If I had been there, you would never have been alone."

There it is again. Somebody pointing out that my friendship with Dylan was one-sided. Was it always that way? Was I so blinded by love that I chose to overlook it? "I appreciate that."

Fernando reaches a hand and places it on top of mine. "I can't make up for the past, but as long as I'm around, you'll always have a standing invitation to spend time with me." His fingers gently brush against my skin. "Once the gang meets you, they'll want you around all the time too."

"Thank you," I whisper. My body feels like I've been sitting in a sauna. Steam would be billowing out of my ears if that were possible. "Twenty-something Ava wishes she could've met you a couple years ago."

"Ditto. I wish that too." He holds my gaze. His eyes are the color of warm gingerbread today. "So, um, going back to the Christmas market . . ." He runs a hand through his hair and clears his throat. "I noticed that Madrid's opened this past weekend. I was gonna ask if you wanted to visit it, but now I don't want to bring up any bad or painful memories. We can skip it and do something else if you'd like."

Again, he's surprising me. I don't know what to say. Men aren't usually so thoughtful or in tune with emotions. Someone like Fernando usually only exists in books or in Hallmark movies. But here's a living, breathing prince among men. Well, ex-prince, if I'm being technical.

"What if I want to go? I'm so tired of living in the past."

He takes a moment to reply. "I'm the genie of the lamp —your wish is my command."

I chuckle. "Is that a quote from *Aladdin?*"

"Sí, good guess. The Genie is one of my three favorite characters."

"And the other two are?"

"Aladdin and Raja the tiger." He relaxes against the plush backing of his seat.

A smile twitches on my face. "I can see the Genie for his humor. Aladdin for his wit and energy. But I'm baffled by why you like Princess Jasmine's tiger."

"Raja's like me. He loves his naps."

I face-palm as he laughs.

"Did you know a tiger averages sixteen to twenty hours of sleep per day? That's my kind of feline."

"I did, actually. Tigers were one of the animals I worked with at the Colorado Zoo when I was doing my residency."

"Really?" He sits taller in his seat.

"Uh-huh. I'm certified as an exotics vet, which means I can work with way more animals than your average cat or dog."

"You continually impress me, *Doctor* B." He emphasizes the R, causing a few goosebumps to appear on my arm. "I'm surprised you didn't want to stay on at the zoo. No offense, but I would've thought that might be more exciting than working in a small town."

"I *loved* working with so many different animals. But I didn't like the zoo's management." I cross one leg over the other. "I looked around for openings at other zoos, but most were on the East Coast. I wasn't willing to relocate that far away. My parents had just moved to California. When Dylan asked me if I wanted to open a practice with him, it seemed like a no-brainer. I thought I'd try out the private sector for a couple years, then go back to a zoo, but it hasn't worked out that way."

"Management's always the problem."

I arch an eyebrow. "Problems for you too?"

"Mm-hmm. Dreams on Ice." He scrunches his nose. "It's a long story, but basically, the company was bought out and the new management was looking to cut costs and increase profits." He shakes his head.

"Ouch. Is that what pushed you to leave?"

"Partly. I already had one foot out the door, but the final straw was when I got reprimanded for reckless behavior."

"What?" I frown. He's the last person I'd ever imagine endangering others.

"Management didn't like me coaching the new skaters on partnering. They wanted them to figure it out themselves."

"How does that make any sense? That sounds more like an accident waiting to happen."

"It doesn't make sense." He shrugs. "I didn't care what they said. I helped out the skaters until they decided not to renew my contract. Anyway, moving to Sequoia Valley was the best thing I could've done. I'm much happier."

"I'm glad. Being happy is the most important thing of all."

"Here, here."

"La Latina is the heart of the old town. It's either the oldest or second-oldest neighborhood in Madrid," Fernando says two hours later.

We stroll down another narrow cobblestone street lined with three-story buildings. We've made so many turns, I've lost track of where we're going. The entire area is a blend of old and modern. There are countless churches and museums, but also a large array of bars, cafes, and tapas restaurants.

"Are you sure this is the right way to your old apartment?"

"Sí. I may be terrible with directions, but I know La Latina as well as my hometown."

"What drew you to this neighborhood?"

"I'd heard it was like a small town. Eighteen-year-old me was nervous about moving from my own town to the big city."

"And how did it actually turn out?" I ask.

"My apartment building was great. I knew all my neighbors by first name. But most of the surrounding properties were vacation rentals."

"That stinks."

"It wasn't too bad. The nightlife made up for it." We make another turn. "This was my street. I lived on the second floor of the orange building over there."

"Did you keep as many colorful flowerpots on the balcony as the owner has now?" I laugh.

"No, I'm terrible with plants. I forget to water them."

"In your defense, I'm sure you were busy."

"Sí, I was practicing on the ice four hours a day. And training another three hours a day at the gym. There wasn't much time left over. Sundays were my only day off, and I used that time for sleeping."

No wonder he's always napping. That's a lot of energy to expend. How much time does he spend at the gym now that he's retired? He still looks like he's in peak physical shape. Does he still practice stuff too?

At the end of the street, I smell garlic, olive oil, and roasting meat. My mouth begins to water and my stomach grumbles. Suddenly, food is all I can think about. "Oh, that smells so good."

Fernando sniffs the air too. "That must be the Garcia family restaurant. They used to serve the best omelets and other local dishes. Do you feel like stopping there for lunch?"

"Yes!"

We enter a building that looks outdated, with peeling paint and faded lettering on the outside. The interior isn't in much better shape. Fernando leads us inside to a small, dimly lit dining room with mismatched chairs and tables with checkered tablecloths. A single ceiling fan hums overhead.

I glance at Fernando skeptically, but before I can say anything, a stout older man with a thick mustache emerges from the kitchen. He's wiping his hands on a worn apron when his eyes land on Fernando. His face lights up with recognition.

"¡Fernando! No puede ser, chico!" the man exclaims, rushing over to clasp his shoulders. The two men have a brief conversation in rapid Spanish. I wish I could follow what they're saying, but I'm only able to pick up a few words here and there. How long has it been since they've seen one another?

Fernando places a hand lightly on my back and switches back to English. "Don Antonio, this is Ava. She's visiting Spain, and I couldn't let her leave without tasting your famous tortilla de patatas."

Don Antonio nods approvingly, waving us toward a table near the window. "Coming right up. Sit, sit! I'll bring you the best we have. Tortilla, gazpacho, jamón ibérico—you'll eat like royalty."

When my omelet arrives, all my earlier doubts are replaced by groans of delight. The tortilla is golden and thick, perfectly cooked with layers of tender potatoes and onion. The gazpacho is also cool and refreshing, the flavors bursting with the freshness of ripe tomatoes and crisp cucumbers.

"We need a place like this in Sequoia Valley," I say as I cut a corner of my meal into small pieces.

"Sí, we do," Fernando agrees. "I've forgotten how much I love Don Antonio's cooking. It's the first time I've been back here in three years. I don't get to Madrid too often unless it's to see family or for a skating engagement."

"You seemed to be in your element when we were walking around. What lured you away from the city?"

He sets his fork and knife down on the plate and wipes his mouth on his napkin. "I loved living here, but when the coach I was training under decided he wanted to relocate to the mountains, the choice was either follow him or find a new coach. My partner at the time, Sylvie, made it clear she was following our coach. Without her, I couldn't skate. So I didn't have much of a choice."

"That must have been a big adjustment to go from living in a big city to a small town."

"It was." He runs a hand through his hair. "Bosque-Beret is a lot smaller than Sequoia Valley. Most of the residents up there were competitive skiers, snowboarders, or coaches. I think during the peak of the winter season, there might've been about two hundred people living there."

"That's tiny!"

"It is." He nods. "There wasn't much to do either. We had a hotel, a post office, a ski shop, the rink, a tiny convenience store, and a petrol station."

"There wasn't even a coffee shop?"

"Nope," he says. "I mean, there was one inside the

hotel, but it was overpriced. A coffee should never cost four euros."

"Could you escape to the next closest town?"

"Nope." He shakes his head. "It was too far away—about an hour by car. And that's without any heavy snowfall."

"Ouch," I hiss.

"Uh-huh." He picks up his cutlery and stabs a piece of his omelet. "Sylvie and our coach claimed it was the perfect training environment since we couldn't get distracted." He sighs. "It was like the cruise ship for me. I told myself I'd try and stick it out for six months, but I barely made it to two." He sighs. "When I broke the news to Sylvie that I wanted to move back to Madrid, we decided to end our partnership. That was the end of my competitive skating career."

"I'm so sorry."

"I'm not." He chuckles. "We were never a good fit to begin with. She was all business, I wasn't. She wanted to go to Worlds and the Olympics, I didn't. Going our separate ways was the best thing for both of us. It led me to the cruise line and allowed her to find someone who shared the same goals she did." He takes a long sip of water. "You look confused."

"I am," I admit. "I guess I'm surprised she wouldn't try and fight harder to save your partnership. It can't be easy starting with a new guy from scratch."

"You're right, it's like finding the right person to date. When you're looking for a partner, there's a lot of boxes that have to be checked. For example, you want someone with a similar technique to yours. If not, it takes months to marry your skills together so you're both on the same page."

"Wow."

Fernando spends the remainder of our meal filling me

in on the challenges of finding a pairs partner. I learn that there are way more female skaters than male partners available and that it's not uncommon for skaters at the highest level to have to relocate and change nationalities to pursue their skating dreams.

In Fernando's case, his old partner ended up moving to France to skate, while he decided not to bother with another partner. He knew he wanted to pursue show skating.

"That's a lot to sacrifice," I tell him. "You have to want it pretty badly to go to extremes like those."

"Indeed. There are times I've wondered if becoming a skater was all worth it. It's made my personal life a mess. But on the other hand, it's also given me a lot of opportunities too, like traveling the world."

Is he alluding to his romantic life? If he is, I'm baffled. This man is a hidden gem. Or as the Cave of Wonders from *Aladdin* might say, "A diamond in the rough." In all the time I've spent with him, he always looks so sad whenever I bring up dating or the past. What happened? And will he ever be able to find his own happy ending?

Chapter Fifteen

After settling the bill and letting Don Antonio know how much we enjoyed his food, we finally arrive at the Mercado de Navidad, the annual Christmas market held in Madrid's main square, Plaza Mayor.

"Does this look like it beats the holiday craft market from back home?" Fernando jokes.

I slowly nod, overwhelmed by what I'm seeing. "So much better."

Although it's still early in the afternoon, the market is bustling with crowds. There are about a hundred booths trimmed in red lights lining the perimeter of the square. They're selling everything from food and drinks to practical jokes. In the center of the Plaza Mayor, there's a towering fifty-foot Christmas tree also decorated with ruby-red lights and glistening gold stars. Loudspeakers play holiday-themed music.

"Where do we start?" I mutter.

"As your tour guide, I say let's go left and make a giant circle."

"Why the left over the right?"

"Because I'd like to try some hot cider." He points to a queue about ten people deep. "If the line's long, you know it tastes good."

"I like your logic." We share a laugh, making our way to the end of the line. "While we're waiting, let's take some couple selfies too. We've been slacking in that department."

"You're right," he groans. "Mamá is pestering me for some photos. I've been stalling. I don't know how much longer I can put her off. She's not a woman I can say no to."

We turn backward, and I loop my arm around his back. We squeeze in together and he snaps a few images of us with the tree in the background.

"How did it turn out?"

He hands me his phone. "See for yourself."

I tap the burst of images. The two of us are smiling and look happy, but to me it's obvious we're a fake couple. "They're okay, but we're too stiff and formal."

He squints at the screen. "You think it's decent enough to fool Mamá and the tías?"

I chew on my lip. "I doubt it."

"How can we fix it?"

I take a moment to consider his question. "We need to be relaxed. Maybe we buy one of the jokes and have the stall owner take some pictures or a video of us opening it up and reading it?"

"I see where you're going with this. We need to be doing stuff where we can be more candid." His eyes dart around the market. "There's a lot of places around here we can play with, like riding the carousel, taking a photo with Papá Noel, and even ice skating."

My pulse quickens and my voice comes out shaky as I say, "Yes, to the first two, but ice skating?"

His face falls when he sees my stiff reaction. Quickly, he adds, "If we go skating, I'll have your back the entire time. I promise, I won't let you fall. But there's no pressure."

Skating with Fernando is tempting, especially when it means being in his arms for an hour or two. However, I also don't fancy making a fool of myself in front of him. "I'll think about it," I say softly.

"That's all I ask."

We've played around the market over the last three hours, capturing photos of us trying everything there is to do until all that's left is stepping foot on the ice.

"Come on, Ava, you *need* the full experience," Fernando says to me. "If there is anything that will convince my family we're a couple, it's me and you on the ice together."

I don't have a counterargument to that, so we head to the rink. He's right. A real girlfriend would absolutely take advantage of having a boyfriend who's a professional ice skater.

My breath hitches as I secure my laces. I can't believe I let Fernando talk me into this. "Have I done this right?" I ask, staring down at the teal-colored plastic rental skate.

He scoots closer and leans over to inspect my handiwork. He slips his hand into the skate and checks the pressure. "This feels secure. Try standing and let me know what you think."

Getting to his feet, he offers me his hand. It takes two seconds for me to feel like I'm wearing a pair of clown shoes that are two sizes too big. My ankles roll inward, and I place all my weight on Fernando. The top edges of the skate dig into the tender skin above the bone. "Um, not good." I grit my teeth.

He helps me sit back down, then kneels, checking the fit again. "What size did you ask for?"

"I think I asked for a thirty-eight. It was weird when I did the conversion on my phone. It said European shoes don't come in half sizes."

"They normally don't, but in skates, they do." He frowns. "What's your American shoe size?"

"Six and a half."

"Then we need to try a thirty-six, thirty-six and a half, and a thirty-seven on you. You usually size down in skates, but with rentals it's a toss-up. Your skates hurt because they're too big. This is an easy fix." He unties the skates and collects them. "I'll be right back."

He walks to the counter in his own rental skates with the ease of a model wearing high heels. His jeans hug his butt, giving him a perfect peach shape. Can he skate in something that tight? I hope they don't rip on him. Although if they do, I'd get a chance to see what's underneath. If it's anything like his arms, I'm sure he's ripped. My body warms like a tea kettle on the stove. I don't really want to share that with the rest of Madrid though. I want to be the only person to enjoy it.

Turning my attention to the ice, I watch as the people glide past me. Some of the skaters are gripping the wall for dear life like I would. They're using their arms to pull themselves along, giving themselves an intense arm workout. A handful of kids hover near their parents, while others are racing one another, weaving in and out of the crowd.

In the center are the experts. One woman in a black dress holds her leg out to the side and slowly brings it into her body for a fancy, fast spin. She whips around so quickly that I start to feel dizzy watching her. I shake my head. How is it possible for a person to even do that?

I wonder what type of skater Fernando is. He's mentioned doing triple jumps in passing, and competing, but until now, it hasn't seemed real. As a pairs skater, I'm sure he's used to lifting people over his head. I shudder. If that's something he wants to try with me today, it's a hard pass. I draw the line at trying to go backward.

My thoughts are interrupted when Fernando returns and plops down next to me. "They didn't have any size thirty-sixes left, but I think the thirty-six and a half will work."

I tug the skates on, and just as he predicted, they fit, although they're a lot tighter than I'm used to. He assures me that's a good thing. It means my ankles are fully supported. Could that have been what my problem was all along? I guess we're about to find out. We snap a selfie, then I follow him to the doorway, waddling like a duck.

"It'll get easier in a minute. You won't have to pick up your feet. You'll be able to glide."

"If you say so," I reply, my voice quivering. I pause in the entryway, inhaling deeply as I wait for a break in the traffic passing by. Holding on to the wall for dear life, I place one foot on the slippery surface, then the other. I exhale. I'm standing. My feet aren't slipping out from underneath me. So far, so good.

I take a few steps, feeling more confident. Can I let one hand go? Hesitating, I glance back at Fernando, who is right behind me. He nods, encouraging me. Taking a deep breath, I release my left hand, leaving my right gripping the wall. I push a little harder and start to glide a few inches. "I'm doing it!" I exclaim. A rush of excitement fills me.

As I turn my head to glance back at Fernando, a kid darts between us. My body stiffens and I lunge forward, losing my grip on the wall. I squeeze my eyes shut, memories of the last time I went skating and fell flashing before my eyes. I wait for the hard impact, except it never comes.

"I promised I wouldn't let you fall," Fernando says, his hands wrapping around my waist.

I exhale deeply, relief washing over me.

"You were doing so well, Ava." As if I'm a rag doll weighing nothing, he hoists me to my feet and steers me away from the crowd. "You're more skilled than you let on. Let's go out in the middle where there's less people." He sends a glare in the direction of the kid who bumped into me.

"The middle?" I sputter. "Away from the wall?" I glance longingly at the plastic barrier.

"Sí, it's the safest place to be."

My breathing quickens. I have to remember Fernando is an expert and I need to trust him, even though my instincts are screaming at me to flee. "Okay," I squeak.

We find a small patch of ice on the opposite side of some orange traffic cones. "Ava, it's okay." His voice is calm and reassuring. He doesn't release his grip on me. "You're safe. I'm going to be with you the whole time. I won't let go until you're ready. You can squeeze my hand or grip my arm as hard as you want."

"I don't want to make you fall."

"You won't." He puffs out his chest. "I haven't lost a student yet." Keeping hold of my hands, he turns backward and says softly, "Relax your body. Skating is just like walking. You move one foot and then the other. One-two." He counts out. "One-two, one-two."

My head goes to my feet. I focus on untensing my

muscles, but it's easier said than done. "Keep your head up, Ava. You always want to look at where you're going."

"Mm-kay," I mumble.

We continue a couple laps around the perimeter. By our tenth or eleventh time around, my body begins to understand how to move and Fernando talks me into easing my death grip on him.

"That's it! Fantástico." We stop. He pulls out his phone and opens the video app, gliding back a few feet from me. "Try skating toward me."

"On my own?"

"Si. Just a few steps." He nods encouragingly.

"I . . . I don't think I can." My body quivers.

"Yes, you can. You are ready." Fernando lowers the phone, and comes toward me, placing a gentle hand on my shoulder. "Repeat after me: I can do this."

"I ca—I can do this," I choke out.

"I've got this."

"I've . . . I've got this."

He lets go and glides backward a few paces. "When you're ready."

If it were up to me, I don't think I'd ever be ready, but if Fernando believes I can do it, I'll try. I dry swallow and wipe my sweaty palms against my jeans. My heart pounds against my ribs. Timidly, I take a marching step forward, followed by another. I glance at my feet.

"Head up, chin up," he reminds me.

I turn my attention back to him and continue three more shaky steps on my own. He stops recording and catches me in his arms. "That's it! You did it! You just skated on your own. Great job, Dr. B!"

He hugs me tightly. I catch a hint of his citrusy cologne. The fabric of his fleece zip-up is soft against my cheek as I rest my head on his chest. My pulse slows, no longer beating like I'm participating in a hundred-meter sprint. We're down to the speed of a long-distance runner. "I'm proud of you. I know how scared you were."

Hearing the pride in his voice encourages me to snuggle tighter into him. "Now would be a great time for a selfie," I suggest, pleased I've bought a few more seconds of being in his arms.

"You're right! Hang on." Maintaining a one-arm hug on me, he holds out his phone, so our cheesy grins are in the frame. There's no doubt these smiles are genuine. "On three. One, two, and three." He quickly reviews it, then shows it to me. "What do you think?"

His expressive brown eyes shimmer like pieces of highly polished chocolates. He's so close, we look like we're about to kiss. It's my favorite picture he's taken of us so far. My breath hitches. "It's good. You have proof I'd pass a toddler skating class."

"You did better than a toddler, trust me." He releases me. "You actually did better than some of our beginner adults too. See for yourself." He plays the video clip of my first steps on my own.

I blink a few times in surprise. My steps don't look as wobbly or clunky as I imagined them to be. On this screen is a woman who appears to know what she's doing. I let out a low whistle. "You had your work cut out for you, Fernando, but dang, I look good."

He clicks the device off. "Do you think you're up for trying a little more?"

It's an internal tug of war. The old Ava is screaming "no" at the top of her lungs. But the new, more confident Ava is clamping her hands over the old Ava's mouth, urging me to give it a go. She mouths *"trust him"* to me, as I have all throughout this trip.

"Yeah, I am. Let's do it."

As we near the end of our session, I marvel at the transformation Fernando has worked on me. For the first time in my life, I'm skating next to a person instead of a wall, confident enough to have a conversation.

It's given me the chance to enjoy the music, lights, and decorations. For instance, I never would've realized that there's a petting zoo, Papá Noel meet and greet, and an arts-and-crafts table for families near the skate rental stand.

"You've really gotten the hang of it," Fernando says as we take a slow, leisurely lap around the rink.

"It's all thanks to you. I'll admit it, you're an excellent coach."

"Gracias, but I can't take all the credit. You're the one who has to put my words into action." He moves closer to me. Our shoulders are nearly touching. "I know how hard it was for you to trust yourself. But I'm glad you did. You're a natural skater, Ava. You learned more in three hours than some people do in two weeks."

His words send a wave of pleasure through my body. "I'm proud of me too."

"Is there any way I could talk you into skating with me when we're back home?"

"I'm open to it." My brain conjures an image of the two of us inside an empty rink, spending a quiet afternoon together as some soft classical music plays in the background. He whis pers how proud he is of me into my ear and plants a series of slow, trailing kisses up my neck. I sigh in contentment and glance at him. "How much do you charge for private lessons?"

"For you, they'd be free so long as you agreed to my terms."

"Which would be . . .?"

"Coffee and dessert with you either before or after the lesson." He winks.

Goosebumps form on my arm. Is he flirting with me? Is he also feeling the attraction that's grown between us since this trip began? How do I respond to him? Should I be equally as flirty back? "*Yes, dummy,*" the new Ava inside me shouts. I lock eyes with him. "You drive a hard bargain, but it's a date."

As the words leave my lips, Fernando's head jerks to the left. His eyes widen and he comes to an abrupt stop. The color drains from his face as if he's seen a ghost.

As I try and stop to see what's going on, I realize I can't. Stopping isn't something we've covered yet. The only way I know how is to grab Fernando or onto the wall. Unfortunately, the wall finds me first and I go flying over it.

Chapter Sixteen

It takes me several moments to catch my breath. OK, I didn't exactly fly. I took more of a Humpty Dumpty-like tumble. I close my eyes. This has to be one of the most embarrassing moments of my life.

It's even worse than the time I was in middle school and didn't realize my skirt had been tucked into my underwear the entirety of our lunch period. My face gets hot reliving that misery too. It may be in the past, but it still leaves a scar. It took half the year for me to live it down. At least here in Spain, nobody except Fernando knows who I am. Once we leave Madrid, this will all be forgotten.

I blow out air. Speaking of Fernando, I hope he's okay. Nothing seems to faze him. Whatever caused him to go into shock like a deer in headlights must've been serious. A cold shiver shoots down my spine.

As I open my eyes, I'm face-to-face with a pair of yellow eyes in thin black slits, appraising me with curiosity. My breath hitches. *Baaaaaaaaaaaaaaaaaaaaah,* a goat cries, then licks my face. It's cold, wet, and rough, like the texture of sandpaper.

I've been licked by a lot of animals in my life, including cats, dogs, cows, anteaters, giraffes, and chimpanzees, but this is the first time by a goat. And it's not an experience I'd care to repeat. It doesn't feel pleasant, especially on my face.

Gah. I must've landed in the petting zoo. I feel the muscles in my back scream in protest as I sit up slowly. The goat isn't the only animal I've attracted. A couple chickens, potbellied pigs, and a pony watch me in amusement too.

The goat bleats again, jumps off the hay bale I'm half sitting, half lying on, and trots over to the other side of the enclosure. I've never been so glad to see hay. It must've broken my fall and saved me from hitting the concrete. Being mindful of the sharp blades of the skates, I bring my knees to my chest and scoot myself so I'm fully sitting.

"Ava!" Fernando shouts. Still in skates, he runs toward me, breaking away from the three workers dressed as elves blocking his path. In an instant, he's kneeling by my side, his eyes creased with worry. "Are you okay? Try not to move too much. A medic is on their way."

"I don't need a medic. I'm stiff, and I'll probably have a lot of impressive bruises tomorrow, but the only thing that's injured is my pride." My eyes rove his body. He's still pale, but some color has returned to his face. "What about you?"

"I'm bueno," he says quickly, clenching his jaw and glancing back toward the elves. "I would've been here sooner, but the petting zoo workers didn't want me back here until the medic cleared you."

I nod in understanding. "I'm sure they were just doing their jobs."

"Still, even if that's the case, they should've let some-body back here. What if you were bleeding or needed CPR? The time they wasted arguing with me could've made all the difference if the situation were serious." He continues ranting about the basics of first aid and how the petting-zoo elves need to be retrained.

My brain zones out. Hearing how concerned he is about me adds to the list of qualities I find extremely attractive about him. Dylan would be hands off. He would've been too worried about being sued for doing something he wasn't supposed to.

Fernando remains with me until a man in a bright-yellow vest and pants approaches us. He removes a backpack and asks me a series of questions in rapid Spanish. Everything he's saying is jumbled in my brain. Fernando jumps in and acts as my interpreter.

After a quick evaluation, I'm deemed fit enough to leave the area under my own power, but advised to rest. Fernando promises the man I will. By this point, we've attracted quite a bit of unwanted attention. There's a horde of people lined up around the petting zoo, staring as if we're the main attraction, not the animals.

"I hope nobody caught my fall on video," I murmur.

"It happened so quickly that I doubt anyone did." Fernando stands and brushes stray pieces of straw off his jeans. He grimaces as he, too, takes notice of our unwanted audience. "Do you want me to carry you? It'll make for a quicker escape than you walking in your skates."

I sigh. As much as I'd rather walk on my own, he's right. "Yes, please. The sooner we're out of here, the better."

He helps me stand, then reaches one hand under my legs and places the other around my back, cradling me to his chest. I loop my arms around his neck. If my back weren't so sore, I'd be enjoying this more. But right now, all I can picture is taking a nice, long hot bath back at the hotel.

We end our visit to Madrid earlier than expected and catch the first train back to our home base of Toledo. Throughout the ride, we're silent, each lost in our own thoughts, staring out the window at the rapidly darkening sky. I think about how much I enjoyed spending the day with Fernando until my Humpty-Dumpty moment.

When I was in his arms earlier today, I didn't want to let go. I wanted to stay there and be cared for by him. With each passing mile on the train, as I relive the moments we've shared together throughout this trip, I realize that I've started falling for Fernando.

I steal a glance at the man sitting next to me. He's leaning his elbow on the tray table, head propped up on his hand. His eyes are closed, and a soft snore escapes, making my lips twitch.

Fernando is my friend, but I'm craving more. I don't want our relationship to be fake. I want it to be real. I want to go on dates and become one of those happy-go-lucky couples you might see in a Disneyland commercial. Except that's the last thing he wants.

After we arrive back at the hotel, I enjoy my long-awaited soak in the tub, then listen to the soothing voice of my favorite audiobook narrator in bed. The exhaustion of the day has caught up with me, and it doesn't take me long to drift off to sleep.

Knock, knock.

I awake with a start, scrubbing my eyes with my hands as I sit up. The red glowing numbers on the clock next to the bed read eight p.m. The knock sounds again. Leaving my nice, warm cocoon, I pad over to the peephole and stare out to see a nervous-looking Fernando. "Hey," I say opening the door.

"Hi." He waves with one hand, shifting his weight from one leg to the other. "I, uh, brought you dinner." He holds up a large paper bag. "I wasn't sure if you'd eaten. I thought we could share a meal together, but, um . . ." His voice wavers as he realizes I'm in my pajamas. "I'll just leave this with you."

As tired as I am, my stomach grumbles as I catch a whiff of cheese, onions, meat, and spices. "What did you bring?"

"It's nothing fancy. Just some street tacos, chips, and fresh guacamole."

"Food is the way to my heart. Especially when it's tacos. Come in, we can eat together." I pull the door open wider. "My stomach says food first, sleep second."

His steps are slow and measured. He gingerly places the bag on the round table by the door and clears his throat. "Ava, about earlier, I'm sorry for everything." His voice is gravelly and raw.

"For what?"

"You crashing into the wall. It was all my fault."

"It wasn't *all* your fault." I rub a sore spot on the back of my neck. "I wasn't looking where I was going. If I had, I would've seen the wall." I leave out the part about not knowing how to stop. I don't want to make him feel any more guilty.

"You're wrong. I distracted you."

"Fernando, I'm really not in the mood to play the blame game." I rub my temples. "If you want to blame yourself, fine. But that's on you. There's no way you'll manage to convince me I didn't play a part in how the afternoon went down too."

"Is your head bothering you?" he asks with concern.

"It's my shoulders and upper back."

"Do you want me to run down to the pharmacy and see if they have any muscle relaxants?"

"No. I can't stand the smell of it."

"I don't blame you, that stuff is strong." His lips twitch. "What about a heating pad? I have one in my room you can borrow."

I sit down on the edge of the bed. "Do you nap with it like a cat and a warm blanket?" I tease, trying to lighten the mood.

"Sometimes. I have arthritis in my knees and ankles. The heat helps make the flares manageable. Especially when I'm traveling or sitting for long periods."

"Oh." Heat rushes up my ears and a horrible thought crosses my mind. "Has it been worse because of all the driving?"

"No," he answers a little too quickly.

"Are you telling the truth, or trying to be a gentleman about it?" I cross my arms.

"The truth. It's been the same as it always is. I have good days and bad days. It's the price I pay for participating in a sport where you are basically jumping on cold concrete. But back-to-back-to-back days don't help the situation."

"Why didn't you say anything?"

He shrugs. "I'm used to it."

I resist the urge to face-palm and shout, "Men!", but settle for taking a deep breath. "If you wouldn't mind sharing your heating pad, I'd appreciate it. I'll make sure I get it back to you before I go to bed. There's one spot I can't reach between my shoulder blades that's been both-ering me."

"Let me go grab it. Don't worry about returning it to

me. I can manage without it for a few days. In the meantime, don't wait for me to start eating. Help yourself. I ordered six tacos. There should be enough for the two of us. They're all carne asada, in case you're wondering."

While he steps out of the room, I poke my head in the bag. Steam tickles my nose, and I can't resist the smell. I reach inside and grab two, excited to see how they compare to back home. I move to the foot of the bed, unroll the foil, and take a greedy bite.

Fernando reappears with a heating pad in hand. "I forgot to grab drinks. I had these two water bottles in my room, but if you want something else, I can run down to the vending machine."

I shake my head. "No, water is perfect. Thanks."

He nods, helping himself to a taco and some chips and sitting on the chair opposite the table.

For a few minutes, the room is filled with the sound of us crunching on chips and tacos. Eventually, I break the silence between us.

"Fernando?"

"Hmm?"

"Can I ask you something personal? You don't have to answer it if you don't want to."

He chews and swallows slowly. "We're beyond the point of you needing to ask for permission. What's on your mind?"

I dip a chip into the container of guacamole I've commandeered. "What freaked you out earlier at the rink?"

Placing his food down, he blinks slowly. "I'm psychic. I knew that was the first question you were going to ask."

"Like I said, if you don't want to answer, don't." I sense he's fighting an internal battle with himself.

"No, it's okay." He takes a deep breath. "Just before you hit the wall, I saw someone I haven't seen in a couple years."

The wheels in my mind begin to whirl. "Who?"

"My ex-fiancée, Isabel."

A large chunk of lettuce and meat falls from my taco onto the foil as my hands start to shake. "Is she a skater too?"

"Yeah. She had a successful career representing Portugal. She won something like six national titles." He runs a hand through his hair. "Last I heard, she was living and teaching in Asia. I have no idea why she'd be here in Madrid."

I stare at the foil, studying all the wrinkles intently. "How long were you guys together?"

"Six years."

"That's a long time," I say slowly, still in shock. I never imagined Fernando would've been in a relationship for so long. Let alone engaged.

"It is." He nods.

"If you want to call her and reconnect while you're here, I can entertain myself for a day or two."

"No." His tone hardens, and his brow forms a deep V. "She's had more than four years to contact me if she had anything left to say and she hasn't. As far as I'm concerned, it's better if we each continue to pretend the other doesn't exist."

He opens his water bottle and takes a long drink. My shoulders tense. "Sorry for bringing it up," I say carefully.

"Don't apologize. You didn't know." He tightens the lid on the bottle and takes a deep breath. "We met as teenagers at a skating camp here in Madrid. We were both big practical jokers, and we constantly tried to one-up one another."

"Uh-oh. I bet that caused a lot of trouble."

He snorts. "It did. We were always in the doghouse with our coaches. But being in trouble brought us closer together. By the end of the summer, I'd fallen for her, and I asked her to be my girlfriend. She agreed."

His voice grows softer. "The first three years, we were lucky. We were training close to one another and were able to see each other every weekend. I proposed on our second anniversary, and she said yes. Around our third anniversary, just after I'd turned professional, the trouble started. Isabel shocked me by announcing that she was moving to Toronto to train. I was happy for her, but hurt she never consulted me."

He closes his eyes. "The distance tested us. For two years, we squeezed in video chats, texts, and calls when we could. Whenever I had time off, I'd fly out to Canada to spend time with her. But she never made an effort to reciprocate."

His eyes open and he looks up at me. "During one of my trips to Toronto, I opened up to Isabel about how frustrated I was. I wanted us to be a real couple. No more long-distance dating. I was more than ready to quit Dreams on Ice, move to Canada, and become a coach if it meant we could go back to the way things were. But instead of getting excited about the idea, she wanted to break up."

"What?" I exclaim. "That doesn't make any sense."

"I had the same reaction. Isabel had recently finished fifth at the World Championships. She saw her results as a sign her singles career was about to take off. She wanted to become the first woman from Portugal to win an Olympic medal in skating. The Games were a year away and she didn't want to have any distractions. Winning was more important to her than us."

My heart aches for him. "Seriously? She was willing to throw away your relationship because of some dumb medal."

He nods. "She's not alone. It's how a lot of people in my sport are."

"What did you do?"

"The only thing I could. I told her to take all the time she needed. If she wanted me to give her space, I would. I wasn't willing to break off the engagement without a fight. As painful as it was to not see her for ten months, if it meant having her as my wife for the rest of my life, it was a small price to pay."

I open and close my mouth. Fernando's just confirmed to me that his heart is made of pure gold.

He continues. "Isabel agreed to my terms. I stepped back and watched her from the sidelines. She had a great season in the run-up to the Olympics and was considered a medal threat. But the thing about ice skating is that falls can happen anytime, anywhere. Even if you're the world's most consistent skater."

"Did she fall at the Olympics?" I guess.

"Yeah. Isabel had a fluke fall in her short program on a double Axel. Unfortunately, it took her out of the medals. Even with her brilliant free skate, she finished in fourth. To say she was devastated would be an understatement."

"Fourth place is the worst. You're so close, but so far."

He shoots me a sad smile. "I tried my best to console her. I thought she needed a mental and physical break from skating. I booked us on a two-week Alaskan cruise. I thought it'd be the perfect way to get away from it all, but that's the opposite of what she wanted. Isabel was determined to jump right back into training and work even harder. Without talking to me, she publicly announced she was committing to another Olympic cycle. I heard about it on TV. After that . . ." His voice falters.

"After that . . . I knew that I'd lost her. When we had lunch the day she returned home from Norway, she gave me back my ring. In her words, she needed to 'go the journey alone.' I tried to reason with her, but she wouldn't change her mind. My heart broke, but I loved her too much to hold her back. I told her I understood, and then she walked away. That was the last time we spoke."

"I'm so sorry, Fernando. That's horrible." It's taking everything inside me not to rush over to his side and offer him a huge bear hug. "I can't believe you had to go through something like that. Especially after being together for so long."

He nods glumly. "It took me a long time to get over her. I eventually tried dating again. I've had two short-term relationships, but both times, they ended with me getting dumped. My heart just wasn't in it. I've given up on ever finding love."

"What if the right woman came along?" My pulse thuds painfully hard against my ribs as I wait to see how he responds.

"It's not gonna happen. Isabel was the girl of my dreams. I don't know if I can ever find someone I'll love more. So it's better not to even try. I've come to terms with being single."

"But Fernando, you deserve to be happy."

"But don't you see, I am happy." He forces a smile onto his face, but it doesn't reach his eyes. "I have my health, a great job, friends that are like family, and my cabin. I don't need anything else."

I open my mouth to fight him, but I sense it's not going to get me very far. Change isn't going to happen overnight.

He deserves to get his own happily ever after. Especially after dealing with a relationship like that. He may say he's happy being single, but he's not fooling me.

Our conversation shifts back around to our road trip as we eat. We decide to play tomorrow by ear and see how we're both feeling. I use his heating pad to release the muscles in my back. It helps, but doesn't alleviate all the aches. My gut tells me tomorrow is going to be rough.

Chapter Seventeen

We decide to leave Toledo late morning to get in a few hours of driving for Valencia. Neither of us is in the mood to return to Madrid.

"How's the stiffness?" Fernando asks as he returns to the outdoor table I'm sitting at near a gas station market. He's got some fresh fruit and nuts for our midday snack.

"As long as I don't move too quickly or try to turn my head, I'm good. The GPS said we only have another hour to go."

He sighs. "With how much discomfort your neck is in, I don't think walking around Valencia is such a great idea."

As annoyed as I am by the situation, he's right. Getting out of bed this morning to walk to the car was tough. If I take a wrong step, the muscles in my back spasm. I can't see myself getting very far unless I have Fernando carry me around the city.

That isn't an option. We can't risk him throwing out his back. He needs to be able to drive. I blow out air. "This whole situation sucks. I want my body to be back to a hundred percent so I can enjoy Spain."

"I'm sorry, Ava," he says in a low tone. "I know how frustrating it is waiting for your body to recover."

Ugh, why did that have to come out sounding like I was whining? Fernando already feels guilty, and now it's like I'm rubbing salt into the wound. "I'm sorry I'm being a grump."

"Don't worry about it." He slides the fruit bag toward me. "It's the pain talking, not you. I've been in your shoes many times. I understand."

"Have you suffered a lot of injuries over the course of your career?" I take a few grapes and pop them into my mouth, chewing slowly.

"No, thankfully. My only major injury was tearing my ACL as a teenager, but since then, I've been lucky. Whenever I'm hurt, it's usually only something minor like a pulled muscle or sprained ankle." He scratches his chin. "We had a great physical therapist on the Dreams on Ice staff who could work magic when it came to putting our bodies back together." He takes a small handful of nuts. "Hmm . . . I bet we could find a massage therapist to help loosen your back."

"Are you volunteering your services to me?" I tease.

"No. I'm hopeless with it." He shakes his head, the tips of his ears the same shade of red as the strawberries on the table. "But the good news is, Valencia is a resort town packed full of spas. I'm sure at least one of them will have a masseuse on staff."

I sit taller. To my ailing body, a spa sounds like heaven. I picture the hot steam room, relaxing on a massage table, and spending the day being pampered by the staff. I've never actually been to a spa, but my sister swears they're worth the splurge. At this point, I'll do anything to get some relief. "Count me in."

"I'll make a call to my tía Yesenia. She'll know where we should go. She travels to Valencia all the time for work." He glances at the time on his watch. "Today's market day in Santa Luz, so she's probably with Mamá. I'll do my best to keep the call short, but they'll both want to say hello to you."

I shrug, ignoring the painful tug between my neck and shoulder. "You can't control what they do, but I appreciate it."

Taking out his phone, he taps the screen and holds it up to his ear. I move on to the nuts and raisins. It's another perfect blend of salty and sweet. One thing I can't get over is how different all the food tastes here. It's packed with flavor. I'll miss it when I get home.

"Hola, Mamá." I hear Fernando's mother reply in Spanish, but he answers back in English for my benefit, which I appreciate. "No, Ava and I decided to head to Valencia instead of Zaragoza . . . Uh-huh . . . Uh-huh . . . Um, two or three more days?"

My attention turns from Fernando to Sequoia Valley. I wonder how my dog is getting on at my sister's house. We've been so busy that I haven't made the time to check in with anyone except Daphne and the clinic, of course, since the day we arrived. I should call my own parents later.

"What? No! Please don't!" Fernando's voice turns panicky. I glance in his direction. His brows are knitted together tightly. "Why? Because that would be too overwhelming for us. Ava and I are still in the early stages of our relationship. We don't need the *whole* family to come to dinner . . . No . . . Yes . . . I'm sure she'll agree with me." We lock eyes. "Hold on, let me put you on speaker."

He sets the device down on the table. "Go ahead, Mamá, she's right here."

"Ava! It's Mamá Alvarez. How are you doing?"

"I'm great. Thanks for asking."

"And my son is treating you well?"

I suppress a giggle. "Yes, ma'am."

"Good, good. I'm looking forward to your arrival in Santa Luz."

"I am too," I say, curious to see the place where Fernando grew up.

"Now, I was wondering if I might be able to get your opinion on something."

Fernando crosses his arms and mouths *wait for it* to me.

I shoot him a curious look. "Sure."

"How would you feel about me organizing a little welcome dinner for you and Fernando?"

He rolls his eyes. *"Little is an understatement,"* he mouths to me.

Picking up on my fake boyfriend's frustrations, I ask, "Er, how many people did you have in mind? I was hoping I'd have some one-on-one time with Fernando's immediate family, like yourself and Mr. Alvarez." He flashes me a thumbs-up. "But if you think a bigger gathering is better . . ."

"No, you are absolutely right. There's no need to invite the whole family."

"I'm glad you're seeing reason," Fernando says, wiping his brow in mock relief. "Anyway, Mamá, is Tía Yesenia with you? I want to treat Ava to a spa day. I need some recommendations on where we should go."

We hear a few muffled sounds. Another woman's voice I recognize as his aunt comes onto the line. "A spa day? How romantic!"

Fernando opens his mouth to correct her, but I shake

my head. "Yes, he's been spoiling me like a princess the entire week."

"Good boy. That's how we raised you," Tía Yesenia says, a hint of pride in her voice. "Fernando, take your woman to the Malvarrosa Resort and Spa. Ask for Ana, the manager. She'll look after you herself."

"Gracias, Tía. I knew we could count on you." He takes the phone off speaker, finishes the conversation with his aunt, and disconnects the call.

"That wasn't so bad," I say, picking out a few more almonds for myself.

"We got off easy, thanks to you."

"How many people would your mom have invited given the chance?"

"Think *My Big Fat Greek Wedding*." He places the phone on the table, leans back in his chair, and stretches. "A small family gathering to Mamá includes everyone who lives within driving distance of their home. About forty people."

"That many? Is your parents' home that large?"

"Sí. My parents run a bed and breakfast. The building has ten guest rooms, a large dining room, and an outdoor patio."

"What happens when your relatives not within driving distance are also invited over?"

"The one time that's happened, for my abuela's ninetieth birthday, Mamá rented a ballroom in one of the local hotels."

I let out a low whistle. "And here I thought having seven people at Thanksgiving was a lot. You win the prize for the largest extended family, maybe ever."

"Nope. That prize would go to our neighbors, the Rodrigueses. They have an even larger family. At last count, I think there were just over fifty of them."

All I can say is, "Wow."

We get out of our seats. Fernando takes care of cleaning up our trash as I move along at a glacial pace.

"Can you give me a crash course on who everyone is before the family dinner?" I rub the stiff spot between my neck and shoulder. "That is assuming your mom will *only* invite a few of your aunts and uncles."

"She'll behave. Especially since you asked her to keep it small." We walk over to the car, and he clicks the doors open. "The hour we have left getting to Valencia should be enough time to cover the basics on the aunties. We'll cover my uncles over dinner."

"How much is there to know?"

"A lot." He starts the engine. "Again, think *My Big Fat Greek Wedding*. My tías have big personalities, meaning there's a lot to warn you about."

"Should I take notes?"

He smirks. "That's up to you."

When Fernando turns into the driveway of the Malvarrosa Resort and Spa, it takes us just over five minutes before we reach the main building.

"Is this a hotel or a palace?" I press my nose against the window, staring out at the mini Versailles.

The building is long and contains four floors, each with sash windows. Leading up to the lobby, there's a red carpet and workers dressed in livery uniforms from a century ago. My favorite detail, however, is the massive fountain with four horses galloping across the water.

"Um, no offense, Fernando, I'm sure your aunt means

well, but I'm gonna be blunt—there's no way I can afford a place like this."

He frowns. "I don't want you to worry about the money, Ava. You told my tía you're being treated like a princess. As your fake boyfriend, I'm treating you to the spa."

I want to say yes to him, but my stubborn pride just won't let me have my way. "No. It's too expensive. I don't want you to drain your bank account for me."

"I want to do this for you." He gives me the puppy-dog eyes.

I'm touched by his generosity, but even if he can afford this place, I still can't bring myself to accept the offer. "I'm a simple girl with simple tastes," I say softly. "I would feel like a fish out of water here."

He sighs. "Okay, you win. I'll turn the car around and we'll go someplace else."

"Do you think your aunt will be insulted if she finds out?"

"If she is, too bad. Today is about you."

During the ride over, I learned that Tía Yesenia is an architect. She's won several awards for her work, and her firm is one of the most highly sought-after in Spain. It wouldn't surprise me if she designed this property.

As we're speaking, one of the hotel valets taps on the window, "Hola, señor."

"Hola." Fernando rolls down the window and speaks to the valet. From what I piece together, he explains that we're turning around and about to leave. The valet nods and takes a couple of steps back, clearing space for Fernando to reverse. He presses the clutch and changes gears, but as we roll backward, the car suddenly jolts.

"Ouch," I hiss as the unexpected motion jostles my neck. I grip the armrests tightly.

Fernando frowns and jiggles the stick. The valet shouts, and we hear the sound of air escaping from the tires. He opens the door to inspect the damage. "Crap," he exclaims.

"What happened?" I don't turn to look, trying to limit my movements.

He rests his head for a moment on the steering wheel and mumbles, "I ran over the spike strip. One of the tires is flat."

A flat tire. I exhale. That's not bad. It could've been worse, like another broken timing belt. I pat him on the back. "We'll get this sorted out. I'm sure a tow truck can take care of it."

"Let's hope so." Fernando brings the car forward and pulls off to the side. I wait in the vehicle while he sorts out the mess with the valet team, taking advantage of the hotel's Wi-Fi to text Daphne.

> Ava: Hey, Daph, sorry I've been MIA. Are you free for a chat this afternoon?

"Well, Ava, it looks like we're gonna be stuck here for a while," Fernando says, returning to the car. "The guy in the valet booth called for a tow truck. They quoted him two to three hours, since we're not an emergency. I thought maybe I could change the tire myself, but the car's tool kit is missing."

"Well, at least we can wait in the lobby and explore. This place is huge."

"It is," he agrees. "But the exploring will have to wait. You'll, uh, be otherwise occupied."

"Fernando . . ."

"Don't kill me, but I also had the valet call the concierge to book you a spa appointment."

I give him a hard look. "We just went through this—"

He places a finger to my lips. "I know you said no a few minutes ago, but if we're here anyway, I want you to be as comfortable as possible."

I exhale. "Do I have a choice?"

"No. Everything's been paid for." He grins.

I exhale deeply. "Fine, I'll do it, but this doesn't mean I'm letting you off the hook." My body is stiff, and I really could use a massage. But I'm going to find a way to split the difference with Fernando. He just doesn't know it yet.

"Noted."

I unbuckle my seat belt. "What are you going to do while I'm at the spa?"

"I'm joining you."

My cheeks burn hot. "You didn't plan on us getting a couples massage, did you?" I sputter. We're a fake couple, but I'm not prepared for us to take it *that* far. Even with a handsome guy like him.

"No!" He quickly adds, "We'll be in separate rooms."

I relax. "Okay, then."

We step out of the car and a hotel worker approaches us with a golf cart. "Mr. Alvarez?" he asks.

"Yes," Fernando says.

"I'm glad I didn't miss you!" The man grins. "I thought I heard the valet mention your name over the radio, but wasn't certain. I'm Javier, your personal concierge while you're with us at the Malvarrosa Resort and Spa. Do you have any bags you'd like me to take charge of while you visit the spa today?"

I blink and stare dumbly at Fernando. Did he book a top-of-the-line VIP package for us to get service like this?

"Uh, we're not going to be here that long. Just a few hours," he says.

The concierge blinks slowly. "Oh. I was informed by the hotel manager this morning that you'd be staying with us for two nights in the presidential suite. Am I mistaken?"

Presidential suite? Us staying here? He must have the wrong people. Alvarez is a common last name, after all.

I glance from the concierge to Fernando, who appears just as puzzled as I am. "I think I know what's going on," he says. "I need to get in touch with my aunt to clarify a few things." He reaches for his phone. "In the meantime, would you mind taking Ava up to the spa?"

"Of course." The concierge smiles. "It would be my pleasure. Señora, if you'll please follow me." He gestures to the golf cart. I take a step forward, but then look to Fernando for permission. I hate to leave him alone.

"Go on, Ava. I'll be right behind you."

Although I feel some guilt, the allure of having a massage to relieve the deep ache in my back is too much to resist.

"OK, I'll see you soon."

Chapter Eighteen

I spend three glorious hours in the spa soaking in a mineral spring, sitting in a steam room, and receiving a massage from a woman with magical hands. She turns my body to putty, working out all the knots in my muscles. I've never felt better. As I emerge from the locker room, Fernando is waiting for me in the reception area.

"Somebody looks happy." He laughs. "I take it you had a good time."

"The best. I'm glad you forced my hand. I didn't know how much I needed it."

"Your back is feeling better, then?" he asks.

"Much." We slowly walk side by side out the glass doors to one of the many garden areas. "How was your massage?"

"I can't tell you. I didn't end up getting one. I've been playing phone tag with my aunt and waiting on the car people."

That's right. I'd forgotten about the whole thing with the concierge and the tow truck. I stop walking. The lightness I felt a few minutes ago has been replaced by a harsh return to reality. "I'm sorry."

"It's all good. I have my trusty old heating pad. It works as well as any masseuse." He shoves his hands into his pockets. "Anyway, I have some great news and some bad news to share with you."

"Okay. Give me the bad news first. I'd rather get it over with."

"When the tow truck driver turned up, it turned out we had two flats instead of one. I was hoping the shop it's been taken to would be able to put on a new set of tires today. But when I spoke to the mechanic, he let me know the ones we need are special order. It'll be three days before he can get them in."

I inhale air sharply. "That stinks. Our schedule was already ambitious. Spending two extra days here isn't what we wanted, but there isn't much we can do about it. We can't drive without tires."

"Well, we could return the rental and get a new one. But the fees for returning it in its current condition are going to be astronomical." He shifts his weight from foot to foot. "It's better to wait it out."

"No, I agree. What's the good news?"

"Do you remember when the concierge mentioned us staying here for two nights?"

I nod.

"Well as it turns out, Tía Yesenia is giving me an early Christmas present. We have an all-expenses-paid stay for the next two nights."

"All expenses paid," I repeat.

"Uh-huh. She reserved the best room at the resort for us. We don't have to stay here if you don't want to, but I thought considering the circumstances . . ." He trails off.

"I'm not one to turn my nose up at a gift like that. If

your aunt has already paid for everything, we're staying. Unless you think we shouldn't."

"Why wouldn't we?" His tone shifts to confusion.

"I don't know. Maybe you'd want to enjoy your gift alone."

"No. Tía Yesenia was crystal clear that this was for the pair of us. Remember, she thinks we're a couple."

I nod. "We'd better make sure we take more photos here so we can show them to her when we meet."

"Definitely." He pulls out a key card from his pocket. "Come on, let's go check out the room. Javier said the private elevator is near the reception desk."

I dry swallow. A private elevator to the presidential suite. Is this really my life right now?

The door swings open to the living room and my jaw drops. This is hands down one of the nicest rooms I've ever seen. "I think my whole apartment could fit inside here." I walk over to the window and draw the curtains back. The entire wall is a window that overlooks the ocean. The water is a stunning turquoise color, filled with tiny dots of seabirds, surfers, and boats.

Spinning around, I take in the remainder of the room. There are two couches, a recliner, a glass coffee table, a fireplace, and an entertainment set with a large TV. The dark-green walls are tastefully decorated with seascape portraits of what I'm guessing is the Valencia area.

I continue my tour, entering the dining room next. The wooden walls are adorned with a hundred different seashells. There's a long rectangular table that could fit about ten people, surrounded by light blue chairs. The place settings are made from crystal and fine china. I pick up a wineglass and turn it over in my hand—there's a pattern of tiny seashells. "I wonder if this is all handmade."

"It wouldn't surprise me," Fernando says, casually leaning against the door frame. "This is the nicest suite I've ever stayed in, but I just noticed we may have a slight problem."

I return the glass to the table and face him. "What do you mean?"

"There's only one bedroom."

"Oh." My mouth drops open. Of all the possible problems, only one bed has never crossed my mind. One of my rules for us traveling together has been that we have to have separate rooms wherever we're staying, but I guess that's about to fly out the door.

"Um, I think we can manage. That is if you don't mind me claiming the living room sofa," I say.

"Nuh-uh." Fernando's brows knit together. "The bedroom is yours. If anyone is going to be sleeping on the sofa, it's me."

"But this is your Christmas gift. You should have the bed."

He shakes his head. "You're the one with the sore back. Not to mention you're supposed to be the princess. I'd never steal the bed from you."

Here we go again. Both of us being stubborn. "What if one of us got the bed tonight and the other tomorrow?"

"I suppose it's the best compromise we'll be able to come up with." His jaw stiffens. "But it won't stop me from trying to convince you to keep the bed."

"You can try all you want." I chuckle. "I'm good at holding my ground."

"So am I." He crosses his arms. "Challenge accepted."

We stare at one another for a solid thirty seconds, neither wanting to break first. Eventually, I give in. There's too much I want to see and do. "Did the concierge happen to give you a list of the hotel amenities? This might be the only time I'll ever get to spend in a place like this. I don't know about you, but I'd like to take full advantage of every offering."

"A girl after my own heart."

His words send a warm, tingling feeling through my body.

"It's all on the hotel app." He whips out his phone. "The username is Alvarez and the password is our room number, 3013." He hands me the device. "Let me know what interests you first. I was thinking about going snorkeling this afternoon, but there's also golf, a pottery class, and wine tasting, just to name a few of the activities."

"Snorkeling in winter? Isn't the water too cold?"

"You forgot who you're asking." He smirks. "I work in an ice rink for a living. With a wet suit, the cold doesn't bother me."

I cock my head. "You're one of those people who does polar plunges aren't you?"

"Guilty as charged." He chuckles. "You're welcome to join me."

"Thanks, but no thanks." I shiver. "Ice-cold water is for drinking, not swimming in."

"It's not *that* cold. Maybe sixty-three degrees?"

"That's cold enough." He shrugs, and I pop open the app, log in, and begin swiping through the electronic brochure. My eyes bulge. Fernando saying there were a *few* activities offered by the resort is the understatement of the century. There's page after page of various offerings. I glance up. "It could take us a month or more to try everything they have here. I'll have to make a top-ten list."

He nods and checks the time on his phone. "We still have a couple hours of daylight. If you're not interested in snorkeling, would you mind if I went?"

"Knock yourself out. While you do that, I think I'll head to the beach. It may be too cold to swim, but it's warm enough to sit out and soak up the sun while I make some calls home."

Fernando flashes me a thumbs-up. "I'm gonna go change. I'll meet you back here in a couple minutes. We can walk down to the beach together."

I grab my swimsuit from my suitcase and step into the guest bathroom. Although I normally would've donned the black one-piece I've had for a couple years, Daphne insisted I update my swim attire and swap for a bikini for this trip. I can still hear her voice. *Everyone in Europe wears a bikini. If you wear a one-piece, you'll stick out like a sore thumb.*

I stare at the white floral print. It's another leap out of my comfort zone. I don't typically wear something so girly or white. I dress for comfort. When I'm not in scrubs, I live in my black leggings, a T-shirt, and a hoodie. I take a deep breath and slip into it, sliding a blue sundress over it.

"You ready, Ava?" Fernando calls out a few minutes later.

"Coming, I just need to wash the sunscreen off my hands."

Once my hands are clean, I reach for my hat and sunglasses and enter the living room. "Do you think—" I'm frozen in my tracks. I need to dive headfirst into the cold ocean, pronto. Fernando is wearing nothing but a pair of fitted swim trunks that don't leave much to the imagination. All those times I've wondered what was under his clothing, and now, I officially have my answer. He's a lean, mean, ripped machine.

"Do I think what?"

"Uh . . ." I fumble for an excuse. "I should put sunscreen on my back too? I couldn't reach it. I mean, I'll probably just be lying in a chair and not exposing that much skin, but better to be protected just in case." I force a laugh.

It's hard to focus when every tiny movement he makes shows off the way he's built. His chest, arms, back —all of it looks like it's been chiseled out of marble. His broad shoulders taper into a lean waist, and when he shifts, I catch a glimpse of his abs. They're a little soft, but I can still make out six squares. My brain short-circuits.

And this is him *after* retiring? What kind of shape was he in when he was competing? I always knew he was strong —lifting humans over your head takes a lot of muscle and power—but now I can see it. And wow. Just wow.

"I would if I were you. Even though it's slightly over-cast, you can still burn easily. Do you want some help with your back?"

"Yes, please," I squeak. "Let me grab the sunscreen bottle."

I flee to the bathroom, practically collapsing against the wall the second I'm out of sight. I need to calm down. It's just a man's body. Nothing I haven't seen before. Except . . . it's not just any body. It's a fitness-model-meets-figure-skater kind of body, and pretending otherwise is pointless. I snort softly to myself and fan my face, taking a few deep breaths before I head back out.

"Here it is. Sorry for the hold up," I say a minute later, waving the bottle. "I forgot I'd repacked it."

Fernando gestures to one of the dining chairs. "Sit. It'll be easier."

I awkwardly shimmy out of the top of my dress and settle into the chair, exposing my back. A second later, I hear the squirt of the bottle, and then his hands are on me, spreading the sunscreen with a touch that's somehow both careful and confident. His palms are warm, and he uses just the right amount of pressure, like he actually knows what he's doing.

"You lied to me," I mumble, eyes fluttering shut. "You said you were lousy at massages. You're not."

He chuckles. "This doesn't count. It's not a proper massage."

"Say what you will. Now that I know your secret, if I wake up with a bad back tomorrow, I'm putting you to work."

"Or you could visit the spa again."

"I don't want to make your aunt spend more than she already has."

"Ava, don't worry about the money. In fact, Tía Yesenia would be offended if you didn't take advantage of another day at the spa if you want it. *She* certainly would." I hear the cap being replaced on the bottle. "I think she intended for these next few days to be treated like we're on a couple's retreat."

"That would explain the bed situation." My eyes widen. "We're supposed to be a couple who've only known each other for a few short weeks. If you ask me, it's pretty bold for her to assume we're on that intimate a level." I pull the top of the dress back over my swimsuit.

"My tía is determined to do everything in her power to speed up our relationship. She wants to see me happy and settled."

I want those things for him too. Although, I'm not sure about the settled part. "Remember, you'll be the first woman to meet the family since Isabel."

My stomach muscles clench. I had forgotten about that. "Your family is going to think that we're a hop, skip, and jump away from getting engaged."

"I know." He places his hands on top of his head.

"We're going to have to ramp things up from a simmer to a boil. We'll have to get comfortable with more hand holding, kissing, sharing inside jokes—the things actual couples do."

Which I don't mind in the least. We may be fake dating, but there's nothing fake about how my feelings are growing for this man. If he needs me to be here for him, I will. I make a note to call my hotel in Barcelona to cancel my reservation. All my plans for my second week here are going to have to be placed on hold.

"I don't know, Ava. I'm starting to think this whole idea was stupid. I should just come clean to my family." The muscles in Fernando's body have tensed. He carries his stress in his shoulders. He's also chewing on his lower lip again, a nervous habit I've noticed he does when he's worried about something.

"Do you want your aunts off your back or not?"

"Yes, but—"

"No buts." I cut him off. "We're doing this. It's settled. End of discussion." I'm in my determined mode and bold enough to pat him on the pecs. They're rock-hard. "Now, let's go. We're wasting time being up here."

The resort's private beach is massive. There's a long stretch of pristine, fine white sand along a piece of beautiful untouched ocean. The tide is low right now. Near the shore, I spot some exposed tide pools and long, straggly strips of seaweed. A few seagulls cry overhead.

There are two rows of beach chairs shaded by umbrellas about twenty feet from the water's edge. Since it's early December, there's a noticeably thin crowd. I count about ten people. It's a welcome relief. I'll be able to make a call to my sister and not have to worry about bothering anyone.

I remove my phone from my pocket and tap Daphne's name. She answers the video request on the third ring. "Good morning, Daph. How goes it?" She's dressed in her bathrobe. Her back is turned to me, her attention focused on the stove. She scoops a pancake out of the frying pan and deposits it onto a plate, turning off the burner.

"It goes." She hides a yawn with her hand. "Where are you?" She squints at the screen. "Is that the ocean?"

"Uh-huh. I'm just outside Valencia." I flip the camera around, panning the length of the beach.

"It looks so pretty." Daphne sighs. "I wish I could be there with you right now." She pulls her robe tighter around her body. "We had our first snowfall last night. I'm not looking forward to going outside and shoveling the driveway when I take the kids to school."

"Can you talk Brian into doing it for you?"

She shakes her head as she sits down. "He's out of town until Tuesday. Anyhow, I've been dying to get the four-one-one on your trip. How has everything really been going? I can't believe you decided to rent a car and drive yourself around! No offense, but you're the last person I ever expected to do something like that."

"Things have been good." I turn the camera back to me and selectively fill her in on some of my adventures.

She chews and swallows a bite of her pancake. "Well color me impressed! A week ago, you'd never left the country, and now, you're a pro."

"How's the office redecorating going? And my Max?"

"Your dog is fine, and mums the word on the office."

"Daphne, come on, that's not fair. Throw your poor sister a bone."

"Fine." She sips her coffee. "I let Vicki pick out the paint color for the break room."

I wrinkle my nose. "What color?"

"That's all you're getting from me. You'll have to wait and see."

I roll my eyes. I get that Daphne wants me to be surprised, but I do want to make sure everything is on track. This is my business.

"Ava," my sister starts, "don't be like that."

"Like what?"

"Annoyed with me. I do interior decorating for a living. And more importantly, I've known you since the day you were born. Aside from Mom, there's nobody who knows your likes and preferences better than me. Trust your big sis. Your only job right now is to soak up as much Spanish sun as you can and enjoy being man free."

I nearly choke as she says that, but turn it into a cough. "You're right."

Daphne studies me for a moment, then leans in closer to the screen. "Ava, you're enjoying this trip as a *solo* traveler, aren't you? Please tell me you didn't pick up a random guy to get over Devon."

"You mean Dylan. And no, I haven't." It's not a complete lie. Fernando isn't a stranger. I swallow hard.

"Good." She relaxes. "Because I want you to—"

"Ava! I was looking for you." I close my eyes and slip lower down the chair. "I've locked myself out of our room, do you mind if I borrow your card key? I couldn't get a spare from the front desk without an ID." Of all the times for Fernando to materialize, it has to be now.

"Ava, who is that?" Daphne asks. "It sounded like a guy."

"Oh, I'm sorry, I didn't realize you were on the phone."

"It's just my sister," I say quickly, opening my eyes and shoving my hand into my pocket.

"Ava, who is that?!" Daphne repeats, her voice more tense.

My hands close around the thin plastic card. I pull it out and shove it into a dripping wet Fernando's hand just as he leans over and waves to my sister. His smile is wide and unassuming. "Hola. You must be Daphne. I'm Fernando. It's nice to finally meet you."

"Likewise." Her tone is polite, but there's a hint of anger she can't hide from me. "Except I'm afraid my sister has been holding out on me. She hasn't said anything about you."

I'm a spider tangled in her own web of lies. Daphne's eyes look like they want to shoot lasers at me. I wish I could disappear.

Chapter Nineteen

"So, Fernando, how long have you known my sister?" Daphne gives us her full attention, now wide awake.

"Oh, a few weeks. She saved my neck by helping my friend's cat."

My heart is hammering so loudly against my chest that I can barely hear Fernando's words.

"You live in Sequoia Valley?" She drums her fingers against the table.

"I do now. I work at the ice skating rink. But I'm originally from Barcelona."

My sister's face relaxes and she lights up. "Wait a second, you're *Coach* Fernando! You taught my son, Brody."

"Brody . . . Brody . . . he's about four years old, this tall" —Fernando holds out a hand—"and likes to hum the Mario Brothers theme song?"

"That's him!" Daphne exclaims. "You were his favorite coach! He was really bummed to find out you weren't teaching the next level. Don't get me wrong, he likes Coach Leslie, but he loved you."

I can't believe what I'm hearing. Fernando taught my nephew? And Daphne is suddenly fine with everything?

"He's a great kid. One of my best listeners in the level-one group. A real natural on the ice, just like his aunt." He winks in my direction. "Tell Brody I'll be back soon. The only reason I'm not teaching this session is because I knew I'd be gone for a month."

"I will! He'll be ecstatic."

He waves and steps out of the camera's view. "I'd better get back up to the room so I can shower and change. I'll see you up there, Ava. Thanks for the key."

"I'll, um, text you when I'm on my way up so you can let me in."

"Sounds like a plan."

He walks up the beach toward the lobby doors, his brown locks ruffling in the breeze. The sunlight catches on his broad shoulders and the easy lines of muscle along his back. His swim trunks sit low on his hips, revealing a glimpse of a lean waist and another peek at the abs you get from actually doing the core exercises the rest of the world usually skips.

I catch myself openly staring at the flex of his strong legs and the effortless way he moves, like the beach was made for him. I'm so distracted, I almost forget I'm still on a video call. I force my attention back to my sister before she notices.

"I. Can't. Believe. You. And. Fernando. Are. A. Thing!" Daphne gushes, leaning closer to the camera.

"What?" If I weren't already sitting, I would've fallen out of my chair. It's the last reaction I ever expected Daph to have. "You're not gonna give me a lecture on hiding things from you? Or being around men so soon?"

"No. Because I know Fernando's a good guy and would

never take advantage of you. I didn't recognize him in the Speedo, but the man is a legend among the moms at the ice rink! He's one of the most patient and friendly coaches on staff. A real puppy dog." Her eyes glaze over. "It's common knowledge that he's single and doesn't date. There have been so many people who've tried to be the one to break his dry spell. But he always shoots them down. Until now. If there were one guy I would ever set you up with, it's him." She shakes her head and refocuses on me. "How serious are you two?"

"We're just friends. We aren't really dating. We're putting on a show so we can get his family off his back," I sputter.

"Whoa. Back up. Fake dating? Meeting his family?" She lowers her chin. "Tell. Me. Everything."

And just like that, she goes from protective older sister wanting to tear Fernando apart to one of his staunchest supporters. I wonder if somewhere between the hotel's driveway and the beach, I entered the Twilight Zone.

Daphne refills her coffee and listens intently as I fill in the gaps from earlier. I tell her about bumping into Dylan a few times, my chance meeting with Fernando at the Denver airport, and our adventure driving across Spain together.

"Your vacation sounds like the plot of a B- or C-level rom-com. I wouldn't believe it if I hadn't heard the details straight from your mouth."

"Is that a movie you'd go and see?" I ask purely out of curiosity.

"If you were starring in it or if I wanted something running in the background while I was cooking, totally."

I snort.

"You asked. I'm just being honest with you. Between

work and the kids, I don't have time for movies and TV. It has to be something that really entices me."

"And that would include . . .?" Daphne does live a busy life. And with my niece and nephew being as active as they are, I don't know how she has time to fit in as many activities as she does.

"Any movie with Chris Evans, something based off a book I love, or something with hockey."

"Hockey? Not football or soccer?"

"No." A blush creeps up her cheeks. "It has to be hockey. The players are"—she fans herself—"dreamy. Especially when they're in suits."

"Does Brian know you have a thing for hockey guys?"

She nods, not willing to let any more info slip out. That's fine with me, because I don't think I even want my brain to go there. I clear my throat. "Going back to Fernando, I need your advice. What's your take on how I should handle his family? I want them fully convinced we're the real deal."

"Ava, as cliché as it sounds, be yourself. You don't need to do anything special. The way Fernando was looking at you earlier is totally different than the way he interacts with any other person at the ice rink. It's soft and tender. Not to mention the way you responded. You can't tell me you feel nothing for that man."

"I . . . I like him. A lot."

Daphne raises an eyebrow. "Your face says it's more than a lot."

I puff out my cheeks. "Fine. I have a serious crush on the man."

She smirks. "Use that to your advantage. Don't force what isn't there. The chemistry you share will be enough."

"Do you think Fernando can get there on his end?"

Daphne shoots me a "do you really need me to point out the obvious to you" look.

"Never mind," I mutter.

We chat a little longer, then I call my parents. After I disconnect with them, I take a few moments to stretch and listen to the calming sound of the ocean waves breaking against the beach. Is Daphne right? Does Fernando see me as a woman he might consider breaking his rules for? I guess I'll just have to wait and find out.

Our two nights at the resort pass too quickly. Despite my first impulse of wanting to try all the amenities, I spend most of my time relaxing beachside.

"The initial plunge is the worst. The key is to keep your body moving. It'll adjust," Fernando says as we walk into the water.

I inhale sharply. It's like I've stepped into a freezer. Despite wearing booties and a full-body wet suit, the chill still seeps into my bones. "Cold," I say, shivering.

"It'll be worth it once you see what's under the water."

I rub my hands over my arms and will myself keep walking. The water is just above my belly button.

Fernando lowers his face mask. "This is a good spot. There's a steep drop about thirty feet from here. It's tempting to go and explore the reef, but don't. The resort equipment manager warned me yesterday that the current is strong and unpredictable."

My thoughts flash to getting pulled out to sea and surrounded by sharks. "I'll be a good girl."

"Are you ready?"

"As I'll ever be."

Fernando and I stick the breathing tubes in our mouths and duck under the water. Another gasp escapes from my lips. My face goes numb. But I quickly forget about it all as a sea turtle flaps its fins, effortlessly gliding past us. Its amber orbs are trained on us as if we're the best source of entertainment it's seen this year.

As I continue to study my surroundings, I notice red and orange sea stars and purple urchins lying out among the thick patches of green seaweed swaying with the waves, as well as schools of colorful fish.

Fernando swims up beside me and taps my shoulder, pointing to the surface. "How are you doing?" he asks, releasing his snorkel.

"Really good. It's hard to believe that a world so different than ours can exist twenty feet off the Spanish coastline."

"So it's worth braving the cold?"

"So far, yes," I admit.

"Glad to hear it." He chuckles. "On the next dive down, see if you can spot some of the seahorses in the seagrass. They camouflage so well that I didn't notice them until today."

We pop back under. Fernando moves through the water quickly, pointing out the seahorses. He's so agile. If he weren't an ice skater, I could see him being a swimmer. He has the height and lanky build for it. I wonder if that's a sport he ever considered.

It's scary just how many thoughts I'm having about Fernando these days, and lately, even dreams. Last night, we were ice skating together again. This time, it was an outdoor rink under the stars. Fernando was so handsome in a fitted black shirt and pants. Holding hands, we glided together side by side as he whispered in English about how much he loved me, followed by Spanish.

It was a dream that felt so real. I could feel the chill through my clothing, hear the sounds of our blades crunching against the ice, and sense the warmth of his body next to mine. The Ava in my dream was a much better skater than I am in real life. I've never been more motivated to take up ice skating as a hobby.

I lose track of time snorkeling. We spend the remainder of the morning in the water. Eventually, a few gray dorsal fins appear above the waves about twenty feet from us. I swallow hard and point to them. "Fernando, look," I say, my voice shaking. "Do you think that's a shark?"

"No." He squints. "I think they're dolphins, unless sharks travel in groups, which I don't think they do."

I breathe a little easier. "Animals can surprise you. They're resilient and don't always follow the rules, like lions. Did you know non-alpha males have formed coalitions with other males to make hunting easier?"

"You never cease to amaze me with how smart you are *Doctor* B." He shakes his head. "If it were a shark, don't worry, I'd protect you."

"My hero."

We exchange twin grins.

Then, like somebody popping a cork of champagne off a bottle, we hear a sharp blast of air being released, followed by a few high-pitched clicks and squeaks as a pod of six dolphins pops their heads out of the water, joining in on our conversation.

"What do you think they're talking about?" Fernando asks.

"I'm not fluent in dolphin, but if I had to guess, I'd say

they're wondering why these weird sea creatures have legs instead of tails."

They come within a few feet of us but maintain their distance. Sticking our heads underwater, we watch the pod work together to hunt a school of silver fish. They're wicked fast and able to change direction at a moment's notice, just like how I imagine Fernando is on the ice.

Eventually, I start to get tired. Back on shore, we sit on the sand and continue watching the pod for a little while longer from a pair of beach chairs.

"They're putting on a show for us," he says.

"Yeah, they are." I set my arms behind me and lean back, sighing in contentment. "Seeing animals out in the wild doing what they're supposed to be doing makes me so happy."

"That's how I feel when I'm out on the ice," he says in a low tone.

A comfortable silence envelops us for a minute.

"If you had to pick your favorite animal, Ava, what would it be?" Fernando asks eventually.

"My favorite? That's a hard question. I have a lot." I giggle.

"Like?"

"If it's a domestic animal, I prefer dogs and cats. For small mammals, I'd say otters and red pandas. If we're talking large mammals, my list would have to include elephants, lions, and tigers. Reptiles and amphibians are tricky."

"I love how your brain works. I should've known you'd group all your favorite animals into categories." He laughs. "What if I challenged you to pick just one?"

"Only one?"

"Yup. Only one."

I sit up and bring my knees to my chest. "Um . . . I guess it's red pandas. I love their little faces."

He scratches his chin. "I've never seen a red panda. You'll have to show me a picture when we get back inside."

"I will. Your mind will be overloaded with cuteness. What about you? What's your favorite animal?"

"Would it surprise you if I said koala bears?"

"Yes." I pictured him as more of a wolf or lion kind of guy.

"When I was touring Australia, I was lucky enough to get up close and personal with a couple koalas for some of our media spots. They were so docile. It didn't take much for them to win me over."

"Are you aware they average twenty hours of sleep a day?" I snigger.

His eyes widen. "They do?"

"Uh-huh."

He snorts. "It figures I'd pick an animal that enjoys naps just as much as me."

I laugh.

"I hate to end it here, but we have to check out by one." Fernando sighs. "If we want to fit a shower in, we should head back now. It's almost noon."

"Where did the time go?" We stand and brush the sand off our bodies.

"You, uh, still have a little sand on your cheek," Fernando tells me.

I use the back of my hand to brush it. "Better?"

"No, it's still there." He glances at me. "May I?"

I nod.

Tenderly, he reaches up and brushes a patch of skin under my eye. His touch sends a shiver of delight through my body.

"There. It's all gone now." His voice is as soft and smooth as velvet.

"Thanks," I whisper.

We stare at one another a few moments longer. The Adam's apple in his throat constricts. "Ava." He starts moving an inch closer to my body. "I've, um, been doing a lot of thinking recently, and I'm ready to, er . . ."

"Yes?"

"To, um . . ." He breaths deeply. "Why is this so hard?" His eyes flutter and he tries again. "I'd like to, um, make you my number-one friend," he blurts out quickly. "And by that, I—"

"Fernando! Ava! What fortunate timing!"

We jump back from each other, and our heads snap in the direction of the pathway leading up to the lobby.

Sitting in the driver's seat of a golf cart in a red pantsuit, like a fox who's found a free meal, is a woman I recognize as Fernando's aunt Yesenia.

Chapter Twenty

It takes a few seconds for my body to calm down. I'm dying to ask Fernando why I've suddenly propelled to the top of his friend list, but for now I'll have to wait. I exhale deeply and school my face in a way I hope doesn't appear too frustrated.

After all, not only is his aunt the one who's footing the bill for the last few days, but she's also one of the people we need to convince that we're the real deal. My hand reaches for Fernando's. I shuffle closer to him, lace my fingers to his, and squeeze tightly, reassuring him I'm ready for the show to begin.

"Tía Yesenia!" he calls.

She backs the golf cart up and redirects it down the path, parking next to us. She points to her cheek. "I'm still wet, I don't want to get your suit dirty," Fernando says.

"Don't let that stop you. Clothing can be cleaned. Go on already. Give your favorite tía what she wants. I haven't seen you in over a year!" He does as he's told. Directing her attention to me, Tía Yesenia holds her arms open and looks at me expectantly. "You too, Ava. You're practically part of the family."

Her words cause Fernando to cough. He drops my hand, and I wrap my arms around Tía Yesenia. Over her shoulder, I mouth *"relax"* to him. He gives the slightest bob of the head.

Greetings exchanged, I return to Fernando's side. He drapes his arm around my shoulder and pulls me closer to his body. "What are you doing here, Tía? Did Mamá send you?"

Tía Yesenia laughs. "I'm not here as her spy. I have a meeting with the hotel's management. I'm presenting some concept drawings today for the expansion wing. Meeting you here is just a coincidence."

"Mm-hmm," he says, not totally convinced.

"Would you two care for a ride back to the lobby? I'm heading that way myself."

"We'd love it," I answer, knowing she wants time to speak to us.

"Fantástico. Ava, you sit up front with me. Fernando, you can have the back."

I take my seat next to her. "Thank you again for gifting us the chance to stay here. The last two days have been a dream."

She perks up in her seat, backing up and starting the cart toward the main building. "It was nothing. I just hope you had some quality alone time together. Goodness knows you won't get much of it when you reach Santa Luz."

"Tía, what do you mean?" Fernando asks.

"Your mamá has quite the schedule planned for you two."

"But that's not what we want." He groans. "Ava is only

staying with us two or three days at most. She has her own plans."

"Fernando, we talked about this," I gently remind him.

"No, Ava. Mamá can't take over our visit."

Tía Yesenia glances in the mirror at her nephew. "If you want to try asking your mamá to change her plans, good luck. She's been the most stubborn member of the family since the day she was born." She laughs and looks to me. "My sister was two weeks past her due date when she was born. My own poor madre was beside herself. The only way Julissa was coming out was by C-section."

"Now I know which side of the family that particular personality trait comes from." I giggle.

Fernando crosses his arms and huffs.

"Was he stubborn as a child?"

"Sí. More so than any of my other nephews. I remember when he was about five years old. His cousin had started taking ice skating lessons. He decided it looked like so much fun that he wanted to take them too. But both his parents said no, he was too young. But I knew my nephew wouldn't budge. Every day for weeks after school, he'd find a way to tag along with his cousins to the rink, watch the class, then practice what they had learned when he got home." Tía Yesenia turns the cart. "His madre has some videos of him skating around the house in his socks. I'm sure she'd be more than happy to locate them for you if you're interested, Ava."

Twin patches of pink appear on his cheeks. "She doesn't want to see those."

"Yes, I do!" I exclaim. "Especially if you were a five-year-old cutie pie."

"Were?" he challenges. "I'm still a cutie pie."

"Most of the time," I tease.

"And what am I when I'm not?"

I take a moment to consider his words. "You're a koala bear because you're always napping."

He smirks.

"You still take long naps?" Tía Yesenia asks.

"Sí," he says.

Tía Yesenia shakes her head. "So, Ava, tell me, how did you and my nephew get together?"

"Tía, I've already told you this stuff," Fernando whines.

"No. All I've heard from you is that you had a girl-friend. Just like your tíos, you leave out all the details." She rolls her eyes. "Now it's Ava's turn to fill me in."

My body shakes in silent laughter. Fernando mutters under his breath in Spanish.

"Your nephew and I officially got together last month, but before that, we were friends. He was a regular volunteer at my veterinary clinic. Every time we talked, I'd wish we could spend more time together. I waited for Fernando to make the first move, but he never picked up on my hints, so I asked him out on a date, and he said yes." I cross my fingers behind my back, hoping Fernando doesn't mind I've fabricated a few more details than we'd talked about.

"You know me, Tía, I'm terrible at picking up on a woman's body language," he adds.

Tía Yesenia laughs. "I'm glad Fernando's picked a smart go-getter. You've given me hope that maybe you'll be the one who finally gets him to settle down and start a family."

My ears burn and I cough a little.

"Tía," Fernando warns.

"What? I'm preparing you for what the rest of the family will say. We want to see you happy and have some babies to spoil."

"I want to see him happy too, but we're still in the 'getting to know you' stage." I rub the back of my neck. "Marriage and kids are the last things on our minds."

"Sí. What Ava said."

"It's never too early to have that conversation." Tía Yesenia pulls to a stop outside the lobby. She turns off the engine and sighs. "But forgive me if I've overstepped. I'm just an excited tía."

"I know you mean well, Tía," Fernando says gently. "Give us time. Like Ava said, right now, we're focused on learning more about one another and growing and developing what we have. I'd like to hope Ava is the one"—his eyes meet mine, sparkling with warmth, then return to his aunt—"but I can't give you any answers about the future yet." He kisses her on the cheek. "Thank you for the ride."

As he says that, even I find myself glimmering with hope that I could be the one. He sounds so convincing. An army of butterflies stirs in my stomach. Every time I've thought about Fernando recently, I've seen him as being more than just a friend. I want our fake relationship to become real.

"Yes. Um, thanks." I offer her a return hug, forcing myself to focus on the present.

"Are you two leaving for Santa Luz after you check out?"

"I think so. We need to check on our rental car first. It's still with the mechanic."

She nods. "Well, if you don't get it back by two, send me a text. You can have the rental agency pick up the vehicle and I'll take you home with me."

Fernando promises we'll keep her up to date. She waves and drives off.

As we ride the elevators back up to the suite, he runs a

hand through his hair. "We're almost out of time, but you can still back out of being my girlfriend if you want."

"Nope. I'm not going anywhere," I insist. Especially now that I've realized what I really want. "I liked your aunt a lot. She was blunt, you'll never mistake what she means or wants."

"That's how *all* my family is." He leans against the elevator wall. "They're loud and say exactly what's on their minds."

"Good, I can handle it."

He arches his eyebrow, but doesn't say anything.

"It's funny. My family is the complete opposite of yours. I can't wait for you to meet them." I face-palm. "Fernando, I didn't mean for that to slip out. I don't expect you to meet my family. Outside my sister. Since you've already met her."

He holds up his hand. "Ava, we're under a lot of stress. I think we'll both misspeak a couple times over the next few days." My gaze meets his, and I see the sincerity in his eyes. "Although for what it's worth, I'd be more than happy to meet the rest of your family."

The doors open and we step out.

"Go ahead and take the first shower. I'm gonna text my sister," I say.

"I'll be quick."

"It doesn't make any difference to me. Take your time."

I open the balcony door and step outside, letting the cool breeze tickle my face. It's so easy to pretend Fernando and I are a couple that at times I can't believe it's not real. Is this how method actors feel?

What is Fernando feeling? He's admitted that he finds his aunts intimidating. Seeing him stand up for himself and say we're taking this relationship at our own speed made me want to applaud, then kiss him senseless.

Even if it's all a farce. He shouldn't be scared of them or even have to put on a show. At the end of the day, it's his life to live. He's the one who has to be at peace with his choices. And if he wants to stay single forever, he should be able to. Although I do hope he changes his mind down the road. As the song goes, one is the loneliest number.

Our rental car is ready after lunch. We don't take Tía Yesenia up on her generous offer, instead departing Valencia for Santa Luz on our own around one.

"Is it terrible if I'm relieved?" I say to Fernando as we leave the city limits and head along the coast to his hometown. The scenery is breathtaking and reminds me of the Pacific Coast Highway from back home. We're driving along a road that runs parallel to the ocean. There's a vast expanse of azure-blue ocean from the road to the horizon that I can't stop staring at.

"Nope, I am too. We deserve a little quiet time to ourselves before we have to face my family."

"Do you think what your aunt said is true? Is your mom really gonna have plans for us the second we arrive?"

"Si, Mamá will have made plans." He blinks slowly. "But I have no problems telling her we have our own. We can slip away for some quiet time or do some sightseeing whenever you want."

My stomach does a somersault. "Are you going to take me to another Christmas market?"

"That's an option." His lips twitch. "There's also some

Roman ruins, the beach, and the big-cat wildlife sanctuary in Santa Domingo."

"Oh, that sounds amazing!"

"It is. The sanctuary's up in the hills about a half hour from Santa Luz. They have pumas, lions, tigers, jaguars, and Iberian lynxes."

"Count me in." I elbow him lightly. "Any adventure involving animals is an automatic must-see."

"Good to know for future reference."

He keeps his eyes trained on the road, casually resting his left arm on the door's armrest. However, I see traces of stress in his body language. He's sitting more erect, and there are a few more lines under his eyes than earlier in the week.

"Your tía Yesenia was fun," I start. "Is she a lot like her sisters, your other aunts?"

"Mm-hmm. They all are."

That's not the reaction I was hoping for. I chew on my lip. How can I get him to loosen up? Before I know what I'm doing, I reach out and brush two fingers along the length of his forearm. Except instead of being reassuring to him, he jerks the car to the right.

For a terrifying moment, I picture us sailing off the highway straight into the ocean. My breath catches and my heart pounds erratically.

"Sorry," he murmurs, immediately correcting the car. "You caught me off guard."

I'm shocked and confused. What have I done to have him react like that? Less than five minutes ago, the mood was light, and we were talking about our plans for our downtime. And now it's like he'd rather be anyplace else than near me.

We drive along in silence for a few more minutes until

he finds a turnout, stops the car, and cuts the engine. Opening his door, he steps out. I watch as he places his hands on top of his head and paces, speaking to himself under his breath.

I open my own door to get some air. A cool sea breeze hits my face. It smells of salt, brine, and mud. Cars zoom past us on the highway. I sit and watch helplessly, waiting for him to signal to me he's ready to talk. All I want to do is take him in my arms, but as it currently stands, that's the last thing he likely needs or wants.

Ten minutes pass. Fernando walks over to the metal barrier protecting anyone from tumbling off the cliff and into the ocean below. Judging that it's safe to approach him, I slide out of my seat and take a series of slow, cautious steps in his direction.

"Fernando?" I call out. He continues to gaze out at the ocean. I plant myself next to him. My hand hovers above his shoulder, but I'm afraid to touch him again. I run my hand through my hair instead.

"I'm sorry if I scared you back there. It's the last thing I ever wanted to do," he says.

"Do you want to talk about it?" I ask softly.

"Not really." He slides his hands into his pockets. "But we probably should."

The word "we" catches my attention. "Is it something I've done?"

"No. It's all me." His shoulder hunch and he takes a deep breath. "I thought I'd be able to handle having a fake relationship with you, but the truth is, I never should've agreed to any of this."

"Oh." All the muscles in my body tighten. I'm suddenly on high alert.

"You're an amazing person, Ava. I've had more fun with

you over the past week than I have in a long time." He slowly raises his head. Our eyes meet, his wide with concern. "You've moved to the top of my friend list, but friendship is all I'll be able to ever give you. That's all our relationship can ever be."

As he speaks, the little dove of hope I had that Fernando and I could become a real couple flees and flies out over the ocean. All the feelings I've developed for him over the last week will have to be suppressed and vacuum sealed back to the state they were before I left Sequoia Valley.

"Lately, I've been feeling like we're slipping past the friend zone and into a place that crosses the boundaries I've set," he says.

I squeeze my knees together. He's hit the nail on the head. We *have* begun to cross that fine line between the friend zone and the dating zone. He's not the one who's responsible for it though. I place the blame on myself. Why did I have to fall for another friend? Ugh. I should've learned the first time around.

"I understand." My voice comes out rougher than intended. "And you're right. I *have* fallen for you, Fernando." I find my body starting to quiver. "I'm sorry if it's become a problem." I look away from him and stare out at the vast ocean, watching the waves break against the rocks. My insides are being ripped apart like a piece of wrapping paper, but strangely, it doesn't hurt as much as it should. I'm numb.

He clears his throat. "I think at this point, it might be for the best if we told my family that you and I broke up. Continuing this charade is going to be painful for both of us. And the last thing I want is for you to have to suffer because of me."

"No, Fernando." I lift my chin. "I'm stronger than I look. This does hurt, but I can push my feelings aside and pull this off. Just like I do at work when I have to help a person who has to make a tough decision about their pet's future."

A small piece of my soul is torn away whenever I have a person who can't afford further treatment for their pet, have to give them a grim diagnosis, or when I have to put an animal down. As much as I want to run to the corner and bawl my eyes out, I have to stay strong and be professional. I can't cry about it, otherwise, I'd never be able to get through the rest of my day. My emotions don't get released until I'm home alone with Max.

Fernando appraises me. "And knowing it's fake won't be too painful for you?"

"No."

I watch his chest rise and fall as he processes. "Okay. I'll trust you."

Chapter Twenty-One

For the remainder of our trip to Santa Luz, we act as if the incident by the side of the road never happened. But neither of us has the same enthusiasm or excitement we held a few days ago. An hour outside of town, our conversation dries up and Fernando flips the radio on to fill the silence.

Lost in my thoughts, I replay some of the events from over the past few days. I think about the Alhambra, enjoying the orange ice cream in Seville, and finding out Dylan was engaged in Toledo. It's amazing how a week can feel like a lifetime. So much has happened.

With each mile we pass and every city we visit, I've shed a little more of the old Ava. Regardless of how confused I am emotionally, I'm proud of myself for being able to hold everything together and know that while I'm hurting, I'm still helping out a friend.

Fernando exits the highway and turns onto a main road. There's a long stretch of hotels and white sand beaches. I can see why this town is considered a hidden gem.

"Welcome to Santa Luz," he says.

"It's lovely." I look out the window. Although it's cloudy, there are plenty of people out and about. Some are dressed in bikinis or trunks for swimming, while others are walking their dogs. But most people we drive past are in wet suits. "Is surfing a big thing around here?"

"Sí. This time of year, we have some of the larger waves in the area."

"Huh, I never would've guessed that."

Fernando maneuvers the car into the left lane and turns onto a narrow road. The cobblestones shake the car, reminding me of a series of speed bumps. Wild bushes stick out from the hills on his side of the vehicle. On my side are a series of compact sand-colored flat-fronted buildings.

He comes to a stop in front of a building with a sign labeled "Pequeña Casa de Luz" in gold and turquoise writing, and turns off the engine.

"This is it. My parents' home," he says tiredly.

"The little house of light?" I guess at the translation.

"Sí. They thought it would sound better than the Casa de Alvarez. It has about ten rooms."

We step out of the car. I scrunch my nose. "Are they small rooms?" The building may be three stories tall, but unless the property extends out to the back, I have no idea how you'd squeeze ten rooms in.

"Hmm? Oh, they're about the same size as what you might find back in America. The bed and breakfast is actually made up of three of these buildings. When Mamá and Papá renovated the place, they didn't want to lose the character or the original features."

"Oh, that makes more sense."

He pops open the trunk and begins pulling out our luggage just as the front door swings open. "Ava! Fernando!" Mrs. Alvarez cries. "Welcome home. We've been waiting for you. You're an hour later than we expected. Did you get stuck in traffic?"

Mrs. Alvarez is about my height, five-foot-six, and has curly hair that's pulled back into an elegant updo. She has the same dark-brown eyes, hair, and skin coloring as her son.

"Something like that," he responds. "Is Papá inside?"

"Sí, he's watching football." She rolls her eyes. "It's the big match between Madrid and Barcelona."

"I should've known." Fernando snorts. "In other words, we won't see him until the game is over." Closing the trunk and turning to face me, he adds, "Papá's team is Barcelona. We could have a volcanic eruption, and he still wouldn't leave his office. Nothing else matters when a game is on."

"Unfortunately." His mother sighs. "I'm sorry he's not out here to meet you in person, but I promise he'll come and find you as soon as the game is over."

"It's okay. I understand. My brother-in-law is the same way when hockey is on. It's like speaking to a wall."

Fernando's mom wraps an arm around my shoulder. "Please, come inside. And call me Mamà Alvarez. You must be famished. I have some fresh snacks and sangria waiting for you. Leave the bags for Fernando."

I glance over my shoulder, but he shakes his head, mouthing, *"Do as she says,"* to me.

We enter the building. The ground floor is smaller than I imagined, but has a warm and inviting ambiance. A set of four windows, all made up of stained glass, flood the area with plenty of natural light. There's a rich-red sofa and a quirky glass coffee table adorned with seashells and a small stack of magazines.

We continue through to an outdoor patio, where two

other women are seated at a long rectangular table. I recognize them as Tía Yulia and Tía Maria. Yulia is the youngest sibling. She has shoulder-length blond hair, square glasses, and bright-green eyes. I wouldn't know she was related to Mamá Alvarez if Fernando hadn't told me.

Maria, on the other hand, looks the most like Fernando's mom. She keeps her brown hair long, pulled back into a braid that hits her midback. She's wearing jade-colored glasses and a matching green silk blouse.

Both aunts stand, come over, and hug me. They lead me to the table, and I'm seated between them like a queen holding court.

"Ava, we've been waiting so patiently for you to arrive. Fernando's kept you to himself for too long," Tía Maria starts. "How has your trip been so far?"

I help myself to a fresh caramel empanada and take a bite, letting the sweet apple settle on my tongue as I compose my thoughts. "It's been great. It's my first time in Spain, and I wasn't sure what to expect, but Fernando's been an excellent tour guide."

"I bet he has." Maria glances in the direction of the door, where Fernando's mother has him trapped.

"Yesenia mentioned that you made the first move. I'm glad you did. Left to his own devices, Fernando would never have had the courage to ask you out," Yulia teases.

"I don't know, he's pretty brave," I say defensively, offended they're not giving him more credit.

Tía Yulia shrugs and moves on, asking about my family. Soon, it becomes apparent that those first couple of questions were just the warm-up. Over the course of the next hour, Yulia and Maria push me into the deep end of the pool, covering the hard-hitting topics.

We discuss how many kids I think I may want in the

future, which is three. They promise not to tell their nephew what I say. Then they feel out if I'd consider settling in Spain when I marry Fernando. Not if. When.

I try my best to give non-answers, but the sisters make it hard. They're gifted at finding ways to redirect the questions I'm reluctant to answer, like an expert team of lawyers. I appreciate that they're looking out for their nephew, but it's still a shock to the system how much detail they want.

"Mamá, I think we have more than enough food here." Fernando enters the patio carrying a tray of flaky rolls in each hand. He scrunches his nose as he looks for an empty spot to place them. "If you bake anything else, we'll have to open a stall at the market." Walking over to me, he places a hand on my shoulder. "If you need any more help in the kitchen, Tía Yulia or Tía Maria can lend you a hand. I've neglected Ava long enough."

Fernando leans forward and places a soft kiss near my ear. The sensation sends a wave of pleasure through my core. The three women eagerly watch us, sighing contentedly. "Do you need an escape?" he whispers so quietly, I barely hear him.

"Yes," I say through my teeth. I'm overwhelmed. I need some quiet time to reset and recharge.

"Before it gets too dark, I'm going to give Ava a tour of the neighborhood. We'll be back before dinner," he announces.

Not waiting for the aunts to get another word in, I stumble to my feet. Some of my muscles cramp from sitting for so long. I ignore the pulling sensation and loop my arm through Fernando's.

"Take your time, you two. Dinner can wait for you." Tía Yulia winks.

"That was . . ." I search for the right word. "Intense. I know you warned me your aunts would be intrusive with their questions, but I didn't expect it to be like that. My brain's turned to mush."

Fernando and I are walking side by side down one of the narrow side streets a few blocks away from the B&B. The buildings are a similar sand color, and if I didn't know any better, I'd think we were back where we started.

"I'm sorry you were stuck alone with them for so long. I tried to escape the kitchen, but Mamá had other ideas. I came as soon as I could."

"You don't have to explain. It's the same way with my parents. Just please tell me you'll be around for round two."

"I will," he confirms. "Dinner has already been made, and as far as I'm aware, there's nothing else left to cook."

"That's a relief." I exhale.

Fernando rubs the back of his neck. "If you're too tired, I could make excuses that you've had too much excitement for today and need to rest."

"Nope, we aren't pulling the 'get out of jail free' card yet." I don't want to leave him to the sharks. Acting as the protective metal cage is the whole reason I'm here. "I'm curious. If you hadn't brought me, what would your aunts have done when you arrived?"

"Set me up on another blind date."

"On day one?"

"Uh-huh." He strokes his jaw. "The tías don't waste time."

"Have you told them how you feel about dating and their meddling?"

He nods. "Yeah, right after the breakup with Isabel."

I frown. "And they didn't respect your wishes?"

"They didn't believe I was serious. They can't get it in their head that I'd purposefully choose to be single when everyone else in the family is married. All that happened out of that conversation was that they pulled back on the number of dates they set up."

"That's not right. They have to see that not everyone can fit into a cookie-cutter mold and want what they want."

"No," he says softly. "But as I've learned over the years, you have to pick and choose your battles. It's not worth the energy fighting them. I'm only home once a year. I'd rather spend my time here making them happy than being at odds with them."

His perspective is so positive, even though I know the whole situation is wearing on him. It goes to show how different things are culturally here in Spain compared to back home in the States. I can't think of many people who'd put the happiness of their family first instead of themselves. It only serves to grow my attraction to him. "You're a good son and nephew, Fernando."

"Gracias. I try to be."

At dinner, I'm seated between two of Fernando's teenage cousins, who spend the meal practicing their English skills with me. I attempt some Spanish, but quickly realize the dialect the kids speak doesn't come close to what I learned in high school. I soon abandon all attempts in favor of English. By the time dessert rolls around, the teens have moved on to doomscrolling through their phones.

Fernando drops into the spare seat next to me before anyone else can claim it. "How did you find Alejandra and Valentina?"

"They were sweet, but the novelty of having an American here wore off when we exhausted the questions about food and TV and they found out I'm not a soccer fan." I giggle. "I never realized how much of a following it has over here."

"Whichever *football* club you support is a major deal," he emphasizes.

"Even if I know nothing about the sport?"

"Sí. Our family is divided. Half support Barcelona and the other half support Madrid. Whichever team you choose is the tiebreaker."

"And who do you support?" I ask, poking him in the chest.

"Barcelona, of course. They're the hometown team." He sits taller. "Just because I skate doesn't mean I don't enjoy watching football. I watch whenever a game is on, which isn't often. Most of the time the networks only show the English Premier League."

"As your girlfriend who knows nothing about sports, I'll go with whatever team you like. So I guess by default, I'm a Barcelona fan."

He grins. "That'll make Papá happy."

"Is now a good time to meet him?"

Fernando glances at the end of the table, where Mr. Alvarez has just joined the family and is speaking to Tía Maria's husband as he makes a plate for himself. "I guess now is as good a time as any."

We stand up and walk toward them. I have my first opportunity to study Fernando's father. Mr. Alvarez looks to be in his mid to late fifties. Although he's balding, he still has a youthful look about him. He has the same olive skin and chocolate-brown eyes as his son. Now that I've seen both Fernando's parents, I notice that he favors his dad's side.

By contrast, the man next to him, his uncle, appears to be a few years younger than Fernando's father. He has light-brown hair, a neat beard, and blue eyes.

As we approach, Fernando's uncle elbows Mr. Alvarez in the ribs. The two men stop and turn their attention to us.

"Hola," they greet us.

"Hola, Tío, Papá. I'm excited to introduce you to someone very special." Fernando kisses my cheek. "This is Ava, my girlfriend."

"Hola. Encantado de conocerte," I manage, hoping I've said "it's nice to meet you," and not something else that was totally rude or wrong. Who knows with this dialect.

"Bienvenida, Ava. Welcome," Mr. Alvarez starts, but then his attention wavers. His face breaks out into a smile, and he waves. "Ah, Isabel, you've made it. Come and join us."

What the heck? At hearing that name, goosebumps form on my arm, and I blink a few times. I spin around and see a woman with red hair pulled back into a low ponytail. She's wearing black leggings and a fitted pink zip-up jacket.

She floats up to Mr. Alvarez, who stands to hug her. "Jorge, it's been too long."

I swallow hard. My hand reaches for Fernando's, but he doesn't take it. His are balled into fists. His cheeks and neck are flushed a deep shade of red. His posture is as stiff as a two-by-four board.

"Your parents, they're doing well?" Fernando's father asks, releasing her.

"Sí. They're same as ever, still running the family bakery. They send their regards."

"Good to hear." He nods and clears his throat. "Your timing is perfecto. My son only just arrived in Santa Luz today. I'm sure you two have lots of catching up to do." He winks.

Isabel lifts her chin and locks eyes with Fernando. "Yes, we do."

"Isabel," he says gruffly. His hands open and close, and his frown deepens. "You shouldn't be here."

Her eyes widen and she splays a hand on her chest. I can't tell if she's purposefully being dramatic or if she's genuinely surprised.

"Fernando! Where are your manners?! She's a guest," Mr. Alvarez says, his voice rising.

"They flew out the door when she cut me out of her life." Fernando's voice stays deadly quiet as he turns to face his father. "And if we're speaking of manners, where are yours, Papá?" Fernando wraps his arm protectively around my shoulder and pulls me closer to him. His chest is heaving. "I brought Ava here to meet everyone, and instead of getting to know her, you brushed her aside for Isabel."

"Fernando," Isabel says, "be reasonable. It's time to let go of the past. There's no reason to hold a grudge."

"I don't hold grudges. I just choose not to associate with people who make it clear they don't want me in their lives. You've had more than five years to contact me if you wanted to talk. Well, time's up." His voice remains calm.

"Isabel, ignore him. He doesn't know what he's talking about," Mr. Alvarez says.

"No, Papá. I've never been more certain of myself. Any love that may have existed between us is gone." He shakes his head. "I know you've always wanted me to come home, run the bed and breakfast, and marry Isabel, but that isn't ever going to happen. My life is in America with Ava."

Mr. Alvarez's lips thin. "There is nothing for you in America that Spain doesn't have."

My eyes dart between the three of them. I don't know what to say or do. I feel like a dog who's been placed inside a kennel, watching people toss a ball back and forth.

"Isabel!" Mamá Alvarez says, coming up to us slightly out of breath. "This is a surprise."

"Papá invited her over," Fernando says in a flat voice.

"I see."

"Hello, Julissa," Isabel says.

"Hola," Mamá Alvarez replies. "Sorry to interrupt, but Jorge, you're needed at the front desk. Carlos is ready to take his dinner break. It's your turn to cover for him."

"But Julissa . . ." he says.

Mamá Alvarez lowers her chin and gives him a stern look. He mutters something in Spanish, shoves his hands into his pockets, and takes a deep breath. "Yes, dear." He takes a few steps toward the door. Then as if he's only just noticed I'm still here, he stops, his cheeks flushed. "Ava, I'm sorry for ignoring you. If you're free, I'd like to get to know you better later."

I bite my tongue, offended by how he's treated me so far. "Okay," I manage.

Mr. Alvarez shuffles inside.

"Jorge will apologize *properly* later," Mamá Alvarez interjects. "Fernando, Isabel, I'll leave you two to talk. Ava, please come with me."

"Mamá, we don't need to chat. She's leaving," Fernando says.

"Some things never change. You've always been stubborn." Isabel huffs. "Look, I get you're still hurt, but I've come all this way to see you. The least you can do is hear what I have to say for old times' sake."

"Fernando, please," his mother says.

He pinches his lips together. "Fine. I'll do it for you, Mamá."

Satisfied, Mamá Alvarez nods. "We'll be in the kitchen when you're done."

Like a sheep being herded by a collie, Fernando's mom guides me to the kitchen, leaving her son and his ex-fiancée alone. I can't believe she's supporting this. I want her to know how angry it makes me, but I can't seem to find my voice.

Chapter Twenty-Two

A blast of warm air hits my body as we enter the kitchen. It's a medium-sized room filled with a mixture of modern and vintage appliances and a large peninsula with three barstools, two occupied by Tía Yulia and Tía Maria. Mamá Alvarez nods toward the remaining one, indicating I should take a seat.

"Can I get you some water?" she asks.

I shake my head. "No, I'm fine."

Tía Yulia pops up from her seat, walks over to the refrigerator, and pours herself some sangria. "She'd be better off with something stronger."

Mamá Alvarez rolls her eyes. "They're just talking, Yulia."

Tía Yulia holds up her hands. "I'm just saying, you know what happened last time. When she broke my poor nephew's heart, it took him months to piece himself back together."

"I remember." Mamá Alvarez frowns. "But I think it's safe this time. They've both grown and matured."

"How do you know?" Tía Maria asks.

"I don't. But I'm choosing to trust her," Mamá Alvarez says in a tone that indicates it's the end of the conversation.

"Well, if she misbehaves, Julissa will let Isabel's parents know about it." Tía Yulia snickers.

I'm happy to hear Fernando's mom is looking out for him. She's not Team Isabel like Fernando's father seems to be. "I will take some of that sangria," I say, rejoining the conversation.

Tía Yulia nods and pours a glass for me and each of the other ladies.

"I missed most of what happened out there, but it doesn't take much detective work to piece it together." Mamá Alvarez accepts her drink and places it down on the peninsula untouched. "Jorge was out of line inviting Isabel to dinner tonight. And for not treating you with the respect you deserve."

I manage a polite nod. Hot lava flows through my veins when I consider Mr. Alvarez's actions tonight. "I don't care about how he's treated me, but I'm worried about the impact he's having on your son."

"It's no excuse, but my husband has a hard time letting go of the past. He's never gotten over my son's breakup or the fact that he's chosen to call America home over Spain," Mamá Alvarez says.

"Fernando is a grown man. Whether he calls the States home or Spain, it's his choice." I take a long sip of the sangria, savoring the sweet taste of the peaches and straw-berries, willing it to cool my growing temper.

"We all agree with you, Ava," Tía Yulia says. "Living in America has changed my nephew for the better. He's happier than I've ever seen him, and he even managed to find you! The only person who doesn't seem to understand that is Jorge."

"Besides, Fernando's never expressed interest in taking over your bed and breakfast businesses," Tía Maria says to Mamá Alvarez.

"Do you own more than this place?" I cock my head to the side.

"Oh yes. Jorge and I have about fifteen properties all over Spain."

"And they're all *highly* successful," Tía Maria adds.

Huh. That must be the real reason Mr. Alvarez is upset. He wants Fernando to inherit the family business. I think I'm beginning to have a better understanding of what's going on now.

The clock chimes seven times. I glance at the window. The patio is deserted. Isabel and Fernando have disappeared. I take a final sip of my sangria and set it down. "If you'll excuse me, I need to find Fernando."

I may have agreed to push my feelings for him aside, but that isn't going to stop me from checking on him. No matter what, we'll still be friends. Thinking about the hurt he might be feeling sends waves of dull pain through my chest. I need to know he's okay.

I push the stool back and stand, suddenly realizing I have no idea where he might have gone.

"He's probably in his old room," Tía Maria muses, reading my body language.

Tía Yulia walks over and sets a hand on my shoulder. "I'll show you where it is."

We pass through the lobby and up four flights of stairs toward the roof. "I thought the building only had three floors."

"It does." She points to a blue door at the end of the hallway. "The attic was converted into a loft for my nephew. He's always preferred the quiet and the view. Odds are, you'll find him standing on the balcony." She gives me a parting hug, then gently pushes me toward the door. "Good luck, Ava."

Taking a deep breath, I open the door and groan as I spy another few stairs. I've definitely gotten my steps in for the day. Climbing four-and-a-half flights has my leg muscles trembling and crying out for me to take a break. At the top of the landing, there's another door. I knock twice.

"Vete. Quiero estar solo," Fernando mutters.

Those words, I know. They translate to "go away" and "I want to be alone." But as is often the case, we can't always have what we want. It's time for some tough love. I knock again. There's no answer. Reaching for the door-knob, I turn it and start to open the door at the same time it flies toward me.

I gasp and stumble backward, teetering toward the stairs, but Fernando's lightning-fast reflexes steady me. The next thing I know, my body is pressed against his. We're both panting. I feel each breath as his chest rises and falls. "I didn't know it was you. I thought you'd be Mamá or Tía Yulia."

"You can be mad all you want at me," I say, lifting my chin and meeting his gaze. "But I'm not going to leave you alone."

"You're an exception to the rule. I'll always welcome *you*, Ava." His words cause something in my stomach to flutter. He moves me away from the stairs and releases me. "I should've come to find you once Isabel left. I didn't mean to leave you to fend for yourself."

"I wasn't alone. Your mom and aunts found me." I glance to the door. "Can I come in?"

"Sí, sí." He steps out of the doorway and gestures for me to follow.

Inside, the room is tastefully done up. The lower floor contains a desk, sofa, and TV. A sleek black wrought-iron staircase leads up to the room's sleeping space and only window. There's a king-sized bed, a side table with a quirky Salvador Dali-inspired lamp, and a dresser.

My attention goes to the creamy white walls, where there are three life-sized photos of Fernando. One of them has him standing on top of a podium next to a woman with dark hair, holding a gold medal.

The second is of him wearing a prince costume against a darkened background. His feet are turned out and he's smiling widely to an invisible audience. The spotlight hits his face in just the right spot, illuminating his high cheekbones.

The last picture is of Fernando with his arms looped around a pair of skaters, each with gold medals looped around their necks. His eyes are glowing. It's my favorite image of the three.

"Wow, these are bold."

"Mamá had these printed and put up for me. I thought they'd be a lot smaller than this, not six feet tall. But she wanted something to 'fill the room,' she said." He runs a hand through his hair. "The three photos each represent a milestone moment in my skating journey. Winning my first national title, getting a job with Dreams on Ice, and becoming a coach."

I continue to study the portraits. In each image, I can see some subtle changes. The first photo has a baby-faced Fernando. His cheeks are slightly rounded, there's no sign of any facial hair, and his shoulders aren't as broad as in the other two images. As a prince, his body has filled out and there are a few fine lines around his eyes and mouth. "What competition is that?" I point to the last image.

"The World Championships." He lowers his chin and studies the ground. "Those are my friends Frankie and Charlie just after they won the title. They were already world-class skaters when they asked me to help them out. They could've easily coached themselves. All I did was offer them some advice from an outsider's perspective."

"Fernando, stop being so bashful! Your friends did not just want your advice. I'm a hundred percent sure they asked you to coach them because you're brilliant at what you do." I shake my head, still trying to wrap my mind around the fact that he can add the title "Coach of World Champions" to his resume. "I bet all your students are stars."

"They are. I have one team I co-coach with Charlie that just won the World Junior Championship title. We have big hopes for them when they move up to the senior division next season."

"Wow. Just wow." I point to the first photo. "Is that woman the partner who caused you to change career paths?"

"Yup, that's Sylvie." He chuckles. "As frustrating as our time was together, seeing that photo of us winning Nationals always reminds me that winning isn't everything. It's why I chose it."

"That's a good outlook to have. And what about the photo of you on tour?"

"That was taken a few days before I retired."

"I can't tell, which prince were you?"

"I wore a lot of hats, or rather, wigs. That day I was Prince Charming. But my favorite character to play was Aladdin."

"I'm starstruck." We walk over to the sofa and sit down. "I'm sitting with literal royalty."

He throws his head back and laughs, revealing the light-hearted, happy-go-lucky man I met back in Sequoia Valley. "I'm more of a street rat than a prince, but I'll still take the compliment."

Fernando shares a few more stories with me about his time with Dreams on Ice before our conversation takes a more serious turn.

"How are you doing? Being surprised by Isabel couldn't have been comfortable."

"I'm okay. It still hurt to see her again, but it wasn't as much of a shock to my system as it was in Madrid." He sighs deeply. "We had a productive conversation. She wanted to clear the air between us."

"After all this time?"

"Yes. There were a lot of things she wanted to get off her chest." He crosses his leg and positions his body toward me. "We agreed that tonight wasn't the best time or place to talk, so we'll be meeting for breakfast."

I swallow hard and squeeze my knees together. It's just breakfast. Fernando is a level-headed man. I'm sure it doesn't mean anything other than he's willing to hear what his ex-fiancée has to say. I do my best to push aside the voice in the back of my head that's telling me Fernando's realized he still loves Isabel and wants to rekindle his relationship with her.

"Your, uh, aunts also said something about your dad that I was wondering about." I fold my hands on my lap. "Is he upset that you aren't going to take over the family business?"

"Sí, that's the gist of it. My parents are close to Isabel's parents. They'd hoped we'd settle here and take over running the B&B." He stands and walks over to a framed photo on the side table, picking it up and running his fingers along the edge. "Except that dream flew out the door when Isabel ended it. Mamá has moved on, but Papá hasn't."

He takes a deep breath. "In his eyes, coaching in small-town America is a huge step down from the B&B. Every time I come home, he looks for ways to convince me I've made a huge mistake and should change my mind. I love the man, but it's frustrating beyond belief."

"He should respect that you are your own man, and he can't make decisions about how you live your life."

"We've spoken about it, but what I have to say goes in one ear and out the other." He sets the frame down. "I've given up trying to change his mind. Just as with my tías, it's not worth the energy to put up a fight."

"I don't know, I thought you did a pretty good job calling him out for snubbing me."

"That was different."

I cock my head to the side. "How?"

"Papá was being rude to you. He can bully me if he wishes, but my friends and girlfriend are off-limits, even if it's a fake relationship."

"I said something similar to your mom about you." I chuckle. "We think alike."

Fernando reaches for my hand and rubs his thumb in small circles over the top. "I guess that's why we get on so well."

My heart yearns to break free of the prison I've entrapped it in, but I'm caught in a loop. I need to stop falling for my friends. Our feelings for one another continue to deepen, but we're forever stuck in the friend zone.

Chapter Twenty-Three

Mamá Alvarez is waiting for me when I return downstairs. She doesn't ask me how my conversation with Fernando went, but she doesn't have to. If something were truly amiss, I'm positive she'd sense it in my body language.

"I have you in a suite on the third floor."

"Oh, um, I'd be happy to stay with Fernando. You don't need to give me my own room," I say, before my brain catches up with my mouth. My cheeks sear with heat.

Fernando's mother smiles, but it's the kind that doesn't invite debate. "You're my guest, mija. You get your own space. Besides, unlike my sisters, my husband and I prefer to keep things old-fashioned under this roof."

"I understand," I say. Physically and emotionally drained, as soon as I enter the suite, and lay on the bed, I fall into a deep, dreamless sleep.

When I awake the next morning, there's a text from Fernando.

Fernando: Good morning, Ava. I hope you slept well. I'm heading off to the rink for the morning session so I can clear my head before I meet with Isabel. I hope you don't mind being on your own for a couple hours. I should be back by noon.

The message was sent at four forty-five a.m. It's about seven-thirty now. Was Isabel on his mind all evening? What are they going to discuss? He's blocked off an awful lot of time to spend with her. I place my phone down and take several deep breaths.

What am I doing? Of course there's nothing going on between them. He hasn't spoken to her since their engagement ended. The only reason they crossed paths is because of Mr. Alvarez. Their breakfast has to be more like a business meeting. Fernando couldn't have been any clearer that their relationship is a thing of the past.

Feeling better, I pop into the shower and change. But not before I send him a quick reply.

Ava: See you when you get back.

I head down to the breakfast room on the ground floor and a few of the B&B guests enjoying the offerings Mamá Alvarez has laid out. There are eggs, tomatoes, omelets, potatoes, and a few bready-looking items. Deciding to stick to what I know best, I choose the omelet.

"Good morning, Ava. I hope you slept well," Mamá Alvarez says, setting down a large pot of coffee on the side table as I fill my plate.

"I did, thanks. The room you gave me is so homey."

"Glad to hear it. I know Fernando mentioned you have

your own plans, but you're welcome to stay with us as long as you like. We make an excellent home base."

"Thank you," I say, reaching for a coffee cup. "Originally, I was planning to head to Barcelona for the last four days of my trip. But now that I'm here, I think two days should be plenty."

"Sí, sí. Barcelona is exciting, but we'd much rather have you here with us." Mamá Alvarez's eyes dance in excitement.

A paying B&B guest interrupts us, asking Mamá Alvarez if she could refill the hot water. She excuses herself while I take a seat, thankful for a few moments to wake myself up. I need to make sure I'm on my A game to continue playing the part of Fernando's loving girlfriend.

A few minutes later, Mamá Alvarez returns and joins me at my table. "My son snuck away before I was up," she says, folding her hands on the tabletop.

"He did. He said he's going to skate this morning, but he'll be back by lunch."

"That's always his favorite place to think." She sighs, not mentioning Isabel. "What about you? What are your plans this morning?"

"I'm not sure. I was thinking of wandering around Santa Luz and soaking in a little sun at the beach."

"You know, one of the most interesting places is the market. My sisters usually go with me, but they're both busy today. It's unfortunate. There's a lot of items on my list and I could use another pair of hands. You wouldn't be interested in coming, would you?"

I thought she'd strong-arm me into going, but at least she's phrased it as a polite request. "I'd love to."

"Perfecto." She claps her hands together. "We'll leave

soon. There are so many people to show you off—er, introduce you to!"

"Great," I say through my teeth. It was a trap. I should've known better than to assume the market would mean one stop. I have to remember I'm not in California anymore. I'm in Spain. People here prefer to visit a baker, a butcher, and other individual shops every few days to pick up their groceries. I'd better make sure I wear comfy walking shoes.

Later that afternoon, I receive a text from Fernando.

Fernando: I'm back.

Ava: *Thumbs-up emoji* Hope you had a great session.

Fernando: I did! Have you already grabbed some lunch?

Ava: No. If you're up for it, I'd love to go out.

Fernando: Great, I'll meet you in the lobby.

I wince at the suggestion.

Ava: Um, is there a more discreet place we can meet?

Fernando: ???

Ava: There are a few people I'd like to avoid for an hour or two.

Fernando: Mamá?

Ava: And your aunts.

Fernando: Should I even ask?

I snort.

Ava: She took me to the market this morning.

Fernando: That's not too bad.

Ava: We went to what felt like literally every shop in town. I shook so many hands that I could've charged people a quarter each and made some serious money.

Fernando: Oh!

Ava: Yeah. I think I've met every shop vendor in Santa Luz. We got back a half hour ago. Your aunts popped into the B&B and wanted to take me on "a few other errands," but I said I wanted to rest first.

Fernando: I'll rescue you from Mamá. Let's meet in your room. We'll sneak out the back.

Ava: That sounds like something Aladdin would say.

Fernando: Who do you think I got it from?

Ava: See you soon, Prince Ali.

"Even though it was a ton of work, you made Mamá happy. She's always wanted a daughter to spoil, and you're the closest she's come," Fernando says as he opens the gate to a restaurant right off the beach.

"I just hope we don't break her heart when we split up. I was thinking maybe we should wait for you to make that announcement once you're back in the States."

We select one of the tables on the patio. A waiter comes out with some water and bread.

"I think you're right. For once in my life, it's been fantastic not to have to worry about being set up by the tías."

"Don't get too excited. My Spanish may not be great, but it looked and sounded to me like your aunts were looking for ways to get us to spend more time together so you can hurry up and propose to me."

He groans and opens the napkin with the silverware and places it on his lap. "At least we can escape to Barcelona tomorrow."

"I'm looking forward to it."

"Your hair looks nice by the way," he says. "I mean, it always has, but I like it when you wear it down."

My cheeks warm as I run a hand through the ends of my hair. One of Mamá Alvarez's appointments this morning was at a salon. I felt awkward standing around waiting for her and agreed to a haircut. As loath as I am to admit this, it was relaxing to have the hairdresser massage my scalp as he washed it, trimmed it, and gave me a few lowlights.

When I saw the end result in the mirror, I couldn't stop smiling. I may have only had two inches taken off, but my hair felt so light. It's the closest I've ever come to a glow up. I didn't think Fernando would even notice. But now that he has, I may consider wearing my hair down more often.

We decide to split a platter of the local seafood offerings. I'm not the biggest fan of crab and shellfish, but since Fernando made the effort to bring us here specifically for those dishes, I bite my tongue and give in. "How was your skating session this morning?"

"It was great! My first coach, Mr. Rodriguez, was there. I can't believe he's still coaching. We spent a long time catching up."

He mentions learning things like flying camels, triple toes, and a death spiral, but they're all lost on me. I make a note to watch a couple SearchTube videos to start teaching myself a little more about his sport.

Not long after, the food arrives. I change tactics and casually slip in the question I've been dying to ask him since he returned. "And what about your breakfast meeting? How did that go?" I ask, helping myself to a piece of fried calamari.

"It was . . . good. Healing, in fact." Fernando's face softens. "Isabel's changed. Our conversation today reminded me why I fell in love with her."

"That's good," I lie. I reach for my water glass and take a long sip.

"We've arranged to meet again the day after tomorrow."

I force a smile onto my face. "I'm so happy to hear that."

"The only thing is, Ava, it means changing our plans

again." He rubs the back of his neck. "I can still take you to Barcelona tomorrow, but if you wouldn't mind, I'd like to clear my schedule for Isabel in case lunch runs long."

"I understand," I choke out. I knew it! It's only a matter of time before he gets back together with her. Fernando's heart has never been up for grabs. It's always belonged to her. That's the real reason he never wanted to be in another relationship. It's romantic. But it doesn't dull the pain. I selfishly wanted him for me.

"You know what, Fernando, why don't you plan to spend the rest of the week with her? A day might not be enough time for you guys."

"Ava?"

"It might work out better for both of us," I lie through my teeth. The tears are threatening to fall. "I won't feel like I have to rush to see Barcelona. And you won't have to rush your visit with Isabel. It's a win-win."

"But Ava . . ." His brow forms a deep V.

"Oh, you know what, it'll also make our fake breakup easier too! She can take my place. You two have a long history together, so it'll be believable if you explain to your family that you still love one another and wanted to pick up your relationship where it left off. You can say the breakup with me was mutual and there are no hard feelings." I push my plate aside, not able to look Fernando in the eyes. "If we do it this way, you'll even get your dad off your back."

"Ava!" another male voice suddenly interjects. That voice. I sink lower into my seat, and the hairs on the back of my neck stand up. Slowly, both Fernando and I turn. Leaning over the fence to the restaurant, wearing a black tuxedo and carrying a huge bouquet of roses, is Dylan.

"Is this a cosmic joke?" I whisper in shock. Fernando

rekindles his relationship with Isabel and Dylan shows up in a tux? "How did you find me?"

He places a hand on the fence and vaults over it. The tails of the tux gets caught by a stray nail and rip. "Ava, I'm an idiot." He kneels down at my feet. "And I've made a huge mistake. Rainy was never the right person! Everything she did reminded me of you. You're the woman I love. Not her! Can you ever forgive me for being a world-class jerk to you? I need you in my life."

My heart thumps rapidly in my chest. I scoot my chair back a few inches toward the wall. I pinch myself, but I'm not dreaming. Dylan has miraculously discovered that he "loves" me. "Why didn't you say anything before you left Sequoia Valley?" I sputter.

"I needed time to figure it all out."

Before coming on this trip, the old Ava wouldn't have hesitated at the thought of telling him I love him too. But I'm not that person any longer. He's treated me like I don't matter ever since he left. My heart can't be toyed with. It belongs to another. Even if Fernando can't love me back. "Dylan, no . . . it's too late," I whisper.

"Ava, please," he begs. "I'll do whatever it takes to prove myself to you. Everybody deserves a second chance." He moves closer to me. "We have a history together. Eight years of friendship can't be destroyed in the span of four weeks. That should be enough for at least five minutes of your time."

I study Dylan's face. His eyes are wide and pleading with me. They remind me so much of a boxer puppy. I know I shouldn't do it, especially after how hard I've worked to get over him, but a small part of me still has feelings for the man. "Five minutes. That's it." I nod to

Fernando. "He's going to be starting a timer as soon as we sit down at that empty table over there."

Dylan opens his mouth to argue with me, but I shoot him my best icy glare, and he clamps it shut. We cross the patio and take seats across from one another. I sit tall and cross my arms against my chest. "What do you want, Dylan?"

"I thought it was obvious. I want you!"

I snort. "You have a funny way of showing it. You stopped replying to my texts. You never called. And then the next thing I know, you're engaged."

"We aren't together anymore. Rainy's personality was too strong for me. I need someone with a softer, gentler personality. Like you."

"Then why did you propose to her?"

"Because at the time, it seemed like the right thing to do." He leans forward in his seat. "But I was wrong about wanting to marry her. You're the only person in my life who's always been right by my side. You get me. I can count on you to bring me a coffee in the morning. To go hiking with me. And to take care of the paperwork so I can make sure our clients are happy. When you move to Fort Collins and join me—"

I wrinkle my nose. He's trying to compliment me, but everything coming out of his mouth sounds like an insult. He didn't want someone with another alpha personality like him. He wants someone who will go along with what he wants. Somebody who's a people pleaser.

The old Ava didn't have a backbone. But the new Ava does. I was too blinded to see Dylan's flaws before. But after spending so much time around Fernando, I know what I want in a man. And more importantly, how I deserve to be treated. "Do you hear yourself?" I look him up and down.

"What?"

"The world doesn't revolve around you, Dylan. There are a few billion other people out there too."

He frowns deeply. "Huh?"

"In the four years our practice was open, you never once brought me coffee. Every time you wanted to spend some time together, *you* picked the spot and the activity. You never wanted to do the things I suggested. And as far as the clinic, I only filled out your paperwork because if I didn't, the patient records would always be incomplete. You always brushed it off and said you'd do it later, but that never happened. You'd always leave right when we closed, and it would be up to me or Vicki to do whatever wasn't done during the workday." I shake my head and rub my temples. "I can't believe it's taken me so long to realize how self-centered you are."

"Come on, Ava, you aren't being fair."

I drum my fingers on the table. "Okay, I'll bite. What's my normal drink order? And when I bought out your ownership of the clinic, name one thing you did to help make the transition smoother."

His eyes widen and he stares at me as if I've grown a second head. "Uh . . . a caramel macchiato?"

"Wrong." I make a buzzer noise. "Care to try again?"

"Green tea latte?"

"That's strike two."

He clenches his jaw. "This is stupid."

To prove my point, I deadpan, "*You* always get the vanilla bean frappe with three extra shots of espresso. Your second favorite drink is a cinnamon bun latte with oat milk. And for the answer to my last question: You didn't do anything. Not a single thing. As soon as the transfer went through, you stopped working. *I'm* even the one who packed up your darn office."

"Ava, I had things to do before my move. I had to pack up my house, find a new apartment in Fort Collins. Make sure I called the utility companies to cancel all my accounts."

I cut him off. "You had months to do that. But you procrastinated. The more I think about it, the more I realize that you haven't changed at all since vet school. You don't need me. What you need is to grow up."

"Ava, be reasonable."

His words send hurricane-force winds shooting out of my body. "That's all I've ever been to you, Dylan." I stand. "There will *never* be an us," I spit out.

Across the restaurant, the timer goes off. "Time's up," Fernando calls out.

As I turn to leave, Dylan reaches for my forearm and spins me around, shoving the roses under my nose. "But you love me."

"I did, not anymore."

Fernando slams his fist on the table and jumps to his feet, causing Dylan to jerk. He walks behind Dylan and yanks him away from me, further ripping his jacket. His chest is heaving and his face flushed red. "You heard her, you're done. Over. Finalizado. It's time to get lost."

Dylan sags as he realizes how much taller and more built Fernando is than him. He drops the bouquet to the floor and tucks his chin to his chest. Fernando starts to drag him toward the gate.

"Wait!" I shout. Both men turn. "Before you get rid of him, there's one more thing I need to know." Dylan shoots me a smug look. "Why did you come to Spain?"

"When I called the practice to ask Vicki about a box I forgot, she mentioned you were going to Spain."

"Okay, but Spain's a big country. How did you find me?"

Dylan's face turns into one of panic and he lets out an audible gulp. "There's an AirTag in your purse," he says so softly, I almost need a microphone to make it out.

"How? When?"

"At the airport in Denver. I dropped it into your purse. In hindsight, it was probably a stupid move."

"You think?" My eyes twitch. "Why did you do it?"

"I, er, wanted to keep track of you. You stopped sharing your location with me when I got to Colorado."

He's an even bigger creep than I thought. "You're lucky I'm not filing a restraining order against you!" I'm seeing red, and if I were a lion, he'd be my first choice of prey. "This is adiós *forever*, Dylan. Don't text, call, or ever try to reach me again."

"Is that clear?" Fernando grunts.

Dylan lifts his chin weakly.

"Get rid of him," I say, gritting my teeth. Marching over to my purse, I remove my wallet, phone, sunglasses, and lipstick before locating the AirTag. Throwing it as hard as I can, I watch with deep satisfaction as it lands in the ocean, hopefully being destroyed in the process.

Chapter Twenty-Four

How could he stick an AirTag in my purse? It certainly explains a lot. I can't believe he'd sink to such a low level to keep track of me. Ugh, I should've listened to Daphne. She knew years ago he was trouble with a capital T. And she was right. When I tell her the stunt Dylan pulled, she'll want to kill him herself.

As I sit in the car beside Fernando, I replay scenes in my head from over the past eight years. In vet school and throughout my residency, Dylan balanced me out. He made sure I didn't spend all my time buried in a corner of the library. He pulled me out of my shell and helped me develop the social skills I needed to be able to confidently speak to my clients. But that's where his help ended. As I grew, he stayed stuck in the past.

Dylan only cared about number one. Himself. He said he loved me. But I doubt it was ever the type of love I craved. I was just a pawn. A stepping stone to another woman, project, job, or whatever else he was after. He had no problem dumping the Queen of Vultures right after they got engaged.

It would only be a matter of time before that was me. My heart wouldn't be able to take riding the Dylan roller coaster a second time. It's already been broken once. A second time would be . . . I don't even want to think about it. There's already a bitter taste in my mouth. "Goodbye, Dylan," I whisper softly.

I swallow hard and shift my attention to the man beside me. Fernando has his hands steady on the steering wheel and eyes focused on the road. It's funny. The paths we've walked in our past relationships are eerily similar.

I pined after Dylan for years, while Fernando loved his Isabel. Neither of us could see their flaws until it was too late. And when they broke us, it hurt as if someone had forced us to walk through a bed of hot coals barefoot. I take a deep breath. At least he'll finally get his happy ending. Isabel is a lucky woman. She'll never find a better man than Fernando. I hope maybe one day, I'll be lucky too. After my trip to Spain, I'm gonna need another vacation from my vacation.

I don't notice until Fernando stops the car that we've left Santa Luz behind us and we're in a dense forest area. The foliage is so thick, it's hard to tell what time of day it is. Only a few patches of sunlight filter through the canopy of trees. Climbing out of the car, I feel how the temperature has dropped. I run my hands over my forearms.

"Here." Fernando slips a fleece jacket over my shoulders. "We have about an hour before the sanctuary closes. We can come back another day and explore some more if you enjoy it."

I don't have to ask where we are. I hear the mighty roar of a tiger. It's a sound that I heard often at the Colorado Zoo. When you stand beside a tiger, only separated by a few inches of thick steel, the sound of its roar reverberates through your bones and reminds you as a human how puny a species we really are. The sound still sends a chill through my body.

"We can have a look at whatever big cats you'd like," Fernando says.

He purchases our admission tickets, and we wander silently from enclosure to enclosure. I can't believe Fernando thought to bring me here. It lifts my spirits to see the animals in wide open spaces, doing natural behaviors like sleeping and surveying their territories from high perches.

"I thought they'd be more active," he says as we pass another exhibit, where the lion is stretched out asleep on top of a pile of rocks, soaking up the winter sun.

"Big cats are like their domestic cousins. They're creatures of the night," I reply.

It's the first time I've spoken in over an hour. I'm happy to have the animals to focus on instead of my nonexistent love life.

We come to the far end of the sanctuary and ascend a set of stairs to a viewing platform overlooking an area with sandy-colored rocks, tall grass, and a water feature. The sign on the right displays an image of the Iberian lynx.

"This is what we're here for," Fernando says as we claim a seat on the bench in front of the glass. "I know this is the cat you were the most excited to see." He squints out at the exhibit. "I don't see anything, but if we wait long enough, maybe we'll get lucky."

"We might, but then again, lynxes are experts at hiding. They're born with those dark spots that help them camouflage seamlessly in their habitat." My own eyes gaze out near the rocks and among the shrubs, searching for any sign of movement or spots. "I would really like to see one. Spain is the only place in the world you can find this particular species."

We hear the chirping of birds and the sound of the water plummeting over the man-made falls to the pond below. The tranquility soothes my mind. "I needed this," I say to Fernando. "I'm not in any mood to be around people right now, except for you."

"I thought the sanctuary would be a nice escape for you. Just like how the ice rink is for me."

"It is. This place is purrrrrrrrrrrrrfect. Pun intended." I pull my jacket a little tighter around my body. The temperature has continued to drop. "I'm glad you were with me when Dylan showed up. It was reassuring to know I had somebody on my side."

"I'll always be on your side," he emphasizes. "That's what fake boyfriends do." He scoots closer to me, so our legs are nearly touching and slips his own jacket over the one I'm wearing. "That man has some serious issues. I hope he listens to you and stays away."

"I think he will." I gaze forward, staring into the enclosure. "He doesn't know about our arrangement. For all he knows, if he shows up again, he'll have to answer to you."

"I'll be ready," Fernando affirms. "Just between us, it was a pleasure to see him squirm. He deserved it."

"He did," I agree.

"How are you doing mentally and emotionally?"

"Would you believe me if I said I'm fine?" I turn my head toward him. "I've had plenty of time to process not having him in my life. When he walked out of the restaurant, my gut told me it was the end of an era. I think I can finally close the Dylan chapter of my life."

"That just goes to show how strong a person you are, Ava."

I wish I could begin writing the next chapter with Fernando, but I know it's not meant to be. Instead, the next chapter starts with me being a more confident Dr. Brown and running my own practice.

We sit for a little while longer. My head makes its way onto his shoulder, while his arm drapes itself over my body, pulling me closer to him. It feels like a warm cocoon. I know I'm flirting with danger, but he's reciprocating, and I can't bring myself to scoot away from him. My eyes slowly flutter closed.

"Ava." I hear Fernando's voice sometime later. "Ava," he repeats.

I hide a yawn with my hand and sit up. I guess I must've fallen asleep. "Hmm?"

"Look," he whispers excitedly, pointing up at the upper left corner of the rock pile. "Is that . . . ?"

"Yeah, it is," I breathe, now fully awake and leaning forward in my seat.

Crouched down at the top of the habitat near the waterfall's edge is the elusive lynx. Its ears have long fluffy black fur. Its main coat contains a series of spots similar to a bobcat or cheetah. But its most impressive feature is its bright-yellow eyes. The lynx is gazing directly at us as if we're on exhibit.

"It's so beautiful." I take out my phone and snap a few photos. "I wish I could get closer."

"I don't know about that. Those paws are large, and I bet they come with equally sharp claws. I wouldn't want to be scratched by them."

"The lynx would be more afraid of you than you are of him," I tease.

"Hmm . . . if you say so." He doesn't sound totally convinced.

The bushes around the lynx crackle and sway. A moment later, another lynx appears, rubbing its head against the body of the sitting one, urging it to stand before it disappears. The sitting lynx lazily pops to its feet, yawns, and sticks its butt into the air, stretching. After giving us one final glance, it, too, disappears into the thicket.

"That was special," I say, grinning widely. "How long was it sitting there while I was asleep?"

"Not long. I only noticed it a minute ago. You were right about the camouflage. I had to take a photo and zoom in with my phone to see if it was really there."

"Well, thank you for waking me up and showing me." I start to lean in to kiss him, but stop short and force myself back to my side of the bench. That was too close. "What time is it? It must be close to closing time," I say quickly.

"You can if you want to. I'm giving you permission."

I blink slowly a few times and return my attention to the gorgeous man sitting next to me. "To do what?"

"Kiss me."

I lower my chin to my chest and stare at him with wide eyes. Have I heard him correctly? He licks his lips. They're full and a perfect shade of cherry-red. "That's not a good idea." I shake my head. "You're with Isabel. I can't be the reason you two break up again."

Fernando inhales sharply. "You think I'm getting back together with Isabel?"

I blink a few more times, now fully awake. "Aren't you?"

"No," he says emphatically.

"Oh." A chorus of gospel singers starts singing at the top of their lungs inside my head. Fernando is still single! "Back at the restaurant, you mentioned lunch with Isabel and clearing your schedule. I just assumed . . ." My voice trails off.

"We were an item?"

I nod.

"I can see where you might get that idea." He rubs a hand over his jaw. "At breakfast today, Isabel and I decided to be friends again, but that's it. I made it clear that any romance between us has fizzled out." He sighs. "Anyway, the reason I wanted to clear my schedule to meet her for lunch is to discuss a skating show she wants my help putting together."

"A skating show," I say slowly. I hang my head. "I feel so dumb right now."

"No, Ava, you're not dumb. Before we were interrupted, I wanted to tell you that we weren't together."

He takes my hand in his. "Since the day you helped me out in the clinic, I've been attracted to you. The more time I've spent with you, the deeper that infatuation has grown. I thought I'd be able to stick to my rules and avoid ever falling for someone. But I've failed—miserably, I might add. Because since we landed in Lisbon, all I've wanted to do is kiss you senseless and make you my *real* girlfriend."

My breathing increases. My stomach begins to perform somersaults. That's what I've wanted all along too. "But what about yesterday in the car when you freaked out on me?"

"That was one of the dumbest moves I've ever made." He pinches the bridge of his nose. "It was a last-ditch effort to convince myself I shouldn't risk another relationship. I didn't want to get hurt again. But all I managed to do is make myself more miserable. I'm tired of being alone. I want to be happy again and spend my time with a woman I've grown to care deeply for." He cups my cheeks with his hands. "I realized today that I can't run the risk of losing you to another man. I want you for me. I want to spoil you rotten, teach you to skate, and learn all about animals from you."

His words cause my brain to go fuzzy. I don't need to hear anything else from him. And I don't want to wait any longer. Leaning forward, I greedily plant my lips on his and kiss him. Deeply. His arms wrap themselves around my back, while mine loop around his neck, and he pulls me into his body. Despite only having a light long-sleeve shirt on, he serves as my personal heater.

I've waited so long for this second kiss. Unlike our first time, we're not putting on a show. There's nothing fake about this. It's like my body has been dropped in a glass of expensive champagne. Everything within me feels like it's sparkling, and I'm filled with bubbles of delight. His lips are so silky soft. His cologne is fresh, a muted lemon scent.

As we break apart, I giggle. "How is it you're always so warm?"

"That's just how I am."

We nuzzle our noses and kiss again at a much slower pace. I allow my brain to completely shut off, my emotions to run wild, and my body to do as it pleases.

We only leave the sanctuary when some of the keepers come through and tell us they've been closed for over an hour. Oops. When you've been enjoying yourself so much, there's not much else that matters in the world.

With my fingers laced through Fernando's, we slowly

meander to the exit and back to the car. "Well, at least we don't have to pretend anymore in front of your family."

"I was under the impression you weren't pretending even when everything was fake."

My face flushes. "Okay, I wasn't."

"Well, if we're admitting the truth, neither was I." He licks his lips. "I was looking for every possible excuse to play the boyfriend card with you."

I elbow him lightly in the ribs. "You should've told me sooner."

"I know. I could've saved us a lot of time and trouble." He sighs. "It won't happen again."

"It had better not because I'm not letting you go anywhere." I giggle. "You're *my* boyfriend. Nobody else's."

"I could say the same for you." He swoops his arms under my legs and lifts me up as I laugh wildly, wrapping my arms around his neck. "I have no intentions of letting you go anywhere either. You've captured my heart. I hope you like being spoiled rotten because that's exactly what I intend to do with you. I'm a man who's been starved for love for too long."

He gives me a peck on the cheek and puts me down at the car. We return home, both smiling widely and feeling as if we're floating along on a magic carpet ride.

Chapter Twenty-Five

The remainder of my stay in Spain passes too quickly. Now that we're officially a real couple, I scrap my original plans and dive headfirst into Fernando's world. His mamá continues to parade us around to every cousin, great-aunt, and second uncle within what seems like a hundred-mile radius. I've never eaten so much in my life—or been kissed on the cheek so many times by strangers calling me *mi amor.*

His aunts give us a little more breathing room and only monopolize us at dinner. We spend a lot of time watching old home movies and looking through his family photo albums. Spoiler alert: Fernando was an adorable kid.

His dad eventually apologizes. He makes an effort to get to know me better, but he's still not my favorite person. I'm still angry about how he treated Fernando by bringing Isabel here. Nevertheless, we form a fragile truce while watching a Barcelona match together. I hope in time, the frost between all of us will thaw.

We only get to Barcelona on the last day. Which is a shame since it's the city I end up enjoying the most. At least

I know that with a Spanish boyfriend, there's a good chance there'll be a return trip in my future.

Saying goodbye to him is difficult. Knowing that he'll be back in Sequoia Valley again in two weeks is the only thing that allows me to board the plane home. It's then and there that the dream world I've been living in for the last two weeks disappears and it's back to reality.

"How does it feel to be back in the good ol' US of A?" Daphne asks as I stand crouched in the kitchen scratching Max's belly. His tail wags almost violently side to side. My hands are covered in slobber from all his licking.

"Weird," I answer honestly. "I know I wasn't gone that long, but it feels like a lifetime ago. So much has happened. I left here planning to spend time by myself getting over Dylan."

"And now, here you are with a tan in the middle of December and a sexy, hot ice-skater boyfriend." Daph leans against the door frame and crosses her arms. "You're going to be the envy of every female at the rink! Especially the moms."

I grimace. "I hate being the center of attention." There's one thing that hasn't changed.

"It won't be that bad." She laughs. "The ladies know Fernando wouldn't pick just any person to date. It would have to be somebody extra special."

"Like someone who knows next to nothing about ice skating or sports in general?" I say in a hopeful tone.

"Exactly. Somebody just like you."

Max rolls upright and barks in agreement. I continue to scratch him firmly under the chin. "I think you'll like him just as much as I do, boy. Fernando is a dog man." He barks again. Daph and I share a laugh.

"Max was a good boy while he was here. The kids loved

having him around. Just, er, don't be surprised if he's gained a little weight. I didn't catch it until the other night, but the kiddos have been feeding him some of their dinner under the table."

I stand and brush my jeans off. "Is that true, boy?" He continues to pant, giving me a wide-eyed, innocent look. "Well, it could be worse. It just means no more treats for a while." I sigh as I attach his leash to the clip on his collar. "Even if Christmas is right around the corner."

"What are your plans for the rest of the day?" Daphne asks.

"After I drop Max off at home and pick up the mail, I'm gonna swing by the clinic. I'm anxious to touch base with my friend Laura and see what you and Vicki have been up to."

"I'll come with you. I want to see what you think about the updated decor."

I arch an eyebrow. "What about the kids?"

"Brian's off today. He can watch them for an hour. Let me grab my keys and my coat."

I settle Max in his kennel in the back of my truck, then slide into the driver's seat as Daphne pops into the passenger side.

"Have you given any thought to Christmas?" she asks. "Are you planning to come over with Fernando? Or is it going to just be the two of you?"

I start the engine and back up, shifting gears. "He won't be back until New Year's. As of right now, I'm planning to do what I always do. Spend Christmas Eve with you and the kids, and Christmas Day with Mom and Dad."

"Mm-hmm." Daph nods.

I steal a glance in her direction. "What?"

"Nothing. Nothing," she says a little too quickly, fidgeting in her seat.

"What is it that you want me to ask you about?"

"I suck at trying to keep a big secret from you." She snorts. "I thought I'd give you an early present and hint that I know your *boyfriend* changed his plane ticket and will be home for Christmas."

I inhale sharply. "But I already took him away from spending a lot of his time with his family. Christmas should be spent with them." I scrunch my nose. "Who's your source?"

Daph ignores the question and clicks on the radio. "Oh, I love this song." She hums along and dances in her seat to the tune of Mariah Carey's "All I Want for Christmas."

I roll my eyes. I'll have to steal her phone and scroll through her text messages to find out. But the likelihood of me being able to do that is slim to none. The device never leaves her side.

"Well, do you at least have a date for when he's getting in? Maybe I can pick him up at the airport."

Daphne zips her lips closed.

Frustrated to no end, I ignore the temptation to double park, tell her to get out, and make her walk the rest of the way to the clinic, but that still won't get me any answers. I remind myself to be nice. It's the holiday season, and Daph is my only sister. Ava 2.0 is supposed to be more understanding and patient. Except when it comes to matters involving Fernando. She's as greedy as the Grinch.

There's a nervous energy swelling inside of me, like a storm brewing beneath the surface. I'm dying to know what else she's keeping from me. Knowing that he'll be home also means I need to rush out and pick up a few little Christmas gifts. I chew on my lip. I've gotten to know the man well, but there are still a lot of mysteries left to uncover. Should I reach out to his friends at the rink and ask for their advice? I shelve the thought for later as we pull up to the practice.

I park in my reserved spot in front and cut the engine. "You redesigned the sign and logo too?" I say, slowly sliding out of the car.

"Uh-huh. The old sign was just text. It was faded and the colors were all wrong. Talk about being ineffective. You needed something eye-catching that screams you're an all-animal vet practice. Something that would make people stop and look."

"This definitely does that," I say, continuing to stare at the neon sign. It contains hot-pink, yellow, and blue lights with the words "Sequoia Valley Animal Hospital" in swirly letters. There's a dog, cat, and turtle standing on either side of the text wearing stethoscopes and headlamps, and a bird perched on top of the Y. "I love it."

"Glad to hear it." Daphne rubs her hands together. "Wait until it gets dark. That's when the sign really stands out."

As we approach the front door, my sister sticks her hands over my eyes. "Daphne!"

"I don't want you to look until I make sure everything is set up perfectly. I only get one shot at impressing you. If I take my hands away, do you promise not to look until I tell you to?"

"Fine," I huff.

She releases me and runs around the reception area, her shoes squeaking against the floor. I hope the inside is a little more toned down and the walls aren't hot-pink or sunshine-yellow.

"Okay, everything's good. On the count of three, you can look. One, two, three!"

My eyes flutter open and I gasp. The clinic doesn't resemble the same space I've worked out of for the past four years. It looks more like a play area than a waiting area.

The walls are thankfully a muted sky-blue. The seating area has been divided into three distinctly different spaces—one for cats, one for dogs, and another for other pets. Each is a different pastel shade.

"It was all Vicki's idea to add the fake grass, the fire hydrant, scratching posts, cat tree, bird perches, and fish tank. She thought if you had a patient who could burn off some of their energy before they were taken to the back, it would help them relax." Daphne snaps her fingers together. "Oh, and she said she'd have no problem making sure the reception area stays clean."

I let out a deep breath. "That's good, because things like the fake grass are going to be high maintenance."

"That's what I told her, but let her figure that out. Come on, there's a lot more to show you!"

She escorts me over to the nook that used to serve as the customers' coffee bar. It's been replaced with the specialized food we carry.

"This is a much better use of the space," I say, running my hand over the newly installed shelving units. For once, it doesn't look like a closet has exploded. Everything we carry has a dedicated space.

"Agreed. We decided that each waiting area should also have its own coffee, tea, and water bar. That way a pet owner doesn't have to cross over into 'enemy territory.'" Daphne makes air quotes. "The last thing you need is for a big dog like a Great Dane to stir up a parrot, iguana, or whatever other animal you have waiting to see you."

As we approach the reception desk, I see the rows of filing cabinets we previously had crammed into the space have been removed. In their place is a clean white wall with the new logo and a list of the prices for our basic services. There's also a glass display cabinet advertising my monthly low-cost vaccine clinic and pets available for adoption.

"Vicki digitized all your patient files. We kept them in case you wanted access to them. For now, the cabinets are in your office, but I'm hoping you'll let me haul them out of here. They're clunky and don't fit the new aesthetic of the place."

"I'll keep that in mind." I shake my head. "What I can't wrap my head around is how you've managed to achieve all this in just two weeks."

"It was a lot of early mornings and late nights to work around when the clinic was open, but totally worth it," my sister says with a gleam in her eyes. "And we're not even done with the tour yet."

We continue our field trip through the exam rooms, break room, kennels, my office, and the storage room. I'd hoped the exam rooms would get a new coat of paint, but I never imagined that literally every room in the clinic would receive an overhaul.

"So what do you think? Do I get the Dr. Brown seal of approval?"

I'm at a loss for words. All I can do is nod as a few tears slip out, and hug my sister tightly. "It's the best Christmas present ever. Thank you," I say softly.

"You're welcome. And I hope you don't mind, but I'm featuring it on my website."

I release Daphne. "Feel free. You did all this work; the world should see it."

"And Vicki—let me tell you, she has a real eye for

design. I told her if she's ever looking for a career change, I'd be happy to hire her."

"No offense, but I hope she turned you down." I laugh nervously. I just offered the temp vet tech a permanent position and made an offer to have Laura join the practice. The last thing I want to worry about is filling another vacancy. The receptionist is one of the most important people here.

"Don't worry, she did. She said you are, quote, 'the best boss lady she's ever had' and she wouldn't go anywhere without talking to you about it first."

"That's a relief. I need her too much."

After dropping my sister off, I decide to take a detour to the Sequoia Valley Ice Sports Complex. I'm deeply curious to see what Fernando's second home looks like. And have some questions for his friends. I have a few ideas about Christmas floating around in the back of my head that I'd like to run by them.

I walk up to the entrance just as a light dusting of snow begins to fall. There's a queue about thirty people long waiting to enter the building. I wonder if I'd be better off coming back another time when it's not so crowded, but then I remember Christmas is only two weeks away. The rink is going to continue being crowded until the end of the year.

I join the end of the line. To my relief, it moves quickly. Ten minutes later, I've reached the cashier's window.

"Hello, how can I help you? Are you here to skate or here for the holiday show?" a woman wearing a Santa hat asks.

"Hi. Um, the holiday show?"

She nods and punches a series of buttons on her computer. "It'll be five dollars, please, unless you brought an unwrapped toy to donate."

"No, I didn't." I reach for my wallet. "Do you take cards?"

"We sure do." She processes the payment and directs me to rink number two.

"Just out of curiosity, how much is the public skate?"

"Ten dollars for adults or twenty dollars per family no limit on kids. Both include skate rental and a locker. Did you want to purchase a ticket for that too?"

"Thanks, but not today."

I enter the lobby into what looks like a winter carnival. There are five towering Christmas trees, a games area, an arts and craft area, a photo booth, and a Santa meet and greet. It gives me a very different vibe than the rink in Madrid. It's more relaxed and focused on catering to families, not just on making money.

All in, I paid twenty-five euros in Madrid to skate, plus five euros for a locker. I can't imagine a family of four, like Daphne's, paying over a hundred euros for the same experience. It makes it easy for me to see why Fernando might enjoy working here so much—he gets to be a big kid.

Rink two is freezing. But with the number of people packed in the stands, about two hundred, it doesn't take long for me to warm up. I find a seat on one of the highest rows, not certain what to expect. Everyone around me is chatting excitedly.

"Do you think Coach Frankie will skate with Mr. C?" a girl to my left asks her dad.

"She will, dummy, didn't you see her practicing during the freestyle session yesterday?" her brother says, poking her shoulder and sticking his tongue out at her.

"Robbie, don't call your sister a dummy. And what have I told you about how you should behave in public."

I focus my attention back on the ice as the lights go down.

"Ladies and gentlemen, welcome to this year's Sequoia Valley Figure Skating Club Holiday Show. All contributions from tonight will be donated to the Laka Wakahanra Children's Hospital." The crowd applauds. "For our opening act tonight, please welcome to the ice your reigning World Champions, Francesca Tomlinson and Charlie Welch, or as you know them, Coach Frankie and Mr. C!"

The show lasts an hour and a half. I'm a novice when it comes to these types of things, but after watching some of the coaches and advanced students perform, I'll admit that I've never been more inspired to pop over to the rink's pro shop and purchase myself a pair of skates.

Making my way down to the ice, I approach the blond skater with thick curls I recognize from the food truck at the antique market. "Hi, Gemma," I call out, feeling awkward. She's a woman I've spoken to for less than two minutes, and here I am addressing her as if we're old friends. "Um, you may not remember me, but I'm a . . . friend of Fernando's."

Her face lights up with recognition. "Dr. Brown! I remember you! I'm so glad you made it tonight! Fernando is going to be so disappointed he missed you! He's on holiday in Spain right now."

"You can call me Ava, if you want." I shift my weight from one leg to another. "And yes, I know. We crossed paths. I just got back from there." I swallow hard. "If you have a minute, I wanted to just ask your advice on something."

"Of course!" Her large blue eyes sparkle. I can see why she would've made a perfect Cinderella. She looks and sounds like a real-life princess, especially with the Scottish accent.

"I need to get him a Christmas present and have a few ideas, but want to run them by one of the people who knows him best before I do anything."

"Absolutely. I'm more than happy to help."

"Here's what I have in mind . . ."

Chapter Twenty-Six

Christmas Eve arrives two weeks later. The weather in Sequoia Valley has continued to stay bitterly cold. All the forecasters predict a white Christmas, which may sound fantastic, but it also makes getting into and out of town impossible.

All the highways that go through the mountains are closed. Unless you're traveling between one of the neighboring towns of Grizzly Springs or Lake Wakahanra, you're stuck wherever you're going to spend the holiday.

I'd hoped Fernando might be able to make it through before the roads closed, but all my instincts are telling me it isn't going to happen. Not that I was even supposed to know about it. As disappointed as I am about spending the holidays apart from my boyfriend, at least I still have my family.

I send Fernando a text when I wake up, opting to play along as if I'm in the dark about what his plans are.

> Ava: Hola, Fernando! Happy Christmas Eve! I hope your weather is better than ours. You're missing one big storm.

I part the curtains on my apartment window and send him a photo of the blanket of white snow.

> Ava: I bet you'll be at the beach this morning or somewhere nice and warm. My phone said Santa Luz was going to be a nice 65 degrees. Do you guys do a big celebration? Also, please tell your family I said hello and wish them a happy Christmas Eve from me too.

Setting my phone aside, I see to Max, then pop into the kitchen to take care of some baking. I volunteered to take charge of dessert for the evening, which means I'll be making apple and mince pies. I crank up the music, pull out my pans, and get to work.

Everything goes pretty smoothly until my power shuts off. "Ugh," I cry. "I *just* put my pies in the oven."

Frustrated, I pick up my phone, ready to text Daphne. As the screen lights up, I see a missed call and text from Fernando. He's my first priority. The pies can wait.

> Fernando: Happy Christmas Eve to you too. Let's trade. I'll give you the beach weather for some snow. Especially if it means that when I get home, we can sit in front of a roaring fire, sip on some hot chocolate, and watch some of those cheesy Hallmark movies you were telling me about.

"I wish we could do that right now," I say to Max. "It's

much better than being here in the dark." I continue to read his message.

> Fernando: We don't do anything big for Christmas Eve, just Christmas Day. Right now, I'm planning to pop over to the inn for an hour then help Mamá in the kitchen. She likes to put together a special dinner for the B&B guests. I'll pass your greetings along. Everyone already misses you and can't wait for you to come back. Are you free to video chat later?

> Ava: We can make plans for a chat, but I can't make any promises you'll be able to see me. I just lost power and I'm sitting in the dark. Hoping my sister still has hers going. I'll get back to you soon.

I tap on Daphne's name and type another message:

> Ava: Hey, sis. Hope your morning is going better than mine. Please tell me you still have power.

My phone chimes a few seconds later.

> Daphne: *Sad face emoji* Nope. I was about to ask if you did.

> Ava: Nope.

> Daphne: Well, I guess that means we're headed to Mom and Dad's place. I just got off the phone with them. They're still good to go. I doubt the power will come back on anytime soon. Dad said Mom's already baking up a storm.

Ava: I hope she doesn't make pies. I'd
just stuck mine in when everything went
down.

Daphne: You're actually baking them?
You didn't pick them up at the store?

Ava: Nope. I wanted to try something
new.

Daphne: Look at you! I'm proud! And
also happy to take them off your hands.

Ava: Even if they taste like crap?

Daphne: Uh-huh. And they won't.

Ava: I appreciate the vote of confidence.

Daphne: *Smiling emoji* Anyway, do you
have enough emergency supplies on
hand—flashlight, candles, water, etc.?

Ava: Remember who you're talking to.
Yes, I have plenty of supplies.

Daphne: Just checking.

Ava: Are the kids doing okay?

Daphne: They're fine. They're making
some decorations for Santa. I'd better
check on them now.

Ava: Sounds good. See you later.

Closing out the message, I retrieve my pies from the oven, place them on a rack, and give Mom a call. She picks up on the second ring.

"Hi, Ava, I knew it would only be a matter of time before you called," she says in a cheery voice.

"Daphne said you and Dad are unaffected by the power outage. Do you mind if I come over a little early and use your oven?"

"Of course, honey. Whatever you need. I should be done prepping dinner by one. Any time after that is fine."

"Do you want any help?" I ask.

"No, I have everything under control. I want you to relax."

I laugh softly to myself. There isn't too much I'll be able to do without power. "Okay, I'll be over at one. Oh, I'm planning to bring Max too."

"That sounds good. We always love having him around."

"See you soon," I say, then end the call.

I glance from the kitchen to Max, sitting in his oversized fleece bed. "Well, boy, what should we do now? I can read on my tablet, stream a movie on my phone, or we can go for a walk. You tell me, what's your choice." At the word "walk," he pops out of the bed and sits obediently by the front door. "You're too smart for your own good." I laugh. "Okay, let's get your booties and sweater on, then we'll go out."

It's still snowing when Max and I leave my apartment, but that doesn't stop my seventy-pound dog from reverting to a puppy. While we take a nice long walk around the deserted park across the street, he experiences the zoomies and runs around with boundless energy. My arm gets a good workout as I struggle to control the leash. At least it helps keep me warm.

"Somebody's going to sleep well," I joke as he finally begins to slow down. I kneel to give him a good pet and some water. Despite the cold, he greedily laps it all up. Once he's finished, we cross the street and head back to the complex.

"What do we think, Max? Should I come back out here and build a snowman? Think there's enough powder for it?"

"If Max won't do it, I volunteer."

"Fernando!" I scream, racing toward my doorstep. He's dressed in a white puffer coat and black pants. There's a little scruff on his jaw and dark rings under his eyes, but he's still one of the most handsome men I've ever seen. He holds out his arms, and I rush into them. "You're here!"

"I got in last night just before the roads closed. Talk about good timing. I'm your Christmas present. I just didn't have any time to put a big novelty bow on top of my head." He brings me in for a kiss.

"I've missed you so much." I bury my face in his chest as we break apart.

He chuckles. "Your sister and I have been working together. The plan was to surprise you at dinner tonight. But when I saw your text, I figured I'd come to your rescue. I still have power at my place."

"My hero." I giggle. "I hate stealing you from your family, but I'm glad you're here."

"Mamá and the tías told me I needed to be here as soon as I explained I wanted to spend our first Christmas as a couple together."

"What did you have to promise them?" I ask, tilting my head to the side.

"That we'd be back for a longer visit next year."

"That's something I think we can definitely manage."

As we try to separate, I realize that we're stuck together. I glance down. Max has managed to wrap his leash around our legs.

Fernando laughs.

"Maximillian! What have you done?" I groan.

"That's a fancy name."

"Growing up, I used to love *A Goofy Movie*. Max is the name of Goofy's son." I incline my chin toward my chocolate lab. "This guy is full of mischief, so it seemed like the perfect name."

"Hmm, I haven't seen *A Goofy Movie,* that's one you'll have to watch with me. Maybe even today." We start to unwrap ourselves. "Do you guys care to come over to Casa de Alvarez and warm up?"

"Please!" I reach inside my pocket for my keys. "Last time the power was out, it took forty-eight hours to restore."

"Well, you're welcome to stay with me as long as you'd like. I have plenty of room in my cabin."

"Do you think I could use your oven too. I have these pies—"

He holds up his hand. "Of course. Mi casa es tu casa."

Free of the leash, I enter my apartment to grab my backpack and the bag of presents for my family. Fernando's gift is also sitting under my little Charlie Brown tree. I'd planned to ask him to come over when he got back, but now that he's here, I want him to have it. I add it to the top of the bag.

We pull up to Fernando's cottage. It's a two-story royal-blue structure with a small porch and a single window trimmed in gold Christmas lights overlooking the front. A white picket fence surrounds the front garden. Although it's covered in snow, I can see a few pointed red hats peeking out.

"Are those gnomes?" I guess, stepping out of the car.

"Sí, they are. Good eye." He opens the trunk while I open the door to the back seat. Max pops out and starts investigating the new territory. "My friend Tim gifted them to me. He collects Chia pets, but I wasn't a fan. So as a gag gift for my birthday last year, he gave me a collection of garden gnomes. I thought they were funny, so I put them in the front yard."

"Are any of them ice skaters?" I tease.

"If you're asking . . ." He takes his phone from his back pocket and swipes until he finds a photo of the garden in summer. "Three of them are. The other two are sloths."

"Sloths?" I scrunch my nose.

"Another one of Tim's quirks. They're his favorite animal. I'll fill you in on the full story later."

I study the image, then hand the device back to him. He helps me gather my stuff from the car, and we make our way inside. A long entryway leads to a cozy living room. There's a TV, huge L-shaped couch draped with several blankets, rustic coffee table, and a six-foot-tall living Christmas tree near the fireplace.

"I'm impressed you had time to put this up! And it's still alive. Considering you've been away."

"I got it last night." He places the bag of gifts down. "A part of my plan was going to be asking you here after dinner to help me decorate it while we ate dessert. But now it looks like I need to make a few changes to the agenda."

Butterflies flutter in my stomach. I stare at him in awe, touched by his level of thoughtfulness. Not only did he spend the last two days traveling to be back in Sequoia Valley for the holidays, but he did it for me. Me. If that's not one of the ultimate grand gestures, I don't know what is.

Max barks and claims a place on the sofa, interrupting my thoughts. "Down, boy. This isn't our home. You can't just jump up onto Fernando's furniture whenever you feel like it."

Fernando laughs. "Aww, leave him. He's fine. It's not a home unless it's lived in. I'm not the type of person who cares too much about keeping furniture clean. There's already some coffee stains on it, crumbs in the cracks, and who knows what else hiding under the cushions."

My heart grows even bigger.

"So do you want to decorate the tree? I have some hot chocolate and cookies we can enjoy to give us some energy."

"Let's do it."

Fernando gets a cozy fire going, as I place my pies in the oven and send a quick text to mom.

> Ava: Hi mom! Change of plans, I won't be coming by at 1 after all. But will still be there for dinner. I'll fill you in later.

We spend the next two hours having a blast hanging lights on the tree and trimming it with the leftover ornaments he picked up from the craft store.

"It looks like something a five-year-old would've put together," he says with a sigh when we finish. "Nothing matches."

"That's what makes it unique. I love it. It's just like us."

"It is?" he asks, placing the last of the ornament boxes to the side.

"Yeah. When we were in Spain, we didn't have a plan. We hoped for the best and things worked out beautifully. With this tree, the same rules apply. I love that from every angle you look, you see something different. No two ornaments are the same."

He walks over and kisses me on the cheek. "I love your positivity, Dr. Brown," he purrs. "How did I get so lucky to have you in my life?"

"You walked into my clinic, that's how." I spin around and clap my hands together. "Now that you have a tree, you need some presents." Walking over to the bag, I pull out the top two boxes. "It's not much, but these are for you."

He studies me with wide eyes. "Ava, you shouldn't have."

"Yes, I should have. You deserve it. And it's not like it's anything too fancy. They're homemade." He stares at the green paper decorated with candy canes, running his fingers over it. "You can open them now if you want."

"I can?"

"Yup. Unless you want to save one for tomorrow. But if I were you, I wouldn't want to wait."

"You're sure?"

I nod. "Go on."

We sit down on the couch next to Max. Soft holiday music plays in the background as logs crackle in the fireplace. Slowly, Fernando peels back the layers of paper on the first gift to reveal a recipe book I've put together for him.

"The Book of Pies," he reads aloud, then carefully opens it. With each flip of the page, the corners of his lips twitch up wider and wider.

"I went around town and collected the best pie recipes

from everyone I knew, including two pies from the Lucky Dog Dinner. Gemma made me promise I wouldn't tell you which recipes they are, but I bet you can figure it out."

"Thank you, Ava, it's one of the most thoughtful gifts I've ever received. I can't wait to try them out."

He sets the book aside and opens the second gift. It's a picture of us taken at the Christmas market in Madrid.

"I went through a hundred different photos trying to decide which one to have printed for you before I finally settled on this one. I know it's the day I face planted, but something else special happened before that."

He lifts his chin and locks eyes with me. "And that was . . . ?"

"It was the day I realized I'd fallen head over heels for you, Fernando. I knew that even though I'd agreed to a fake relationship, I wanted it to become real."

"That's the same day I knew my feelings for you were real too." Placing the frame down on the table, he reaches over and takes my hands in his. "Thank you so much for these gifts. They're the best things I've ever received. Happy Christmas Eve, Ava."

He gives me a kiss, and I feel like I've been transported to the land of the Sugarplum Fairy in *The Nutcracker*. Everything about it is magical.

L ater, Fernando disappears into his bedroom and returns with a large box.

"If we're exchanging gifts, it's my turn to spoil you." He sets the package on my lap.

"But I thought you were my gift," I mumble, my cheeks warming.

"I am." He puffs his chest out. "But this is something practical we can both enjoy," he says with a wink.

I hesitate, then rip open the paper. I've never had the patience to keep the wrapping paper nice. "Wow, my own skates!" I bound out of my seat, hugging him tightly. "Thank you!"

"These come with lessons from me too." He grins. "I can't have my girlfriend getting hurt. I'm going to turn you into a pairs skater."

"We have a loooooooooong way to go until that happens." I peck him on the cheek. "But either way, thank you. I can't wait to try these out. I wish the rink were open now. It's too bad they'll be closed until next week. I'm off work and actually have the time."

Fernando's eyes twinkle with mirth. "What if I had my own personal rink?" Smugly walking over to the back sliding door, he pulls open the curtain to reveal a flat portable rink that's about twenty feet by twenty feet. "It may not be the best quality, but ice is ice."

I smile widely. "I'm game if you are, *Coach Fernando.*"

We spend the rest of our Christmas Eve skating together on the ice until it's time to head over to my parents' place. It's hands down one of the best holiday experiences slash dates I've ever had.

It's hard to believe that only a few weeks ago, Dylan had shot me down and I was sitting at home eating a pint of ice cream, trying to get over him. I never thought my heart would heal. And I certainly never pictured myself having an ice skater as a boyfriend, but fate works in mysterious ways. It doesn't follow a timeline, and it doesn't allow you to pick who you'll fall in love with. It just happens.

Both Fernando and I still have a lot of growing and learning to do together, but one thing is for certain: I've finally broken out of that loop. I have a friend and boyfriend who loves me for being me, and I don't plan to ever look back.

"Hey, Ava." Fernando points up at the doorway, just short of us entering my parents' house.

"Mistletoe," I breathe.

"Shall we?"

He doesn't have to ask me twice. Under the sparkling lights and falling snow, we share a Christmas Eve kiss. "I love you, Fernando," I whisper into his ear as we take a moment to breathe.

"And I love you too, mi amor."

<h1 style="text-align:center">*Epilogue*</h1>

An entire year has passed since Fernando and I became a couple. It's a week before Christmas again. And here I am at the ice rink, about to skate in the holiday show with him.

"Just take a few deep breaths, Ava. You've got this," Gemma tells me as she adjusts my hair one final time.

Internally, it's like I'm being chased by a stampede of wildebeests. My heart is racing. All my muscles are twitching. I can't stand still. "How do you guys do it? You make it look so easy."

"Years of practice." A small smile graces her lips. "It wasn't always easy. Trust me."

With a final flourish, she tucks the ponytail behind me, then gives me a hug. "You're ready."

"It's go time," Frankie says, popping her head into the makeshift dressing area. "Aww, Ava, you look just like Princess Jasmine."

Heat sears my cheeks. "Thanks."

"Just remember to breathe and skate just like you and Fernando practiced. He's waiting for you."

I remove the skate guards covering my blades and manage to walk down the hall on jelly legs to the entrance to the ice. The cold air sends goosebumps up my arms as Gemma takes my jacket from me. My hands brush down my costume. I'm in a gorgeous turquoise dress trimmed with some gold accents and peacock feathers. Gemma personally designed for me.

"Princess, about time you showed up." Fernando appears on my left side, clad in white pants and a white jacket trimmed in gold. "Are you ready for this?"

"Not really, but either way, I'm doing it."

"You'll be magnifico," he whispers into my ear, then he kisses me. A tingle of delight spreads through my body, helping to calm a few of the nerves. "Trust your coach."

"And now, please welcome to the ice Coach Fernando and his princess, representing our adult skating program, Dr. Ava," the MC announces.

Fernando grabs my hand firmly, and we skate out onto the ice and assume our starting position in the middle. The music begins and I let my muscle memory take over as he leads me through the pattern of forward and backward crossovers, two-foot spins, bunny hops, and waltz jumps I've worked hard over the past year to perfect.

As the program progresses, I relax and settle in. It helps that the man I love is right beside me. Fernando floats across the ice with the ease of a swan skimming across the water.

"Are you ready for the grand finale?" he asks through his teeth.

I nod.

Slowing down, I arch my back and cross my legs, and allow him to lift me, trusting he won't let me fall. If you'd asked me a year ago, I would've laughed at the suggestion of being six feet up in the air, and called you crazy, but now, it's become one of my favorite moves.

We skate together every evening after work. Although I know Fernando is exhausted by six p.m., he never complains. He's always full of encouraging energy, with a goofy smile on his face.

Speaking of work, after the redesign and our new website launched in January, the clients began to trickle in. At first, growth was slow, but by summer, I had more people than Laura and I could handle. Word has gotten out that there's a vet in town who doesn't charge an arm and a leg to treat animals.

As a result, my staff has grown from just Vicki to include a new receptionist, four vet techs, and even a third vet. I'm proud to say we're an all-female business and were selected as this year's Sequoia Valley Business of the Year award thanks to all the positive reviews we've received.

The hardest part about growing was letting Vicki go. But I knew she was meant for bigger and better things. Although she'd talked about wanting to become a vet tech, she found her niche as a junior designer working for Daphne. I have to say she *is* talented. And she still helps out at my monthly clinics.

As our program music crescendos, Fernando sets me down and we hit our ending pose.

"Well done, Dr. B," he says softly into my ear.

We stand upright, take our bows, and leave the ice, high-fiving Charlie and Frankie on the way. The rink's newly crowned Olympic champions are the closing act.

"That was so good," Gemma gushes, pulling me into a firm hug. "Tim took a video. I'll have him send it to you as soon as we get home."

"Don't forget about me." Fernando pouts.

"You were your normal self." Gemma rolls her eyes. "Your performance was good, just not as brilliant as Ava's."

"I meant, I want a copy of the video too," he says.

"Oh." Her cheeks color.

"Anyway, do you mind if I steal Ava for a second? There's something I need to ask her."

"Sure."

Fernando takes hold of my hand and leads me to the coaches' room. It's empty, but there are bags, jackets, and costume pieces scattered about.

"What's up? Do you have some corrections and feedback for me, Coach?" I tease.

Fernando remains quiet. He removes something from a hidden pocket and slowly gets down to one knee. My mind goes blank, and my hands fly to my mouth as I realize what he's about to do.

"Ava, in the short year we've been together, you've managed to make me fall in love with you more than I ever imagined was possible. I thought love was something I'd never be lucky enough to experience again, but you showed me how wrong I was." From behind his back, he pulls out a black velvet box. Inside is a princess-cut diamond on a gold band with smaller baguette diamonds. "Will you make me the happiest man alive and become my princess?"

"Yes!" I shout.

He smiles as wide as a prince discovering he's been named the heir to a kingdom, flashing all his pearly whites. As he stands, he slips the ring onto my finger. It's a little big, but nothing that we won't be able to take care of by resizing it.

"Prince Fernando, you've made me the happiest vet alive."

He grins. His eyes are shining as bright as a Tiffany diamond. We move toward each other without thinking, being pulled by something magnetic. We lean in and our lips meet. They're soft and silky.

His hands find my waist, as mine slide up his chest and around his neck. I can feel the warmth of his skin through the fabric of his costume and the steady rhythm of his heartbeat mirroring mine. Everything else falls away. All that exists is us.

He tilts his head slightly, deepening the kiss, and I melt against him like I've been waiting my whole life to be in this exact place.

"Fernando, Ava, are you in here?" Leslie, Charlie's sister, bursts into the room a moment later, sounding frustrated. "I need you two for the finale. You can kiss all you want later. Right now, you're on my time."

We slowly break apart.

"Leslie, not now." Fernando groans. "I *just* proposed."

"In here?" She wrinkles her nose. "Why didn't you do it somewhere more romantic like the rink's garden area or even after your performance?"

"Because I wanted it to be private and in a place where I thought nobody would disturb us."

I giggle, covering my mouth with my hand.

"Well, you chose wrong. Anybody could walk in here. You're lucky it was me." She huffs. "Anyway, I can stall and give you guys two minutes, but then I need you lined up for the finale and bow."

"Fine. We'll be right there."

"You'd think they'd at least lock the door," Leslie mutters on her way out.

"Ignore her," Fernando says, licking his lips. "Now where were we?"

"Right here." I gaze into his eyes, ready to kiss him again. My mind is focused solely on this man. Forget the finale. I'm dreaming about our future and the whole new world we're about to create together.

Dear Reader

Thank you for taking the time to read "Caught in a Loop."

You can find the bonus content for this book here:
https://tomitabb.com/caught-in-a-loop-bonus-content/

If you enjoyed this book, please take a moment to leave a review on Amazon, Goodreads, Bookbub, or whatever platform you may have discovered this book on. It helps Tomi connect with readers like you!

Love her books? Become a part of her treasured community here.

Stay connected with Tomi by scanning QR code, or by visiting her official website.

Https://TomiTabb.com

About the Author

Tomi's publishing journey began in 2020 with the release of her debut novel, *Dancing With a Royal*. Although she's always loved writing fictional stories, Tomi's background is in academic writing. She holds an MA degree in History and is currently pursuing her doctorate degree in the same subject.

In her rare free time, Tomi enjoys figure skating and hunting for new pumpkin flavored foods to try. It's one of the many reasons fall is her favorite season.

Tomi is a California native where she resides with her family and one very spoiled cat.

Website: TomiTabb.com

Also by Tomi Tabb

The Unexpected Royals

-Dancing With a Royal

-Jiving With a Royal

-Designing for a Royal

-More Than a Passing Shot

Friends of the Unexpected Royals

-Designs on Love

-Engineering Love

Novellas Related to the Unexpected Royals Series

-Pointe Shoes and Sugar Plums

The Skaters of Sequoia Valley

-The Rules of the Rink

-The Sloth Zone

-Caught In a Loop

The Royals of Isola Nostrum

-The Great Austen Adventure

-For the Love of Dinosaurs

Historical Romance Novellas

-The Mysterious Mr. Marcellus

Acknowledgments

Caught in a Loop was a story that I decided to tackle just as I found out I was expecting my first child. It will forever hold a special place in my heart because of this.

Writing while you are expecting is a challenge. There are days where the words came flowing out of me, and other days where I felt exhausted and could only get a few sentences on the page. It was truly a roller coaster end to 2024 and beginning to 2025.

Then, just as I felt like I'd found my stride, my daughter arrived and life as I knew it changed again. Finding time to do anything has been especially tough. Especially when I had to return to work and my grad program.

I may be producing fewer books for the next few years, but becoming a mom is the best thing that's ever happened to me and I wouldn't change it for the world.

I'd like to start out by thanking my amazing family for supporting me over the last year. Whether it was child care or a shoulder to cry on, you've been with me every step of the way over the last year and I could not have done this without you.

Next, I'd like to thank my editor extraordinaire Joanne Lui. You're not just a whiz with turning my manuscript into a diamond, but you've also become a good friend of mine. Thank you for always being there.

To Brooke Gilbert, my rainy day partner in crime.

Thank you for your continued encouragement and support as our lives have changed over the past year.

To Charity Chimni, thank you for your eagle eyes and catching all of my silly mistakes within my stories.

To my beta readers, thank you so much for your feedback and helping this story evolve through the first three drafts. It's been such a treat to watch Fernando and Ava's story evolve each time I hear from you all.

Finally, to my wonderful treasured community of readers, thank you for your support. It means the absolute world to me that you are there and enjoy my work. I literally would not be here if it wasn't for you.